Praise for *SKY ROPES*

"I read. I loved. I fought off tears. There's not a kid who can't find themselves in this wonderful debut story."

—Jerry Spinelli, Newbery Medal–winning author of *Stargirl*

"This is NOT your ordinary camp story. *Sky Ropes* begins with a hurt and damaged heroine whose terrible fear of becoming the 'mean girl' comes out of the real possibility that she might. But it's also possible that she might not—and the tension between those possibilities is tied up with the challenge of the Sky Ropes that terrify Breanna. A complex and intimate and honest novel whose pace quickens and quickens into a breathtaking climb into the treetops, this is a read that redefines the genre."

—Gary D. Schmidt, Newbery honoree, Michael L. Printz honoree, and National Book Award finalist for *Okay for Now*

"From the first paragraph, Sondra Soderborg's *Sky Ropes* whisks the reader along in a brilliant whirlwind of humor and authenticity, heartbreak and triumph. As Breanna navigates the (figurative and literal!) highs and lows of some pretty intense fears, her voice pops and locks off the page in such a vibrant dance of language that I didn't even realize I was reading aloud until I finished the book in one big exhale. Glorious, important, hilarious, and true, this is a story for anyone with big fears, high hopes, and a desire to define the world in their own brilliantly bold terms, no matter what."

—K.A. Holt, author of *House Arrest* and *Knockout*

"Sondra Soderborg's *Sky Ropes* is a precarious walk through the games, pranks, and social hierarchies of [a] middle school team-building camp, real-life practice in Breanna's journey from traumatized child to her own true self. Eventually, as the lockbox under her steeled heart came undone, so did mine."

—Liz Garton Scanlon, author of *All the World* and *Lolo's Light*

SKY ROPES

SONDRA SODERBORG

chronicle books · san francisco

Library of Congress Cataloging-in-Publication Data available.

ISBN 978-1-7972-1564-8

Manufactured in China.

Design by Ryan Hayes.
Typeset in Hoefler Text.

10 9 8 7 6 5 4 3 2 1

Chronicle Books LLC
680 Second Street
San Francisco, California 94107

Chronicle Books—we see things differently. Become part of our
community at www.chroniclekids.com.

TO PATRICIA LEE GAUCH,
MENTOR, FRIEND, AND DAEMON
—SONDRA

CHAPTER ONE

"ALL WE GOT TO DO," NIRAJ SAYS, "IS CATCH THREE RACCOONS."

Breanna laughs loud. Head thrown back, peeling, pink elbows resting on the splintery bleachers of Sugar Maple Park, she's loving this.

Niraj, one bleacher step down, has cooked up his wildest camp prank yet. He rests a finger on his chin, thinking. "Babies probably. They'll be friendlier."

Pascale stands on the ground in front of them, throwing a softball straight up and catching it, *thwump*, *thwump*, over and over. It's nearly dark, but the yellow ball glows in her fingers, gathering light from the tall, buzzy lamps along the park walkway. "Raccoons bite," she says. "If you catch a raccoon, it'll bite you. You'll spend the rest of camp in an emergency room, getting rabies shots." Her ball *thwump*s. "You'd hate that, Niraj."

And she's right. He would hate that. But Pascale is nothing but a sweet pea, trying to reason with Niraj when he's being ridiculous. Not Breanna. She loves listening to this crap. It'll never work, but it's funny.

"Let me finish," Niraj says. "I've got it this time." He's been trying to think of an "epic camp prank"—his words—for the past two and a half months, ever since school got out and the pamphlets about sixth-grade team-building camp started coming in the mail. Camp starts tomorrow, so he's in panic mode. "I'll make three signs—*1, 2, 4*—and run string through them, like necklaces." His hands fly as he talks. "Tonight. I'll make them tonight and that's all we'll need." He looks at Breanna. *We* means her. Her and him.

She shakes her head and laughs. "No way," she says.

Camp is for chumps. She's not going.

"But then what, Niraj?" she asks, egging him on. It just feels good, listening to Niraj. Everything about tonight feels good. She's at home, here at the park, with her friends, Pascale and Niraj, Scott and Mitchell, who left twenty minutes ago. The five of them have played ball almost every afternoon and hung out in the evenings as often as they could. Like real friends. It's been the best summer. The best summer since before Breanna moved to Beecham, when she was barely six.

"Picture this," Niraj says, squaring his hands like he's framing the perfect shot. "There's a big building at camp. I saw it in the pamphlets, a cafeteria, right?"

Breanna nods her head. *Thwump, thwump* goes Pascale's softball.

"We catch the baby raccoons, we put the signs around their necks, and we turn them loose in that big building." He stops to

3

make sure they're both paying attention. Pascale is already shaking her head. "We do it before everybody else shows up, before breakfast, right? The counselors will have to clear out those raccoons." He's grinning wide. "Get it?" he says. "They'll go nuts trying to catch them and when they do, they'll see 1, 2—4!" He looks from Breanna to Pascale and back. "They'll think they've missed one! Epic!"

The idea is wild and clever. Breanna loves it! "Epic, Niraj," she says, laughing hard. "No question about it."

Pascale has stopped throwing her softball. It's too dark for Breanna to see the profound disapproval in her sweet eyes. But it's there. She knows.

"Yes!" Niraj jumps to his feet and the bleachers rattle. "But Breanna," he says—and Breanna knows exactly where this is going. "You know I can't do this without you. You're the prank boss. The prank ninja. The queen of pranks." His brown eyes, catching the light, are pleading. "Come on. You gotta come to camp. You gotta. Gotta. Gotta!"

"Sorry," Breanna says. "You're flying solo. Camp is for chumps."

That's been her line all summer. Her friends hardly argue anymore.

She gets up, stretches her arms out over her head, and sighs. It's time to head home, but she hates to go. Her friends will be gone till Saturday. Six days. To the team-building camp that kicks off sixth grade at Vincent Chin Middle School. She's going to miss these chumps. But she's worked hard not to go, and once she gets through tonight, she'll have succeeded.

Everything about team-building camp as the start to middle school is stupid. For one, it's a terrible way to meet people. Kids from five schools—including Sternmore Academy, where she used to go—will be there, all the sixth graders starting at Vincent Chin Middle School. They're supposed to live together in cabins, she and girls she's never even seen before. Share a shower. Do stuff they don't know how to do. Nope. She is not going to let kids she doesn't know watch how bad she is at canoeing before they ever see the magic way she rifles a softball across home plate.

No way.

Once all the chumps get back, she'll meet new kids in the places you're supposed to meet them: in the halls of school, where she can scare them or crack them up with the lift of an eyebrow. Or in Spanish class, where she knows all the bad words (since her teenage boy cousins were her first and best teachers). Or in the cafeteria, where her laugh is the loudest, and people are always watching her out of the corner of their eye, not sure if she's fun or dangerous. She's both. That's how school is supposed to start. That's how it's going to start for her.

"I better get going," Pascale says. "No raccoons, Niraj. You know that, right?"

Niraj laughs, but he doesn't agree. He's going to make signs— *1, 2, 4*—and pack them in the regulation green garbage bag that they have to bring their stuff in. For sure, he's going to do that.

"I've got to go, too," Breanna says. It's time. Time for the last, careful steps of her summer-long camp-avoidance campaign. The trickiest part is still ahead, she knows.

"You'll show up tomorrow, right?" Niraj won't quit. "It'll be dumb without you."

"I know," she says.

"Uggghhhh," Niraj clenches his fists and Breanna knows that he's upset for real. That's hard—she doesn't like making Niraj feel bad.

Pascale and Breanna walk east, stopping at the edge of the park, where tall sugar maples line the street. They wave at Niraj going south, down the park's lit walkway. Head down, hands shoved deep into his front pockets, he doesn't see them, but they watch him, till he finally dissolves into shadow.

Hard as it is to disappoint Niraj, she is not going to camp.

Silently, Breanna and Pascale walk down Beech Street. It's dark now. The bright moon, almost round, shimmers high above the trees. Only a few stars show through the dark. Pascale points to the tip of the Big Dipper and Breanna nods. Their sneakers scuff the sidewalk.

Another dumb thing about camp is team building. That's the kind of camp it is, team-building. What is that, even? And really, what's the point? It's not like the kids at Vincent Chin Middle School are going to unite to stop a crustacean-alien invasion from the Crab Nebula or something. They're just kids. They need to figure out ordinary stuff, like how to get to third-period Art in the basement. Like how to remember their locker combinations. Like how to hold on to their friends, even the ones—like Mitchell—who they don't have any classes with.

That's enough. It is.

At the corner of Beech and Stadium, Pascale stops. "I'm going to miss you, you weirdo," she says. She wraps her arms around Breanna and hugs her tight. Pascale is so tall, tall and skinny. Breanna only comes to her shoulders.

"You, too." And it's true. She is going to miss Pascale. Hugging, they rock under the streetlight five, maybe six, times. She is going to miss all her friends.

But that's the way things have to be.

Breanna turns left onto Birk, and she's almost home. She can see her little house, halfway up the block and across the street. The bright porch light shines in the dark, a magnifying glass on the chipping gold paint of their old cedar shingles. Coming into the yard, she can see her mom through the big kitchen window, setting a pile of clean plates into the cupboard. She's unloading the dishwasher.

That's Breanna's job.

Her mom does not do Breanna's chores.

It's a very bad sign. For a second, Breanna feels sick.

She makes herself stop panicking. Maybe her mom is being nice. She can be nice. Not when she's sure she knows what's right for Breanna and won't listen. Times like that, she's an unstoppable force. That's how it would go with team-building camp if her mom actually knew. She must not know. Breanna has been so careful all summer, so her mom won't find out and make her go.

Tonight is the end. Tonight, she has to be the most careful of all.

Resting her hand against the rough bark of the oak tree that takes up the whole front yard, Breanna watches her mom putting dishes away. She's got to pay attention to everything and play it all right. In case her mom knows more than she's letting on. She can be nice, but she can also be tricky.

Her mom peers out the window and Breanna steps behind the oak's wide trunk. This tree is a friend. It was her only friend for a long time. She's played in the shade here since she was six years old, setting up monster villages in the roots, watching the other kids on the street bike by, chucking rocks after the ones who looked tough enough to take it. Of course, she didn't hurt them. She just wanted them to stop and talk to her. It never worked. She was lonely in Beecham for a long time. Yeah. It was hard to move here from Detroit, to leave her cousins in Mexicantown and her Gran in Hamtramck. But they had to.

To get away from her dad.

To be safe.

The dishwasher is empty now. She watches her mom pour water from the electric kettle into a cup with a tea bag in it. She watches her sit down at the kitchen table and stare out through the window.

Standing here, hidden from her mom, her hand running up and down the bark of this friendly oak tree, Breanna can admit to herself the one, actual reason that she isn't going to camp. Those other things—meeting new kids in a strange place and having to do team building—suck. But she could handle them. She's the queen of handling stuff that sucks. She's the queen of figuring out how to make the stupidest things in the world not boring. Niraj wasn't lying when he called her the queen of pranks. If she were going to camp tomorrow, she'd have amazing pranks ready to go. And she would pull them off.

It's tempting. Almost.

But the truth is, she's not going to camp for one reason—the Sky Ropes.

The Sky Ropes are a high-ropes course. An obstacle course in the air famous for how high they are off the ground. The highest high ropes east of the Mississippi. The great, big, hairy deal of camp.

It's so messed up.

She is not going to do the Sky Ropes and she is not going to be near the Sky Ropes and she is not going to listen to people talk about the Sky Ropes because that will infect the air she breathes with Sky Ropes poison and that is absolutely not how she is going to spend the next six days of her life.

Starting tomorrow, there is something at Vincent Chin Middle School for the kids who aren't going to camp, probably some boring classroom where they sit and read or something dumb like that. It's supposed to be their choice, whether they go to team-building camp or not. The pamphlets that came in the mail said so. She can't be the only one who isn't going, though honestly, it's okay if she is.

If she's stuck in a boring room alone, nobody will think about her and the Sky Ropes in the same thought. Nobody will eye her up and down and wonder why she hasn't done them. It matters that nobody wonders. She has a reputation to protect. She is fearless.

Fearless Breanna Woodruff.

It is everything to her. Nobody, especially not a world of new kids coming from four other schools, is going to get one tiny hint that she is terrified of heights. Terrified.

She has her reasons.

CHAPTER TWO

THROUGH THE WINDOW, BREANNA SEES THAT HER MOM IS LOOKING down at the cup pressed between her palms. She seizes the moment to dash from behind the big oak to the backyard. The rusty gate creaks as she opens and closes it. But it's a small sound. It could be wind, sighing along branches. Her mom won't have noticed.

The motion-activated light on the back porch flashes on and the whole crummy backyard glows. Tall nettles clog the fence, their dangerous leaves reaching for her as she passes. Those leaves, spiky and sharp. They sting her fingers and her legs when she's burying stuff back here. They're eating up the lawn, growing right into it. In five years, maybe less, it will be nothing but nettles, the worst backyard in the world.

Hands tucked into her sweatpants pockets, protected from those spiky leaves, she edges to the back corner of the yard, where the dirt under the nettles shows the clear prints of her worn-out sneakers. It looks just like she left it this afternoon, her burial mounds undisturbed. It's the night before camp, and her mom doesn't know what she's buried back here.

Pamphlets. That's what's she's buried.

They've come in the mail all summer. Pamphlets about team-building camp. About Camp Horizons, "where young people learn to lead through cooperation and courage." They are bright with colored pictures of kids pretending to have the time of their lives, bright with the towering Sky Ropes and their glistening, dangerous cables. Those pictures are as close as Breanna ever wants to get to camp, thank you very much.

Of course, the garbage wasn't safe. Her mom's been checking the garbage since Breanna pushed her torn-up report card to the bottom of the kitchen trash in second grade. Same with recycling. Her mom checks that, too. She's thorough.

Way back in June, when the pamphlets started coming, Breanna hauled them to Sugar Maple Park to throw them out there. The pamphlets said that even though it's how sixth grade started and attendance was strongly encouraged, every kid got to choose whether camp was right for them. They said camp was all about choices.

Yeah, right.

Whoever said that doesn't know Breanna's mom. If she knew about it, she would make Breanna go, no question.

The third day of Breanna throwing out her little bag of trash at the park, Pascale asked straight out what she was up to. "Nothing," Breanna had said. "Nothing." But Pascale is too smart to lie to.

That's how Breanna started burying pamphlets under the stinging nettles along the backyard fence, where no one would ever think to look.

She touches the packed dirt with the toe of her worn-out Nike sneaker. It's solid. Good. She's almost there. Her plan has almost worked.

The night is cool. A breeze tickles at the edges of her ponytail, pulled through her Detroit Tigers cap. But she's sweating. She's worried—that's the truth. There's still tonight. She still has to get past her mom tonight. No mistakes.

She knows what she's worried about. It's the way her mom's gone silent about school starting tomorrow. It does, across the whole Beecham School District. It's just that for kids starting Vincent Chin Middle School (except for kids like her, doing plan B), camp takes up the first week.

Usually by now, her mom would have said, "Show me the treads." Breanna would have lifted up her feet and shown her the bottoms of her Nike sneakers, slick and smooth and almost worn through. "Okay," her mom would have sighed, that *how am I going to afford this* look on her face that she's had ever since they moved to expensive Beecham, where the public schools are good and where they live fifty miles, fifty full miles, away from her dad and his green Chevy truck.

But it makes sense, her mom not asking this year. She's been super busy, picking up all the extra shifts she can at Glendale Manor, a place for people who can't live on their own anymore. She's covered everybody's summer vacations—something she almost never takes. She's been too busy to drive Breanna to visit Gran in

Hamtramck and eat savory kolaches in her tiny blue kitchen. Too busy to have Aunt Jo and her grown-up boys, Breanna's cousins, over for a barbecue even once. Too busy to keep track of Breanna the way she usually does. Breanna misses Gran and her cousins a lot. She even misses her mom. But her mom being crazy busy has been just what she's needed to work her plan.

Silently, Breanna slips inside through the sliding-glass door on the back porch. She's going to sneak in and ambush her mom in the kitchen. Make her jump.

She creeps noiselessly across the family room, her eyes adjusting to the dark till she can see the shadow of the old blue couch and the TV shelf and the bookcase. In the corner, the computer screen catches the porch light and glows like it's dangerous—which it is. That computer could have ruined everything. But she's covered it. She knows the password for her mom's Gmail account and she's deleted stuff from Vincent Chin Middle School and Sternmore Academy, too, just to be safe. She tiptoes down the dark hallway, inching toward the kitchen, till she can just see the light brown hair, striped with three lines of gray, piled on top of her mom's head.

That head. It's not where it's supposed to be.

Five minutes ago, when Breanna was in the front yard, her mom was sitting on the stove side of the kitchen, facing the window. Now she sits on the other side, back to the window, watching Breanna's every step.

No. No. No!

So many times Breanna has seen her mom like this, sitting, waiting, patient, waiting, a spider, waiting. Waiting to talk to Breanna about something Breanna does not want to see or hear or talk about ever. Like moving. Like a call from the principal. Like camp. Camp!

"Mom!" Breanna bursts into the kitchen. "I'm not going. I'm not. You can't make me." She might as well not mess around. Her mom knows. Breanna can see it in her unblinking eyes, in the firm line of her shoulders, in the way she calmly presses her cup with both palms. She knows and she's been lying in wait for Breanna tonight, even being helpful, emptying the dishwasher like that. Breanna knew it was a bad sign. But instead of paying attention to it, the way she should have, she's walked straight into her mom's sticky web. "It's stupid," Breanna says. "I'm not going."

Silent as a spider, her mom brings her cup to her mouth.

Okay. Breanna has got to calm down and be smart right now. Pascale-level smart. She knows her mom knows something. But she doesn't know what. There might still be time to make the save. She straightens up and stands in the middle of the bright kitchen and stares back at her mom's unblinking eyes. She can wait, too. Her mom might give something away.

Breanna's brain kicks into *get me out of this* mode, one of the places where it does its best work. The thing is, if her mom knows about camp, but only the general idea of it, then maybe Breanna can talk her out of making her go.

But if her mom knows about the Sky Ropes, then it's all over. Her mom will know exactly why Breanna doesn't want to go. She'll see right through the story that her friends believed. *Camp is for chumps* might be true. But her mom won't let her get away with that lie as the reason.

Her mom knows Breanna inside and out. She knows Breanna so well that it's scary. She knows that Breanna is terrified of heights. And she knows why.

Across the table, Breanna eyes her mom. It's like looking into a fun-house mirror. She's almost as tall as her mom, which is not very. Her hair, except for the gray streaks, is the same light brown, thick, medium long. Her face, coming to a sharp point at the chin, is just the same shape. The pale skin, just the same, except that Breanna's is sunburned and peeling. The brown eyes, the same, except for her mom's dark-framed glasses, which magnify the way her eyes never blink, like a spider. The same thickness, the same sturdy arms and legs and belly. Only her nose, high and sharp, is different. That nose. It's the one thing that tells Breanna who her dad is. The one thing she doesn't want to see in the mirror.

She waits, trying to read what's happening. Her eyes stray out the window, where she can see the outline of the big oak tree catching light from the front porch. She wishes she could run her hand along the bark and feel its familiar, rough surface. It calms her down to feel things against her fingertips. She watches the oak tree sigh against a soft wind, and just thinking about the feel of that bark soothes her.

"Your friends are going." Her mom cracks first. That's good.

"So?" Breanna says.

"They'll make new friends. Meeting new kids from other schools is the whole point of this camp."

It's a big part of it, sure. But not the biggest. Maybe her mom doesn't know about the Sky Ropes. "So?" Breanna says.

"They'll find themselves another Breanna. Improved version."

That hurts. She's got to hand it to her mom, she's good. "I'll take my chances," Breanna says. But she feels a sharp bite in her gut. *What if they do? What if they do?*

Palms against her cup, Breanna's mom keeps her unblinking watch. "Took you five and a half years to make those friends," she says. "Doesn't make sense to take your chances." The corners of her mouth turn up, like maybe she's had her fun and this is all almost over.

Breanna doesn't answer. She doesn't want to blow this moment when it feels like things might break her way.

The fridge hums. The clock on the wall ticks.

"Oh, Breanna," her mom sighs and drops her spider eyes and shakes her head and she might be giving in. Breanna lets herself relax, a tiny, tiny bit.

But her mom looks up and her spider eyes focus. "Do you really think that I don't know all about this camp?" Breanna freezes. "Do you really think that the counselors haven't called me and sent me emails that I erased before you did and that I don't know about all the stuff you've buried in the yard, seeing how you tracked dirt inside every single day? Do you really think that I don't know exactly why you don't want to go?" She shakes her head in a way that seems weary with her own daughter's stupidity. "Do you really think that I don't know about the Sky Ropes? Oh, honey."

It's over.

Breanna should have known. She should have never under-estimated her mom or pretended that her mom's silence meant she didn't know. Her mom knows. She always knows.

She knows everything, everything that Breanna doesn't tell her and everything that Breanna hides from the rest of the world. Because she was there when it all happened. Breanna remembers her mom screaming and kicking and pounding her fists and frantically waving the police upstairs to that high-up window in the old house off McNichols, where they lived and where her funny, smooth-talking dad changed into something else, somebody else, dangerous and mean and crazy with the OxyContin that he kept taking after his shoulder healed up. In her head, she can still hear him shouting, "Fly, baby. Fly!"

She was five. Five!

At the table, her mom cradles her teacup. The smell of the tea, ginger and lemon, fills the room. It's a good smell, but it makes Breanna sick. Her mom, waiting like this, catching Breanna in her sticky web. She pulls out a chair and slumps down, too worn out to keep standing.

"Mom," she says, "I can't go to camp. It'll kill me. You know it will."

"I know it won't," her mom says.

"No, Mom. Those ropes. You know I can't." Breanna buries her face in her hands. "You know."

Reaching across the table, her mom picks up the fingers of Breanna's left hand. She pulls them gently down and off Breanna's face and squeezes them with her own fingers, warm from her cup. "You don't have to do those ropes," she says. "That's how this camp works. But you need to be there with your friends and new kids from all over the city." Breanna stares at the white-topped table. She cannot look at her mom. "And you need to feel what it's like to live with those high ropes and know that you're in charge of what you do, that you can keep yourself safe there."

"I can't," Breanna says. "Please, Mom. I'll be too scared. Everyone will see. The Sky Ropes are everything. If I don't do them, people will know. They'll know I'm . . . I'm . . ." She can't even say it. But she has to. Her mom has to know how serious this is. "That I'm a coward." Breanna forces the words out in a whisper.

Her mom squeezes Breanna's fingers. "You are not a coward. You are my brave, strong girl."

Tears well up in Breanna's eyes. "I can't do it," she says. "Please, Mom."

Her mom lets go of Breanna's hand. She lifts her pointy chin, the sure sign that she is done. "You're going, Breanna. You've always been going." Her brown spider eyes are fierce. "You've been signed up for two months. Go pack."

CHAPTER THREE

HOT ON THE BUS.

Hot and loud.

A hacky sack boinks Breanna on the head. "Hey!" she shouts, hucking it back. She is in no mood to goof off right now. Half the windows are open as they swoosh down the freeway, but it must stink in here, all these sweaty kids. Breanna's marinated for half a day, along with the rest of them. She can't tell if it stinks or not.

It must.

Super-annoying kids in the back sing loud enough to hear—clearly—over fifty shouted conversations. Michael Plotz stands up every five minutes to cuss at Lorie Quinn, eight rows back, because she told the girl sitting next to her that Michael was a crappy kisser and now the whole bus knows.

Those kids in the back started singing in Beecham with one thousand bottles of beer on the wall. They're more like croaking now, all the way down to seventeen. What kind of kid would want to sing those stupid words 983 times? How boring would your life have to be to *want* to do that? She cannot fathom.

She is trying her best to use this time on the bus to plot a serious, not-goofing-around prank with Niraj, who sits, bare legs leaving wet streaks on the slippery green seat, across from her and Pascale.

Niraj had been so happy to see her this morning. He bounded at her from across the parking lot, shouting, "You came! You came!"

"Of course I came," she shouted back, grinning a grin that wasn't fake, because the way he was so happy made her happy for one second. It was kind of beautiful. "You think I'd pass up this chance to pull off the world's best prank?"

They've been talking pranks ever since. He's fixated on the raccoons. He brought the signs—*1, 2, 4*—like she knew he would. It's a funny idea and she'd go along with it if it could work. But Pascale said *rabies* and Pascale knows stuff. Breanna is not touching that prank.

Besides, she needs to think of her own prank, something crazy and gutsy and mind-blowing. She's been trying to think of something ever since her mom said she was going. She wracked her brain the whole time she was stuffing her regulation green garbage bag with all the crap on the packing list. Of course, her mom had both—the packing list and the regulation green garbage bag complete with two labels that said BREANNA WOODRUFF—ready to go.

Breanna dutifully packed everything on the BRING TO CAMP side of the packing list. She added a few things from the DO NOT BRING

TO CAMP side, like any self-respecting kid would. Candy—a full-size box of Nerds and a giant Snickers bar from her mom's no-fly zone on the highest kitchen shelf. A tube of medical ointment, which apparently only counselors are supposed to have—her mom's Bengay, to be specific, which is slippery and stinks in a useful, pranky sort of way. Her cell phone, stuffed into socks and buried in the pocket of a balled-up soft, old University of Michigan sweatshirt. All of it is contraband. Cell phones are contraband! How stupid can this camp be?

But her mom. Last night she checked Breanna's bag—checked Breanna's bag!

She went through it, thing by thing, and found all the contraband and piled it up on the white-topped kitchen table and stood guard till Breanna gave up and said she was going to bed.

But Breanna isn't called the prank ninja for nothing. After her mom finally fell asleep and Breanna had tossed and sweated in her sheets for hours, she got up and super quiet smuggled a few other prank supplies into her bag. Water balloons—for mid-dinner entertainment. All three flashlights in the house, plus extra batteries—for midnight reconnoiters. A whole, unopened box of Saran Wrap—for wrapping toilets, counselors' cabins. That could be funny. And Saran Wrap is pricey. Her mom will feel that when she has to buy a new roll.

It was tough sneaking the stuff out of the house this morning because her mom was still watchful, of course. So just getting supplies for even the most basic prank past her mom was an actual, real-deal accomplishment. And it was important. A killer prank matters now more than ever. It will get everybody's mind off the

Sky Ropes and on to Breanna—Vincent Chin Middle School's newest, coolest, gutsiest sixth grader.

It's the one, sure thing she can think of to protect herself from the Sky Ropes.

They've been in this bus, on the road for hours. Breanna sweats on the edge of the seat she shares with Pascale, trying to think. But her brain is useless. It's a standing tube of Campbell's Cream of Mushroom Soup, glopped out and quivering in the pan. No ideas are going to boil up from that.

The bus turns down a bumpy dirt road, tires grumbling in loose gravel. The trees bend over them, sifting sunlight into spotty shade, speckling the dust coming in through the windows. It's pretty here.

That's not right. She is moving closer to the Sky Ropes every second. That is not a pretty thing or a good thing. If she starts thinking things are nice here, she might let down her guard. She cannot do that.

The road winds and thumps. "I wonder if raccoons like Velveeta," Niraj says, his words echoing into the silver water bottle under his mouth that he carries everywhere. Breanna doesn't answer. She's trying to stay focused on her own, actually possible, actually epic prank. They're in the middle of nothing but trees. Trees and trees forever. They haven't passed anything, not even a broken-down barn, for twenty minutes and those annoying kids have started up one thousand bottles of beer on the wall, again.

They pass under a metal arch spanning the road. Welded letters along the top spell out the words Breanna had been sure she'd never have to see: Camp Horizons.

They're here. They're here. She's here.

Breanna feels sick.

Climbing, the bus grumbles over stones and lurches into potholes. Up and up. The road curves sharply. It dips suddenly. But then they are in a bowl of deep green, a valley lined with trees where, over exhaust and dust and sweaty kid stink, everything smells like pine. Breanna breathes in deep. She can't help it, dang it! She loves that smell.

Up and down the hillsides, colors pop—yellow, orange, and red. And there, fringing the top of that third hill, burgundy fall leaves, her favorite. Small brown cabins cluster in the trees. Nestled among them stands a wide building, pale yellow against dark pines. It must be the main building, the one Niraj needs for his raccoons.

Crossing a pocked and muddy lot, the bus slows down. "Ah!" Pascale and Niraj say the word together. Breanna follows their eyes. Out past the building, over the tops of the trees, stretching out behind the hills, the sun is sparking against Lake Ojibwe. Sparking. Flashing. Jumping with light. Nothing in the world can dance like that! Nothing makes Breanna happier.

No. No. No.

She has got to get a grip. She digs her sneakers into the grimy metal floor and touches her fingers to the slick, crummy seatback and looks around. She is on a crowded, stinking, yellow school bus in a place she doesn't want to be, a strange and tricky hell with the power to make her forget—like she did just now—that the Sky Ropes are here, somewhere, hiding in these beautiful, stupid hills, and they are waiting for her, silently waiting for her.

They are going to hurt her.

She is sure.

CHAPTER FOUR

BREANNA THUNKS HER REGULATION GREEN GARBAGE BAG DOWN ON the splintery floor of cabin 17. She reaches deep inside and pulls out her baseball glove, soft and worn, fitting her hand just right. She needs it. She needs to run her fingers over the soft, grainy leather while she sorts this place out.

She shoves the rest of her stuff hard under the bottom bunk. The whirliest, most enormous dust bunny in the world flies straight at her. It makes her laugh. Life-size dust bunnies. Somebody should have put *that* in the pamphlets.

She pulls herself up to the top bunk, the last one in the longer row of beds, closest to the bathroom. The mattress, thin and stained, smells like towels left in the wash five days. Doesn't matter. This spot is officially hers. It has a name card taped to it—

Breanna Woodruff—in black marker and gold glitter. Gold glitter! For real, like this is third grade.

Still, this is her spot. From here, she can keep watch on these girls she's stuck with for the next six days and plan a prank so cool and daring that everyone will forget about the Sky Ropes. That's what she's got to do to leave this camp as Fearless Breanna Woodruff.

She's got exactly no ideas. But she's got time. Six days. She can do this. She has to.

There is one good thing about camp: Pascale is in the next bunk over, top bed. Right there, where Breanna can whisper to her at night, when everybody else is asleep. It's almost too good to be true, but Breanna will take it.

"Hey, friends!" Stacy, high-voiced camp counselor to cabin 17, gets everybody's attention. The small cabin is full, twelve girls plus Stacy milling around in the aisle between the two rows of beds, sitting on the bunks, going in and out of the bathroom. "Welcome! Welcome!" Stacy says. "I'm exultant. I'm over the moon to be here with you at Camp Horizons." *Over the moon.* That's all it takes for Breanna to know that Stacy is a lightweight, not someone she needs to pay any attention to.

"Let's start with a get-acquainted game," Stacy says, handing out pens she describes as having "all the colors of the rainbow." Rainbow pens. Clearly Stacy is the one responsible for the gold glitter. A lightweight lightweight, someone Breanna can truly ignore.

Breanna is done with Stacy. She lies down on her bunk, prepared to *get acquainted* with exactly no one. She's not here to make new friends. Keep track of her old ones, yeah, of course. But not make new ones. She has too much else to deal with.

Except. Wait a second.

From the corner of her eye, Breanna sees Cynthia Albright walk out of the bathroom. Cynthia Albright, Pascale's former BFF, is *also* in cabin 17. Breanna sits up to watch where she goes. She comes straight to Breanna's bunk. Looking at no one, not even Pascale, who is standing right here at the end of the bed, she plunks herself down on the bottom bed.

She and Cynthia are freakin' bunkmates.

This is amazing!

Holding her Detroit Tigers cap on her head with her gloved hand, Breanna peers over the foot of the bed and sees Cynthia's name taped to the bottom bunk. How could she have missed that? She grins at Cynthia, who shakes her head grimly, like she can't believe what's happening.

Breanna can add making friends with Cynthia Albright and recruiting her to the softball team to her camp to-do list. She's been trying to corner Cynthia all summer with no luck at all. Now, Cynthia is stuck in the bunk right below her. She's got six whole days to recruit Cynthia! It's another perfect thing, like camp is conspiring to make her like it. She won't, of course.

Stacy is handing forms to all twelve girls in the cabin. People are moving around, starting to talk to each other. Their voices, loud and high and sometimes squealy, bounce off the wood-beamed walls and rise up into the high eaves.

Breanna is definitely done now.

She sighs, lies back down, and rolls onto her side, facing the wall between her bunk and the bathroom, where the dull green paint chips and flakes. Over and over, she runs her fingers across the baseball glove on her hand, feeling every crease and wrinkle and thin crust of dry sweat.

Seconds later, Stacy says, "One for Breanna." The corner of a piece of paper settles against Breanna's ankle, just above the line of her socks. Twitching her leg, so little that it probably doesn't look like it's on purpose, she flicks the paper off the edge of the bunk. The pen, which Stacy set on the mattress beside the paper, takes more work, an actual kick. But off it goes, hitting the floor with a good, sharp slap.

Stacy, beside the bed, is handing stuff to Cynthia and talking to her quietly. She doesn't react to Breanna's falling paper and pen, which is surprising, since lightweights always take the bait. Breanna rolls to her other side and watches Stacy walk away, watches her step right on Breanna's paper, lying on the splintery floor. That's not what she expected. Maybe Stacy won't be the worst.

Breanna turns her back to the girls one more time. She squeezes her eyes shut and covers her facing-up ear with her baseball-gloved hand to block out the noise. She needs to be thinking about her prank.

"Breanna." It's Pascale. Breanna opens one eye. She'll do that for Pascale.

Pascale, so tall, leans close over the bunk, the tight, black braids along her head right up in Breanna's face. "This better be good," Breanna says.

"Sign my form. Number five. 'Find someone who speaks a foreign language.'" Pascale pushes one of the forms Stacy was handing out at Breanna. Breanna grabs it and starts to read. It's a list of demands. "Find somebody who." Over and over. "Find somebody who has lived outside of the United States." "Find somebody who has a sibling or cousin in the military." Beside each sentence is a line for initials. No girl can initial another girl's paper more than once.

This is not a get-acquainted game. This is torture.

"Number five," Pascale says again. "Sign it."

"'Find somebody who speaks a foreign language,'" Breanna reads aloud. She's spoken Spanish for as long as she can remember. It's what her cousins spoke at home and taught her because they thought it was funny—a fat, white toddler saying *gracias, abuela, casa,* Spanish words all mixed up in her baby English. "Spanish isn't foreign," she says. "I'm not signing." She closes her eyes.

"You're impossible." Pascale snatches her paper away. "Number eight, then. 'Find somebody who likes a sport you like.' Softball. We both like softball. Sign it."

"You only like softball because I taught you how to play."

"Sign my form!"

Breanna sits up, dangling her legs over the edge of the bunk. "Give me your pen," she says. "It better not be violet."

Pascale hands her a pen—it's orange: tolerable—and Breanna writes a giant *B* where Pascale points.

A girl, skinny, muscled, almost as tall as Pascale, pushes through the narrow aisle between Breanna's bunk and the wall. She squeezes up close to Pascale, who has turned to face her. The space between the bunk and wall is so tight that Breanna feels claustrophobic with this new girl here. "What did you two get signed, over here all secret?" she says. Her voice is silky smooth, but Breanna hears a hard edge just underneath. "Which ones can you sign for me? I'm Cami."

Breanna does not like the silky-smooth way this girl talks. People who talk like that are hiding something. You can't trust them—she knows.

Lifting one eyebrow, Breanna glares at her.

Most kids, seeing that eyebrow, get the message—*get lost*. But not this girl. She stands there, just stands there, like she thinks Breanna is going to talk to her.

Pascale, Sweet Pea, steps into the silence. "I'm Pascale," she says. "My friend's Breanna. We both like softball. If you like softball, I can sign number eight."

"Softball!" Cami says, in her silky-smooth voice. "That's my best sport. What team do you play on? I'm with the Lanton Leopards. Tri-region champions this summer."

The Leopards! Holy crap.

Breanna knows that team. It's a fancy travel team. They play serious ball, like Junior Olympic level. She watched some of that tri-regional tournament this summer, watched the Lanton Leopards dismantle the Westland Wizards. They won three in a row in a best of five—one game a no-hitter. Their pitching is legend.

Suddenly it's embarrassing to be wearing a baseball glove. Slipping it behind her back, Breanna eases it off her hand.

Cami leans back against the wall, one leg cocked up. Against Cami's bright, white tank top, long, lean lines of muscle track from her shoulders to her wrists. Breanna bites a hangnail off her thumb and, not thinking, asks, "What position do you play?" Immediately, she hates herself for making conversation with this smooth-talking girl.

"Pitcher," Cami says.

Breanna shouldn't have asked. Those arms already said it. Did she pitch that no-hitter? Breanna can't remember seeing her before.

Breanna's a pitcher, too, a good one, but not fancy travel team level, not like Cami. Breanna tugs down the sleeves of her long-sleeve T-shirt, hiding every inch of her arms. They are strong arms, she knows, but they don't look like it. She's got fat over her muscles. She could play right field, half asleep or picking dandelions, for all her arms have got to show for themselves.

"How about you?" Cami asks, eyes narrowed and unfriendly.

"This. That." Breanna looks away and mumbles. She knows it isn't right, that there's nothing to be ashamed of in her arms or her pitching. But a pitcher for the Lanton Leopards. With arms like that! Cami intimidates her. She does. "You know," Breanna says. "A little bit of everything."

"You pitch!" Pascale butts in. "Don't be humble. That's not even like you." She turns to Cami. "Breanna's so good! She taught me the whole game—how to hit, field, slide home. She's amazing."

"For sweet!" Cami says in her silky-smooth way. She smiles at Pascale with this lift in her lip that looks like a snarl. "What team do you play for?"

Breanna presses the toe of her sneaker hard into Pascale's side. She doesn't want Pascale to answer. But Pascale. She doesn't know that Cami's team is better than theirs by ten million percent.

And Pascale always thinks the best about people. She doesn't know that Cami is making fun of her. Not yet.

"We play Beecham Rec and Ed, Level Six," Pascale says. "We're the Gonzo Gazelles."

Breanna's face turns hot and red. Compared to the Leopards, Rec and Ed is like using training wheels. Their name is stupid, and their sponsor only bought XL T-shirts, too big for everybody, down to the knees on the smaller girls. They look and sound like a joke. She knows that.

But the Gonzo Gazelles are her team, and she loves them. Nobody takes them seriously till about the fourth inning, and by then they've shown what teamwork and brains and hustle and plain hard work can do. They win. They almost always win. No matter how much better the other team's T-shirts are.

The Lanton Leopards have uniforms. Gold jerseys with black spots down the sleeves. Black pants. Black cleats. Breanna notices uniforms. Good uniforms make her jealous, like those are the real teams, the ones that count.

Cami's nostrils flare—out, in, out, in—as if it's all she can do not to bust out laughing. "Rec and Ed," she says. "The Gonzo Gazelles. You guys must be soooo good. We'll have to play some ball while we're up here, Gazelles versus Leopards." She looks straight at Breanna, and Breanna knows that she is the gazelle and Cami is the leopard and they are the only two players in this fight—and it is a fight. Cami's eyes stare hard and cold at Breanna, her lip curled into an undeniable snarl. "I wonder who'll win."

Breanna can taste the superiority that Cami is exhaling. It's in the air, filling up the whole atmosphere of cabin 17. Breanna just met this smooth-talking girl, but she doesn't trust her or like her at all. "I guess we can play," Breanna says with a shrug, hoping she sounds like she doesn't care. "We can get some kids together if you want. Throw the ball around. Sure."

The two girls glare at each other across the narrow space between the wall and Breanna's bunk. Cami's snarl spreads across her whole face. Already, Breanna kind of hates this girl, and it feels like this girl might hate her right back.

"Give me your form," Pascale says coldly to Cami. Cami hands it to her without breaking her intense stare at Breanna. Pascale initials the form and hands it back. "Okay," she says, folding her arms across her chest. Even though it's hard to make Pascale mad, Cami's done it.

Cami does her smiling snarl at Breanna for a few more seconds, then stops. She breaks first—score one for Breanna. Without a word, Cami turns and pads down the aisle of bunks. Her toenail polish is lime green. Lime green. Like poison.

"Well, shoot," Pascale says, facing Breanna. "I walked straight into that one."

"Ankle-deep, Sweet Pea. Ankle-deep."

"It's okay. We'll show her when we play ball."

"Sure. Pitcher for the Lanton Leopards. No problem."

Pascale frowns. She wanders out into the press of girls with forms and rainbow pens. Breanna stretches back out on her bunk. Her eyes track up the red-stained logs that form the corner, thick with yellowing varnish. Where the ceiling should be, there are high eaves instead, exposed logs angling up and intersecting in an *A* at the top. It's cool, cooler than you'd think for this ratty, old cabin.

She closes her eyes to think. Girls are swarming her bunk, trying to get Breanna to sign their forms. Cami must have sent them. She ignores them all.

Four minutes ago, she'd had two camp challenges: the "life-changing" Sky Ropes and a camp prank that makes the Sky Ropes boring. Now she has a third: a smooth-talking enemy, a dangerous pitcher who thinks she can laugh at Breanna and Pascale and the Gonzo Gazelles and get away with it.

Breanna turns her lips up into one little smile.

CHAPTER FIVE

A BELL CLANGS, FAR AWAY BUT LOUD. STACY, THE COUNSELOR, claps her hands, *1-2, 1-2-3*, until everybody (not everybody) joins in and stops talking. "That," she says, "is the chow bell. When you hear it ringing, it's time for chow!"

Stacy says *chow*. Real people don't say that. B-movie cowboys do. Lightweight.

Still, lunch. Breanna hasn't eaten since before the long bus ride—Honey Nut Cheerios, peach Kroger-brand yogurt, a banana her mom made her eat. Since then, no snacks, no candy smuggled in her regulation green garbage bag, nothing. It's late afternoon, well past lunch time. She's hungry. She'll get off her bunk for lunch.

Rolling down, Breanna nearly topples a bit of a girl standing between her bed and the one next to it. "Watch it," the tiny girl says in an untiny voice. "You nearly crushed me."

"Sorry. I didn't see you." Breanna steps back, away from the girl. "You're such a little peanut."

"Don't call me Peanut," the girl says. "My name is Tess. I have a condition."

"Okay, Tess." Breanna puts her hands up and steps farther back. One second out of her bunk and she's already messing up, making some puny little kid with a condition feel bad. This camp is tricky. One second, it seems okay, like she might even like it. The next second reminds her that it's not okay and it won't be okay and she cannot let her guard down, ever.

The cafeteria is a big, wide room in the pale-yellow building Breanna saw from the bus. Old wood paneling lines the walls and brown industrial carpet stretches across the floor. It's worn out and old-fashioned. But it isn't ugly. Not at all. It is alive with light. Along the whole back wall, windows open out across Lake Ojibwe, the deep, blue lake behind camp. It's sparking again, big and close and shining.

Tingling with the joy of it, Breanna weaves through the maze of tables where her camp mates are starting to sit. She stands at the big bank of windows and gazes out, watching the beautiful lake. Seagulls circle. Low waves, foamy white, ripple and crest. The lake stretches on and on, disappearing somewhere out past the horizon, like it might go on forever. The noise of shouting kids and scraping chairs and clattering plates fades, and the slow, steady motion of the waves spills over her brain like liquid calm. She could get lost, standing here.

"Breanna. Hey, Breanna." Pascale calling her name ends this moment. Breanna turns and *poof*! Her calm is gone. She faces a room full of loud mostly strangers who she has to sit down and eat lunch with. She doesn't want to deal with these kids. She doesn't want to know them. She searches the room for her friends.

Her eyes flick across hair and faces and ears. Some she recognizes from Sternmore. Most are new. But there, sitting at a table along the left side is Mitchell, elbows on the table, talking to a boy with black hair. Two tables over is Scott, drawing on a napkin with the tiny pencil that he always keeps in his back pocket. Her friends. Her good friends. Scott looks up, sees her, and smiles. It's nice.

She makes her way to Pascale, sitting at a big round table, near the middle. Niraj is there, too, his straight black hair tucking up where it fringes the collar of his shirt. Hands going fast, he's already talking to whoever sits next to him. Pascale points down firmly at the empty chair beside her. She's saved this chair for Breanna, just her, in this mass of strangers. What a relief.

Kids are going around the table introducing themselves. There's a girl with purple hair whose name Breanna doesn't catch. There's Niraj, too busy talking to know it's his turn. But when he sees Breanna looking at him, he stops. She raises an eyebrow. "Tell everybody your name," she says.

"Oh, hi!" he says, looking around the table like he hadn't noticed anyone but the kid he was talking to before. "I'm Niraj. Niraj Anand."

There's a girl named Rachel. She says her name, "RACHEL!" very loud, looking straight at Breanna, like there's some reason for Breanna to care. Breanna stares back at her. "I'm Cami's friend." Rachel sits next to Pascale and yells across her. "You know. Cami, from the cabin."

Sure. Breanna knows. Cami, the pitcher who thinks she's God's gift to softball. Breanna nods her head slowly, frowning, trying to be very clear that being Cami's friend does not rate with her.

Pascale introduces herself. Breanna says her own name. Almost before she's got the words out, the boy sitting next to her barks out his name. "I'm Max. Max Barrett." His dark hair is straight and flat, except where it stands up over his left eye. He wears huge, black-rimmed glasses and is like the poster boy for Nerdom.

Some dry booger hangs out of his nose. Breanna elbows him and points to the spot under her own left nostril. Max grabs up a napkin and wipes hard and successfully. Breanna's about to congratulate him, but he starts talking first. "Seventeen is a prime number," he says.

"Yeah," Breanna says, raising an eyebrow in alarm.

"You're in cabin 17," he says, looking at her like she should appreciate something here. He waits, as if, given time, she'll figure it out. She doesn't. "I know because this table is top bunks, cabins 17/18." He points to a sign in the middle of the table that Breanna hadn't noticed. Top Bunks 17/Top Bunks 18 it says. They have assigned seats, or tables at least.

"So?" Breanna says.

"Prime cabin," Max says. "Primes in the prime. You know?"

Breanna does not know. She must look confused, because Max says, "Prime people/prime cabin."

Breanna, a carton at her mouth, laughs out loud, spluttering milk. This kid. He might be the king of all nerds. He's so weird that he's funny. Also wrong.

Clearly, he doesn't know about Breanna. She is not prime. Neither are Cami and Rachel. But there's Pascale. He's right about her.

Shaking her head, laughing, Breanna grabs some napkins from a caddy in the middle of the big, round table and wipes up the milk. She sees Rachel, on the other side of Pascale, looking disgusted. Maybe she saw the booger; maybe she knows Max and doesn't approve of anybody laughing at his stupid jokes. But Breanna likes this strange kid. And as for Rachel, she and Cami deserve each other. Breanna knows the type—Rachel the Minion, for sure.

"You're weird," Breanna says to Max.

"You are correct," Max says. "I'm in cabin 18. Not prime. All the boys' cabins are even numbers. Whereas—1, 3, 5, 7, 11, 13, 17, 19, 23—all the primes are girls' cabins."

What do you even say to something like that?

"My partner, however, is prime," Max says. "Even if our cabin isn't."

"Partner?"

"You know," Max says, "the kid we're teamed with for all of camp." Again, Breanna does not know. Max is quick to explain. "Top bunk/bottom bunk. Those two kids who are supposed to stay together." Max talks with his hands. They curl and slap and move almost as fast—but not as gracefully—as Niraj's hands. "Always together in all activities, keeping track of each other. Except not in the bathroom. And not at meals where we sit with some configuration of our cohort cabin, which is 17. We're Team 17/18. We're a cohort. Didn't your counselor tell you anything?"

Apparently not. Or maybe Stacy explained all this up at the cabin. Breanna absolutely wasn't listening. She missed this and *this* is interesting. Important, even. She's got a camp partner, and it's Cynthia Albright! Another one of those perfect things conspiring to make her like this stupid place.

Last spring, model citizen Cynthia Albright damaged the principal's portrait at school, accidentally showing Breanna and the rest of the world that she had an amazing left arm. She's a southpaw. She can aim and she's got distance. Ever since, Breanna has been determined to get Cynthia to pitch for the Gonzo Gazelles. Determined. Cynthia has ignored her, completely. Every call. Every surprise appearance at her front door. Every text—a ton of those. But Breanna won't give up. Six days stuck together at camp? That's a lot of time. Enough to convince Cynthia that being Breanna's relief pitcher is exactly what she wants and needs.

Whoever made them partners is a freakin' genius.

Staring around the room, she finds Cynthia in the sea of tables and watches her. She's sitting very straight on one side of a round table, with Cami just across. If Max is right—and he seems like the kind of kid who is usually right—that table must be bottom bunks, cabins 17 and 18. Cynthia's arms are folded tightly. Her curly brown hair is pulled into a ponytail, with a few loose bits pinging around her face. She looks alone, like there's too much room between her and the kids on either side. It's weird.

Last year, at Sternmore, in that whole throwing thing, Cynthia—who never got in trouble in her whole life before and who was that kid who knew all the answers without even trying and who never let anyone copy her homework—broke the rules. And then, when Breanna's friend Scott got blamed for what she did, Cynthia let it happen. She let Scott sit in in-school suspension for three days, for something *she* did. It was a crappy thing to do. Pascale, Cynthia's BFF, ratted her out in the end. She had to. And so now those two aren't BFFs anymore. They don't even talk. The whole school stopped talking to Cynthia. (Except Breanna of course. And Scott—he's just like that.)

Cynthia is alone. But she makes it look okay, like it's what she wants. Maybe she does. But if she doesn't, Breanna is right here with the perfect solution.

Softball.

Softball will give Cynthia a team, a team with Pascale on it.

Those two. They miss each other, whether they admit it or not. All summer, Cynthia biked around and around Sugar Maple Park and stared at Pascale when Breanna and her friends were there, at softball practice. Pascale would stop whatever she was doing and just watch her. She didn't wave or make eye contact. Just watched. So sure, Cynthia can be an island at her table, can look like she doesn't need anybody, but she misses Pascale. Breanna knows.

Yeah. Softball will give Cynthia friends again, Pascale most of all. Softball will make her famous—the best left-handed pitcher Rec and Ed has ever seen. Breanna will show her. Cynthia won't be able to resist.

Six days. Breanna can do that in six days.

Breanna's eyes skim across Cynthia's table. Other girls from Breanna's cabin are there, too, including that little peanut she nearly crushed earlier, and girls whose names she didn't bother to listen to.

The little peanut—Tess, her name is Tess—is sitting next to a boy. Breanna's eyes stop at him. She doesn't mean to stare. But she can't help it. He is beautiful. His bottom lip is tucked up, like he's concentrating hard. His straight, dark bangs swish over wide, brown eyes. She watches as he drums, rhythmic and complicated, against the table. Maybe it's the way he sways to some song in his head or maybe it's the graceful dance of his fingers, but he reminds Breanna of her big cousin Jorge. Kind, funny, handsome Jorge. He may have been her cousin, but she had a crush on him when she was four.

Max has followed her gaze. "Yep. That's him," he says. "My camp partner. I told you he was prime. He's a real nice guy, hasn't teased me once. Which is more than I can say for the rest of those clowns."

"What's his name?" Breanna asks, her voice too soft, which is straight-up embarrassing.

"James. James Perez. Coming over from Mallet Creek Charter."

Somehow, James looks up and sees Breanna through all this crowd of people. Probably it's because Max, right next to her, is waving at him like the dorkwad he is. James waves back. And James. He looks at Breanna and kind of ducks his head in a friendly sort of way. And he smiles at her. He has a beautiful smile.

Her whole face goes hot. She knows she's turning red. She tears her eyes away and looks down at the table. Thankfully, Pascale is handing off a huge bowl of macaroni salad to her. Breanna puts two big mounds on her plate and starts eating. It's something to do.

Something to look at besides that beautiful, beautiful boy.

There's baby carrots. There's white bread. There's iceberg lettuce with ranch dressing. Breanna keeps her head down and eats. She doesn't talk to Max, doesn't lift a skeptical eyebrow at Rachel the Minion (even though she wants to), doesn't say a word to Pascale. She doesn't dare look up from her plate of food because of where her eyes might go.

Eventually, a counselor guy, hair combed straight back, thin little mustache, thin strip of facial hair down his chin, stands up at the front of the big room. "Hi, everyone," he says into the microphone. "My name is Marcos."

Max jabs her ribs with his elbow. "That's my counselor," he says. "He might be prime, too, but I have insufficient data to be sure."

"Welcome to Camp Horizons," Marcos says. "It's going be a great week of team building, of meeting new friends, of working and playing together, of supporting each other and challenging yourself to do things that you don't think are possible. You will leave here better people, more generous, more confident, and stronger than you are today. I promise."

Promise? Promise?

That is way too much.

Breanna does not need to hear this. She read it all summer long in those pamphlets she wasted so much time burying in the yard. Marcos sounds just like them. *Camp Horizons will change your life!* She tries to block him out, but his voice leaks through. "Bonfires, nature hikes, the Sky Ropes," he says. "Swimming, canoeing, waterfront games, team building." He goes on and on.

It's almost more than she can take. Almost.

But there's something new in what he says, something that wasn't in the pamphlets, at least not in the direct way that Marcos is saying it. It's important, this phrase he's saying over and over: "Challenge by choice."

CHALLENGE BY CHOICE. Breanna hears that loud and clear.

"There are many things to do at camp. But you don't have to do them. You choose. Challenge by choice."

It means, Breanna thinks, that you decide what you want to do and you do that, just that. This is good news. This means lots of kids will skip lots of things, including the Sky Ropes. It means that nobody should bother anybody about what they do or don't do.

She can use this, right now.

"Wait," Breanna interrupts. Startled, Marcos stops talking. "You mean," she says, "that we don't have to do any of this camp crap if we don't want to?"

"Come on, Breanna," Marcos says with a laugh. He knows her name. She's never met him and he knows her name. "There's no crap at camp. It's all great." He steps back and takes a deep breath. "But your question is good. Some things at camp are required. Like team building. Everybody does that." His head tilts to the left. "But for most everything else, you choose what you do."

"So once I do the team-building crap," Breanna says—she feels the eyes of every kid in the room on her, which is what she was counting on—"I'm free?" She grins at Marcos. The room is with her, she can feel it. She wants to use this moment to make sure that Marcos says yes. Once he does, she's sprung. Safe from all of it—canoeing, nature walks, Sky Ropes. Come on, Marcos. Come on!

He hesitates, like he's thinking of the right way to answer, like he knows he might end up on the wrong side of this conversation. He must know that she's got the ear of every kid in the room.

She gives him a little nudge. "I've got a smelly mattress in cabin 17," she says. "What if I choose that?"

Everybody laughs, including Marcos. Including James—Breanna can't help but look.

"No kidding!" Marcos says. "Those mattresses stink!" The room laughs again. This is tipping her way. "Sadly, Breanna, you cannot choose your bunk." He scratches at the strip of hair along his chin. "You don't have to do the activities, but you have to show up."

Dang. She'd been so close to getting him to say what she needed him to say. So close. And now she is going to have to see the Sky Ropes. "What kind of choice is that?" she snaps.

"The kind where two of us"—he points to himself and Stacy—"are mostly in charge of twenty-four of you. We need to know where you are and what you're up to. We work hard not to leave you alone."

"That sounds a little creepy." She gets her laugh, which is the best she could hope for. But dang! Dang! Breanna thought she had something here, she really did—a way to avoid the Sky Ropes completely and make it cool for other kids, listening to her so closely just now, to do the same. She shifts in her chair, restless and uncomfortable. Pascale lightly touches her arm. "It's going to be good," she whispers. Breanna rolls her eyes.

Marcos is deep into talking about the Sky Ropes. "You don't have to do them," he says. "Challenge by choice. But."

Here it comes. There's always that *but*.

"They're great," he says, pausing, looking around. "I mean, powerful. A challenge that can change what you believe you're capable of, what you actually are capable of. If you can possibly do them or even a part of them, go for it!"

The room full of new sixth graders sits silent, leaning forward, paying complete and total attention to Marcos. It feels like every kid here is buying what Marcos is selling. *The Sky Ropes are awesome!*

Except Breanna.

She gets it, this big lie of camp. That some made-up obstacle course in the sky, designed to scare the crap out of you, can make you strong and confident and brave.

As if real life isn't hard enough.

Nope. She is not going to be tricked. She is not doing the Sky Ropes. In fact, she is going to make skipping them cool. She is going to outshine them by pulling a prank so big, so surprising, so unforgettable that kids will talk about it for years. Her prank—not the Sky Ropes—will be the big event of this stupid team-building camp.

Just watch me, she thinks. *Just watch me.*

CHAPTER SIX

NATURE WALK. THAT'S WHAT'S UP FIRST FOR TEAM 17/18. PASCALE shows Breanna on a printed schedule, carefully folded, that she pulls from her back pocket. Even Pascale rolls her eyes. That's how boring it sounds.

No way is Breanna getting out of it, either. Stacy must have figured out that Breanna is a flight risk. She sticks to Breanna's elbow all the way from the main building, across a boardwalk, through a marsh, to the field where they finally stop. Breanna is stuck.

But at least Stacy talked. Now Breanna knows for sure that cabins 17 and 18 are cohorts, like Max, that funny kid from lunch, said. It means the two cabins are paired for all activities, all through camp. They do everything together. Which means James, Max's partner, will be with Breanna every day in every activity. One more thing too good to be true. Sure, she'll take it. This camp can throw all the perfect things at her it wants. She won't be fooled—she's never going to like it here.

Kids stand, slouched, arms folded, in a giant patch of mown meadow. The late summer grass is short and crunchy under Breanna's sneakers. Along the edges of the field, tall, golden flowers wave in the breeze. The hills rise around them. The lake sparkles behind. It's beautiful here, Breanna can't deny that.

Better than beautiful.

From where Breanna stands, she can see a chain-link backstop that belongs to a softball diamond, just like the pamphlets promised. That's why she packed her glove. And it's right there, across the field. Cami, that mean pitcher from the cabin, flashes into Breanna's mind. Breanna can't wait to show her just what a Gonzo Gazelle can do on that softball diamond.

Marcos's voice pulls Breanna away from softball. He introduces Grace, a chunky lady whose hair is shaved short on one side and hangs long, at an angle, on the other. The name tag stuck to her T-shirt says GRACE, CAMP NURSE in big, neat letters. Grace has wide, muscular arms that show under her black tank top. Some of her veins bulge, like a body builder's. As she steps forward to talk to them, she swaggers.

Breanna likes her immediately. She likes the way she looks straight-up strong, not trying to hide it at all. She likes the way she looks tough, like she could snatch Thor's hammer out of Thor's hand and beat him at a game of keep-away. That's how strong she looks, stronger than Thor. Tougher than Thor. SheThor. That's who Grace is.

She has two jobs here—not just nurse but also naturalist. She's going to teach them all about nature on the walk they're about to take. "Our nature hike ends in the event of a medical emergency," she says. Kids laugh. "It doesn't usually happen on the first day," she says. "You won't be that lucky." At least SheThor knows what everybody thinks of this nature hike.

But it's clear in five seconds that SheThor loves nature. Loves it! "Let's look at where we stand right now," she says. She dives right in to the easy-to-miss things all around them. Breanna is suddenly alive to the tiny frogs scuttling through the grass and nearly invisible turtles sunning on the logs and the hundreds of red-winged blackbirds hidden in the cattails.

She's not going to say this out loud, but SheThor makes nature not boring.

The sun is warm. The blue of the sky is so September deep that it's turning purple at the edges. The wind blowing gently from the marsh smells rich and sweet, like an overripe cantaloupe going soft on the kitchen counter. SheThor shows them so many things right here, where they stand, that it's almost too much. The way a river birch is shedding its bark in long, thin strips—defoliating, SheThor says—is super cool. Breanna has to stop listening so she can soak up what she's heard so far, feel it, let it settle into her skin and sink into this little basket over her heart where she stores good things she wants to hold on to.

Not listening, she sees Marcos and SheThor move from kid to kid, pouring something dark into everybody's hands. She puts out her hand when Marcos comes to her. He pours in birdseed, which is weird, a heap of sunflowers in the shell and miniature brown balls and shiny black slivers. Breanna has no idea what to do with it. She strains to hear what SheThor is saying to Tess several kids away. "Anywhere in the field or even back to the boardwalk," she says, closing Tess's hand around her seeds. "Stay close to the tree line or follow the trail up into the woods. You'll be most successful near trees or bushes."

Successful with what? Breanna would like to know.

Cynthia charges past, her seed-filled palm pressed tight against her chest. She speaks quickly to Breanna. "You're my partner," she says. "You have to come with me." Whoa. Cynthia just spoke to her! That's big progress. Breanna follows Cynthia fast back the way they came, past Niraj, past beautiful James, past Pascale, who catches Breanna's eye for a second and smiles. Along the boardwalk, Breanna has to run to catch up. That's how fast Cynthia rushes through the marsh.

On the other side, Cynthia stops so suddenly that Breanna steps on her heel. "What are we doing?" Breanna asks.

"Shhhh," Cynthia says. She has a strange, un-Cynthia-like look on her face, happy and excited and something else, too. Like she's full of wonder, maybe. It's sweet.

They're standing in the path between the boardwalk and main building. Arching trees and thick bushes form a tall canopy over their heads. The wind drops yellowing leaves on Breanna's sneakers. Nobody else is close by. Faraway shouts float in the air, but the kids they left behind in the field are strangely quiet. It feels like they're all alone in this little bit of covered woods. Wind blows. Leaves quiver. Breanna's arms prickle.

"I saw chickadees here when we walked through," Cynthia whispers. "This is a good place." She's talking to Breanna again.

"For what?" Breanna's voice sounds like a shout.

"Shhhhhh," Cynthia says again. "Do what I do." Breanna watches as Cynthia lifts her seeds to the sky and opens up her palm. Her green eyes catch the sun.

All around, Breanna hears rustlings, whistles, chirps, and calls, the trees and bushes fluttery with birds. She sees them, brown, black, stripey, gray. They perch on branches and hop down tree trunks and fly, a sudden *flooooof* of feathers, from twig to twig.

Breanna copies Cynthia, raising her open palm, full of birdseed, into the air.

"It's the little ones, the hoppy black-and-white ones," Cynthia whispers. "Chickadees. They're the ones Grace says will eat out of our hands."

Yeah, right.

But the look on Cynthia's face, open and hopeful. Breanna has known Cynthia for years and never seen her look like this. She hopes the chickadees will come, for Cynthia, at least.

Without warning, a tiny black-and-white bird lands on Breanna's open palm. Surprised, she jumps, and it flies away.

"Did you see that?" she says to Cynthia. Cynthia nods, her face shining.

Breanna holds herself very still and raises her palm higher.

A minute goes by.

Another.

She stands perfectly quiet.

A tiny bird lands on her upturned wrist. Its cold little feet tickle her skin, soft as breath. Slow, like someone has slowed down a movie, slow, slow, slow, Breanna lowers her hand. She wants to see this thing.

Here it is. Right here. Glossy feathers, ruffly chest, black wings striped with white. Its heart thumps. Its black eyes roll. Its tiny beak bobs against Breanna's hand, peck, peck, peck.

The cold little feet resting on the swell of her wrist pulse with her. As seconds go by, Breanna's heart bubbles. She wants to shout, *Cynthia. Look! Look! Have you ever seen anything so beautiful?* But she doesn't shout, doesn't move. Just watches, amazed.

This camp. It has its moments.

CHAPTER

SEVEN

BY THE TIME BREANNA AND CYNTHIA RUN OUT OF BIRDSEED, THEIR
classmates' voices are so loud the birds have flown off anyway.
Without talking, as if they'd never talked at all, they join up with
the group back on the playing field. But Cynthia talked to her. And
they just shared something special together, them and those sweet
little birds. It's going to help Breanna's plan, no question.

Now the hiking part of the nature walk starts. SheThor leads
them up a narrow trail. She names trees as they pass—burr oak,
honey locust, redbud. She names bushes, too—sumac, native
viburnum, invasive buckthorn, which has three-inch thorns and
is everywhere. She stops to show them small things they might
miss, a hawk angling up to the sky with a mouse in its beak, fungus
layering its way up a dead tree trunk, owl pellets half hidden in dry
grass. Breanna is interested in all of it.

They make their way from the field to a trail that winds up a wooded hill. Breanna, dropped back to nearly the end of the line, watches her campmates climb. Near the front, Pascale walks with little Tess, who is her camp partner. Cynthia follows about five steps behind them, like she wants to be with them, but isn't.

Breanna knows she should be walking with Cynthia. She's been told several times now that that's how it works with camp partners. But she wants to be alone on this hike, just her and nature. Right when they started up the hill, she stopped to tie her shoes and waited, crouched down, while Cynthia kept going, staying close but not too close to Pascale. It makes Breanna sad for Cynthia, the way she misses her friend so clearly.

The trail rises up the hill, getting steeper and rougher. Breanna watches her friends pass through an open space above her. Coming up behind them, that awful Cami from the cabin is moving fast, Rachel the Minion nearly jogging to keep up. It's like now that the trail is a little bit hard, Cami has to outdo everybody. Hands in pockets, elbows out, she and Rachel weave past one kid after another, and when the trail is too narrow, it's the other kid who is forced aside.

"Hey," Cynthia shouts as Cami cuts so close passing by that she nearly swipes Cynthia off the hillside. "Watch it!"

Her yell is enough to alert Pascale, who quickly pulls Tess off the trail before the steamrolling girls can topple her. Arms around Tess's shoulders, Pascale looks back at Cynthia and shakes her head. Cynthia does the same, in return.

Maybe they aren't talking, but they just agreed on one thing: Cami (and Rachel with her) is not okay.

Breanna clambers over roots and boulders in the trail. Pebbles eddy out from under her feet. Standing at a dense bush up ahead, SheThor says loudly, "This is an elderberry, native to Michigan. Look for the jagged leaf and the cluster of white flowers in the spring or purple berries now. Both flowers and berries are edible."

Niraj and some boy with tight curls on his head are goofing around and going slow and soon they have dropped back enough to be just ahead of Breanna. Niraj leaps over a boulder. "See that, Trevor?" he says. "I'm a hiking ninja."

"No!" Trevor says, shaking his head so his curls bob. "You've been hiking for like twenty minutes. That is nowhere near ninja level."

"Come on," Niraj says. "We've got water bottles. We've got trail snacks. We've got shoes with good treads." He lifts up his foot to show Trevor. "Ninjas," he says. That's when he notices Breanna behind them.

"Breanna!" he shouts. "Trevor, that's my friend Breanna." There is straight-up excitement on his face and in his voice and for a second, Breanna feels like the queen of everything. "You know," Niraj says to Trevor. "She's the one I've been telling you about. We're going to pull the world's best camp prank together."

"Yeah, we are," Breanna says, smiling and waving a little at Niraj's new friend Trevor. "It's all I'm thinking about." She wishes it were true, but she is freakin' distracted by all this beautiful nature. She hasn't thought about the prank once since SheThor showed them the bark on that birch tree back in the field.

That stops now. Prank now.

Trevor has stopped walking. He looks hard at Breanna. "Niraj hasn't stopped talking about you." He shakes his head, slowly, like Breanna is Baby Yoda, appearing before him in the flesh. "You're a legend," he says. "Respect."

Breanna feels her face turn hot and red. She's embarrassed, but she loves it. Whatever Niraj is saying about her is exactly what she needs to hold on to her reputation and prep people for her incredible prank.

"Dude," Trevor says. "No matter what you're planning, I'm in! Anything. I'll do anything. Okay?"

"You better mean that," Breanna says, grinning. "We'll need you, for sure."

"Cool!" Trevor says.

SheThor, standing on a boulder about twenty feet ahead, is calling down the trail. "Look to your right as you come up this last rise," she shouts. "See that circle of trees and poles and silver cables two hills over?" Breanna feels a sudden clutch in her gut. "That's the Sky Ropes."

No warning.

Breanna isn't ready.

She doesn't mean to look, but her head swivels up and right just like everybody else's, and there they are—the Sky Ropes. They glow. They do. Like they're radioactive.

Everyone gathers on top of the hill, staring at the ropes and listening to SheThor, who is not talking about nature anymore. "Of all the challenges by choice here at Camp Horizons, the Sky Ropes are the toughest," she says. "Everything else is really prep for that."

Gusting wind quivers her voice. But Breanna can hear her, loud and clear. "I did them myself the first time I came here. I was scared. But doing them was important. It was a victory I haven't forgotten." Her eyes move over the kids, hanging on her words. "When you are right up against the choice of whether or not to do it, do it! You won't regret it."

How can SheThor say that? Like she knows what's right for every kid on this hill? Breanna's gut hurts.

Once they finally stop staring at the ropes and start hiking again, Breanna can't think straight. She means to block out SheThor and think of a prank. That's what she needs to do right now. But the Sky Ropes are in her head—only the Sky Ropes, their electric shadow filling her brain.

Ahead of her, Niraj whistles. "Look at that!" he says, staring at the still-visible Sky Ropes. "Three thousand feet high, and we're going to be up there."

"Don't be dumb," Breanna snaps. "They're nowhere near that high."

"Approximately," Niraj says, laughing like he thinks he's funny.

"You're wrong!" She feels mad at Niraj.

"It doesn't matter how high they are," Trevor says. He's shading his eyes, staring at the ropes as he walks. "They won't break. They're so strong, you can drive a car on them and the car won't fall off."

"A car with or without speakers?" Niraj asks.

"With. Definitely with," Trevor says. "We could blast Drake from our speakers up there and the whole camp would hear."

"Yeah!" Niraj says. "That would be cool!"

Breanna forces herself not to look at the ropes, to keep her eyes only on the trail. But the Sky Ropes won't budge from her head. She's seen them now. They don't look fit to hold a bird or your average sixth grader and certainly not her. This is crap. She takes a deep breath and says, "You're being dumb. You can't drive a car on the Sky Ropes." She can hear a small shake in her voice, but she doesn't think they can.

Niraj turns around and looks at her hard, like he hears.

"Dude," Trevor says. "The Sky Ropes are going to be *aaaawesome*."

"For sure," Niraj agrees, moving his eyes off Breanna. "We're going to kill it up there." Suddenly he stops and pulls his Yankees cap off. "Those ropes are crazy high. I'm doing them. But if I fall off and break my head, I'll be mad."

"You can't fall off, man," Trevor says. "That's the way they're made. Even a car can't fall off."

This is a ridiculous conversation. Breanna hustles up the trail, leaving Niraj and Trevor behind. The magic she had felt in learning to see the differences in varieties of oak trees has vanished. Without meaning to, she pictures a car on the Sky Ropes. She hears Drake blasting from the speakers. And suddenly it isn't a car.

It is her dad's truck.

A green truck. The front end crumpled, the left light missing, rust snaking up the grill. Laughing, sitting beside her dad at the wheel, are Niraj and Trevor. From open windows, music blares from the old stereo that doesn't actually work. She sees herself, sitting in the pitted truck bed, her and Pascale and Cynthia and Tess, too. The truck inches along the Sky Ropes, high, high, high in the air.

The front left tire slips and the truck lurches down. The right front tire slides and the back tires spin. The truck hangs low and the beat gets louder and the engine revs and the shred of back tire holding on gives way and the truck is loose and tumbling and below stand Max and James and Mitchell and quiet Scott and the truck is falling faster and her friends don't move and they stand there watching and her dad's green truck slams into them and bursts into flames so bright that Breanna, hiking up the trail, puts a hand over her eyes to shield them.

Holy crap. She just let herself imagine the Sky Ropes and her dad in his green truck killing her and all her friends.

That is not okay.

If she is good at anything, it's keeping thoughts about her dad out of her head. There's a place she keeps those thoughts, a lockbox *under* her heart with seven chains and a padlock. Nothing gets out. Nothing. She doesn't know how what just happened happened.

Breathing hard, she reaches out and pulls a leaf off a bush where clusters of tiny, dark berries bob in the breeze. *Elderberry. Native to Michigan. Look for the jagged leaf.* She runs her thumb and first finger across the leaf, over and over. It's nice. She rubs at the rough edges, the smooth spots between the sturdy veins, the hard little stem. The leaf turns tissue soft and dissolves in her hand.

But it's done its job. Her heart stops pounding. Her breath comes slower. She slams her dad and the green truck and even the Sky Ropes into that lockbox under her heart and chains it up tight.

The rest of the hike is a blank. Breanna can't see the point of knowing how to identify a hornbeam tree or learning the types of shade plants that thrive under oaks. And though she tries, she can't get her brain to focus on a prank. She's got a great prank brain. Always, without fail, it comes alive when she needs it to.

But it won't today. It's back to that gloppy cream-of-mushroom-soup dullness she felt on the bus. Something about this stupid camp is messing with her prank brain. That can't happen. A good prank is the key to leaving this place with her reputation secure.

Fearless Breanna Woodruff. That's who she is.

She needs a spectacular prank, so that everybody will know that and nobody will care whether she does the Sky Ropes or not.

CHAPTER
EIGHT

IT'S A RELIEF WHEN THE HIKE IS FINALLY OVER AND THEY SIT, AGAIN, in the cafeteria, eating dinner. It's a late dinner. Outside the big bank of windows that runs along the back wall, the sun is dropping low along the lake. Breanna stares as the gray-blue of the evening water deepens to azure and a last ribbon of sunlit orange dazzles across it.

A sign in the middle of the table says TOP BUNKS 17/BOTTOM BUNKS 18. It's a different configuration of kids than at lunch. James sits at her table, tapping the round of a spoon against his palm. Her cousin Jorge was like that, always with music in his head. James really does remind Breanna of him. That's a good thing. Jorge is the best.

Pascale is here at her table, too. And Niraj's friend Trevor. He, in fact, sits beside her.

She passes Trevor a bowl of mashed potatoes. He takes them and grins a giant grin at her. "Tell me what we're doing," he says soft in her ear.

"Too soon," Breanna says. "With pranks, timing is everything." If this were Niraj, he would bust out laughing and tell her to knock it off and spill the prank plan. Thank goodness Trevor doesn't know her well enough to do that.

"Dude," he says, loud enough for the whole table to hear, "When I told you I'd do anything, I meant it. I will."

Pascale, sitting on the other side of Breanna, hears that. She gives Breanna a *what are you up to now* sort of look. "Hey, Trevor," she calls loud. "I'm Pascale. I know you're Niraj's camp partner. Niraj is my friend, too." She pokes at Breanna's arm, three times. "I don't know what Breanna is dreaming up, but I'm warning you right now that signing up for one of Breanna's pranks—or whatever it is you're talking about—is going to be way worse than you think. Take my advice. Don't do it!"

"Cool! Cool!" Trevor says, running his hand through his rumpled hair. He's in, no question. Breanna just needs to think of something for him to do.

Marcos, the counselor for cabin 18, stands up with the microphone. "How's it going, campers?" he calls.

"Good." "Great." "Fun," a few kids call back.

Thank goodness Marcos isn't one of those annoying people who forces everyone to answer him loud and together. He moves on. "Usually after dinner, we have free time. We'll explain how free time works tomorrow because it's probably not what you think. But tonight, since it's late," he motions out the window, where the sun is down, "we'll jump straight to our nightly campfire instead. One of the main things we like to talk about here is fear. How we all feel it and how we can build tools to manage it and act bravely in the face of it. Usually, our talks are serious. But not tonight. Tonight we have fun with fear. I'll see you all down at the beach."

Fun with fear. Now that's something Breanna can get behind.

Twenty minutes later, down a long flight of stairs to the wide sugar sand beach along the lake, Breanna sits around a blazing campfire with her team. Marcos stands beside the fire, the shadow of the flames sifting across his face in bursts of light and dark. "Fear can be exciting, right?" he says.

Breanna, sitting on a hard, log bench, silently agrees. Cynthia, her camp partner, dutifully sits beside her. They haven't spoken since the chickadee. But from what Breanna has seen, Cynthia isn't talking to anyone, including Pascale, who, with Tess close beside her, sits in the sand in front of them.

"Who likes horror movies?" Marcos asks. Breanna does, a lot. "How about ghost stories?" Breanna likes those, too. "Tonight, we'll tell ghost stories around this fire." Shivery pleasure shoots up Breanna's spine. This is good.

Marcos starts telling a story, but it's hardly a ghost story. It's about a man named Hyrum who's got a hook for a hand and goes around terrorizing teenagers sitting in cars. Breanna's mind wanders to those teenagers. She bets they're kissing. She thinks of James and stops herself.

As ghost stories go, this one wouldn't scare a baby. Tess, in front of Breanna and curled up against Pascale, is listening, but not even she looks scared.

Still, Marcos has a knack. He circles the fire, light catching his eyes, leaning in close to one kid, then another, his voice so soft you have to strain to hear, then loud, then soft. A scream! Everybody jumps, even Breanna. It's fun.

If she were telling this story, it would be better. There'd only be a hook named Hyrum, no man attached. If you're kissing in a car in the lonely woods, it's way worse to hear a screech against the window and have it be a disembodied hook. Heck, a man with a hook might be looking for directions to Wendy's. Breanna glances at James, his chin resting in his hand, his fingers drumming softly against his cheek. He has kissable lips, a little heart-shaped ridge on top, nice and full on the bottom. He must feel her eyes on him because he looks up and smiles. She smiles back and her face burns hot. What is she doing? This is not like her at all.

Marcos stops talking. The fire spits. Its sweet-smelling smoke spirals up to the stars, a billion brilliant pinpricks. Lake Ojibwe breathes, in and out, in and out, along the shore.

"Anybody else want to regale us with a ghost story?" Stacy asks the group. "Nothing too scary, just fun."

Breanna can't believe her luck. This is exactly what she needs, her first big chance to show this group exactly who she is—Fearless Breanna Woodruff.

Hands go up, but Breanna doesn't wait to be called on. "When I lived in Detroit," she says, knowing those words alone are enough to scare some kids—some folks are just scared of Detroit, which is messed up. She loves Detroit and her cousins and the happy life she had there once. "There were six houses on my street where people still lived. The rest were empty, half of them burned down, the way things went in Detroit." The fire pops and sizzles. Kids are listening. Excitement sparks in her veins like electricity. "The grass around the empty houses was taller than my head. We scared up pheasants when we played hide-and-seek. Wild turkeys flew over our fence and ate the food we left out for Scarface, the three-legged dog we found.

"The summer I was five, seven wild turkeys came to our yard every day. One day, there were four. The next day two. And then none. None." The wind blows smoke across Breanna's face. The coals of the fire glow red. The kids are with her. She can feel it.

"I was playing grocery store with my friend Jackie in a burned-out basement, where we liked to go. But this one time, after the turkeys disappeared, there were pheasant feathers everywhere. In one corner, we found bodies of five dead pheasants. They were shriveled, like all the blood had been sucked out of them." Breanna drops her voice low. "We were scared. We never went down there again.

"Two nights later, Mrs. Perkins's cat, Rascal, didn't come home. The next day, we found her pink collar in the grass. Just that, the pink collar with its little gold bell." She stops and looks around the circle of listening faces—still with her. "No, wait. That's not all. We found her tail, her furry, striped tail. That was in the grass, too."

Near Breanna's knees, Tess gasps. Stacy clears her throat. From across the circle, Max, not sounding scared at all, says, "What did that?"

"Yes, what did that?" Breanna repeats. "That was the question. We didn't know. We sat up nights to watch. My big cousins took turns helping us out; Mr. Bettelman, next door, sat on his front porch with his army pistol." Marcos, standing near the fire, shifts from one foot to the next, looking ready to interrupt. Breanna charges on. "Mr. Bettelman said it was feral dogs. Said he'd shoot 'em before they ran off with a human baby. Not that there were human babies on our street. Jackie's brother was the youngest, and he was three." Tess is trembling against Pascale now. "We watched. We waited. The Greenbergs' German shepherd went missing. But nobody saw a thing."

"Real human babies?" Tess asks, her voice small and pinched.

Pascale glances up. Her worried eyes say *enough already*. Breanna ignores her.

"That's only what Mr. Bettelman said," Breanna answers. "He said a lot of stuff."

"Breanna," Stacy interrupts, "Let's call this."

"No," James says, his voice strong. "We have to know what it was." She can tell that he is into this.

"I'm almost done. I promise," Breanna says. "One night, my cousin Jorge was watching the street. Under the streetlight—the only one that still worked—he saw this thing. This *creature*." She stops to let the word sink in.

"It looked like a dog, a big dog, kind of. But it walked on its hind legs, like a human. Its head was shaggy. A line of black fur ran down its spine. Its sides were nothing but bare skin with black hair sprouting here and here." She touches her left side, the base of her neck, her right leg, like she's pointing to tufts of black hair erupting from her body. "Jorge saw it perfectly. It held something wiggling and furry and still alive in its paws. Blood dripped from its teeth as it sucked the life right out of it."

"Okay. We're done here," Stacy says. She sounds mad. Breanna didn't think a lightweight would have the guts to get mad.

"No!" "No way!" "Tell us!" The kids around the campfire insist, until it's clear that it will be worse if Breanna doesn't finish.

She keeps going. "Have you ever heard of El Chupacabra?" she asks.

"What is it?" Niraj asks, his eyes wide.

"The dog monster," Breanna says, hunching her shoulders and twisting her hands into crooked claws. "I'm not making this thing up, El Chupacabra. Trust me, I'm not." Her voice is a ragged whisper. "It's real . . . and it's everywhere."

"Everywhere?" Niraj asks softly, head turning to one side and then the other.

"For sure," Breanna breathes. "It's here."

Tess pulls in a loud, sharp breath. Kids start talking all at once. James throws his head back and laughs hard and loud. He has a wonderful laugh. Cami, standing in the back, arms folded, looks pissed in the second that the fire lights up her face. Probably she would like to be getting all the attention Breanna has right now. Mean girls are like that.

But this is Breanna's moment. She is in control. Of herself. Of the group. Of everybody's fear. She is Fearless Breanna Woodruff, and now they know it.

They are going to remember this story. They are going to remember her. And they are going to remember the incredible prank that she is going to pull here.

The one she needs to figure out, fast.

Ten minutes later, leaping up the wooden stairs, Breanna feels light and happy and powerful. She hears *El Chupacabra* running from group to group, from the kids around the fire with her to other cohorts spread out ahead and behind, until it seems like everyone is talking about it. "El Chupacabra." "El Chupacabra." Flashlight beams search the bushes. Groups of huddled kids stop and stare at some stir of shadow under the bright moon.

Near the main building, where the girls go one way and the boys go the other, James hurries up behind her. "I love El Chupacabra," he says, shaking his head so his bangs swish sweetly across his eyes. "I've heard those stories since I was a kid. But that was the best one ever. You know how to tell it!"

"Thanks," she says, her face burning hot. James puts up his fist for a bump and they laugh, touching knuckles. Her hand feels hot at the spot where they touched. Walking up to cabin 17, she can't help but run the tips of her fingers over her knuckles again and again. It's so silly, but she's crushing on this boy. That isn't like her. And right now, there's no room for that nonsense. She's got a prank to plan.

CHAPTER NINE

IN THE CABIN, AFTER LIGHTS-OUT, BREANNA'S BRAIN BUZZES. SHE
lies in her bunk, her head on a soft yellow smiley-face pillow that
she got with the giant claw at Quality 16 Theaters. She listens to
the quick click of the crickets and the deep thrum of the peepers.
She can't sleep.

She should be thinking about her big prank, she knows. But
she isn't. Instead, she's thinking about how great it was to tell that
story and feel everybody hanging on her words and how all the kids
in her cohort know who she is now and how James fist-bumped her.
It was perfect.

"Breanna?" A little voice carries up from the bottom bunk next
door. It's Tess, awake, too.

"Yeah," Breanna says.

"Your story scared me." Tess's voice sounds small.

That's not what Breanna wants to hear right now, when things feel just the way she wants them. She knew Tess was scared. She saw her trembling. She saw Pascale's *just stop* look. But she told the story anyway. She loved the way it felt so much that she charged on without thinking twice. It wasn't entirely kind.

Sometimes, when she does things that aren't kind, she thinks she might be mean.

Her dad is mean. He seems nice because he is a real smooth talker. But he is mean. Being like him is the thing she dreads most in the world.

Living with what he did to her and her mom has been the hardest thing she's had to deal with, by far. She doesn't want to hurt anyone like that, ever. She doesn't want to come close.

Telling that story tonight wasn't mean like that, not at all. But she knows she was only thinking about what she wanted while she did it. It was selfish. Selfish and mean go together.

She doesn't need to be a sweet pea. She can't be. But she is going to care and try to do something to make up for it when she's made somebody feel bad. Like listening to Tess, right now. "I'm sorry, Tess," Breanna says. "I didn't mean to scare you." It's not completely true, but it's not a lie, either. "It was just for fun."

"It's not real, right? El Chupacabra?"

"What do you think?"

There's a long silence. Tess might be thinking hard. She might have fallen asleep. "No," she finally says. "It's not real. It's a made-up story, because sometimes it's fun to be scared."

"Yeah. You got it."

"It was a little bit fun." Tess's words are slow and heavy. She's almost asleep now.

Breanna would like to say more. To Tess, or just out loud to the darkness, she'd like to say, *It's fun to feel scared of something not real. Like El Chupacabra. But it is not fun to be scared of things that are real. Like a green Chevy truck showing up to your softball game. Like the Sky Ropes. Like your dad, high on OxyContin and out of his mind.*

She hears even breathing coming from Tess's bunk. She sighs and makes herself stop thinking of her dad. It's time, past time, to figure out her prank. She leans over and opens the blind beside her bunk to look out at the beautiful night and give herself over to her prank brain, which she hopes is working now.

Through the window, the branches of a big oak tree glow waxy silver in the moonlight. Eyes heavy, she studies the thick trunk, imagining how good the rough bark would feel beneath her fingers. Her eyes trace up the tree and along a high branch and then to twigs and finally leaves.

Her eyes fall shut, but she can see the tree clearly, tracking up it, higher and higher. And now she is standing underneath it, still in her bed, but standing outside, the oak above her, so enormous that it stretches into velvet darkness and reaches to the stars, millions of stars, close enough that she can touch them. One, just past the reach of her fingers, winks off. Then on. She moves toward it. It blinks off and on again. It isn't a star at all.

It is the eyeball of a fat rhinoceros. She is near enough to see that now. It paws the ground, its body rippling across the sky.

Carefully, so carefully, Breanna pats him on the shoulder. She is sure he is a *he*, though she can't say why. She rubs his wrinkled forehead, his skin sweet sandpaper beneath her fingers. He tosses his head and bows before her, like she is the Queen of Stars.

"Come on," he grunts. "Let's go."

As if she's done it ten thousand times, she angles her foot on the rhinoceros's lowered head and he tosses her gently on to his back. She wraps her arms around his neck, her legs around his body. With unexpected grace, he lopes into the Milky Way. Shimmery streaks of fiery ice, pink and blue and brilliant white, ignite around them. Breanna shivers. Whether it's the thrill of riding a rhinoceros or the cold, she doesn't know.

The rhinoceros says nothing. He's going somewhere, charging forward, twisting one way, then the other as he dodges piercing shafts of moonlight. His galloping hooves are light as hands, tapping out a complicated rhythm against a table edge. Every dancing step draws them closer, closer to the glowing center of the sky. Below, Breanna can see the tiny oak tree and teensy cabin 17. She can see the lake, like a bird bath. And there, there! The Sky Ropes, nothing but harmless toothpicks in the night.

Up, around, and on the rhinoceros runs, past the North Star, the Big Dipper, Orion's Belt. She knows because he names each one, and more besides—Andromeda, Pegasus, the huge Crab Nebula that they learned about last year. Every step brings them closer to the spot where the universe collapses on a single, swirling point.

They get so close that Breanna sees. The center is a face. The rhinoceros stops. Breanna stares.

James's face.

James. Beautiful boy. His smile, his swishy bangs, his dark brown eyes, pulsing in the stars. Neon bursts of green and orange explode around him.

Here, in the sky, Breanna can stare and grin and be a dope the way she never is in real life and no one will know. Except the rhinoceros, because when she thinks, *James is more beautiful than Shawn Mendes and Bruno Mars combined,* he nods his head and says, "Indeed."

James's face.

Shining in the universe.

For her. Just her.

Of course, even in the dream, it isn't real. "You rat," she says out loud to the rhinoceros. "This is cardboard James. Real James is asleep right now in cabin 18."

"We don't have to stay," the rhinoceros says.

"We do. Run closer," Breanna says. "It's exactly why I came."

The rhinoceros, stumpy legs a sudden blur of speed, turns his horn toward her face and says, "I know."

DAY TWO

TUESDAY

NEXT MORNING, BREANNA'S EYES FLY OPEN. A BIRD TWITTERS
outside. A tree branch scrapes at a screen. She remembers the
dream, James's face shining in the center of the universe.

She doesn't even know him! How embarrassing.

Nobody knows, but still.

Camp is making her crazy. She's got to get out of here, out of
this cabin, at least, and be on her own in the fresh, cool air.

She looks around at the bunks of sleeping girls. Nobody's awake
but her.

Fast and quiet, she rolls off her bunk and crouches down to
grab her soft old University of Michigan sweatshirt from the garbage bag under the bed. She is face to face with Cynthia, whose
green eyes are unexpectedly open.

"What?" Cynthia says, so hazy and confused that she is actually talking to Breanna.

"Heading out," Breanna says. "Don't worry."

"Wait. What?" Cynthia sits up halfway. "I'm your camp partner." She slowly wrestles her feet out of her sleeping bag. "I'm coming."

"You're not dressed. I'll only be gone one second."

Cynthia looks down at her pajamas and reaches for her own garbage bag under the bed. She goes in slow motion. Probably she tells Breanna to wait. Probably she gets dressed as fast as she can.

Doesn't matter. Breanna is gone.

Outside it's cold, a real fall morning in the woods. Breanna can see her breath. Lights are on in a few cabins. The muffly sound of running water comes from cabin 13. A toilet flushes in cabin 5. From faraway, she hears the clap of a wooden cabin door against the frame. Besides that, it's quiet out here.

She needs this.

She half jogs along the wide trail between the cabins. Her worn-out Nike sneakers rustle against a thick layer of pine needles. Up ahead, she sees two birds, almost as tall as her, walking side by side like old friends. The beaks on those birds! Long and sharp and dangerous. Old friends who could poke her eyes out. One of them turns back and studies her, its face blazing orange.

Come at me, she thinks as she gets close. *Come at me and see how that goes.* The one that turned to look at her steps off the path and makes room for her to go by. Smart bird.

She breaks into an actual run, just to run, just to suck cool morning air into her lungs. She runs into the clearing where the pale-yellow main building nestles in the trees. She smells bacon.

She loves bacon! Half tempted to stop, find the kitchen, and sneak a piece right now, she sees someone else has the same idea. Standing on the porch, pulling on the handles of the locked front door is Scott, her good friend, quiet and always hungry. He is already here, first in line for breakfast.

"Scott," she shouts, jogging past. He turns and waves, keeping one hand on the locked front door.

Four fat white geese come waddling around the side of the building. She slows down to watch them. One walks up next to Scott and pecks at the knee of his jeans. She feels the flickering of an idea that might be a prank, and then it's gone. That's okay. If it's anything good, it will light up later. That's how her prank brain works.

She runs again. Mist rises off the grass. Along the boardwalk, bright lily pads and pointy cattails vibrate in the soft marsh current. She lets her hand run along the well-worn wooden handrail, feeling the grain of it in her fingertips. She watches a small turtle clamber up a log. She sees another raise its skinny neck, then plink along on little green legs until it slaps down into the water. It really is beautiful here. Breanna breathes in deep, feeling good, feeling calm and strong.

Now that she's out past the marsh, she knows where she wants to go: to the softball diamond that she saw yesterday at the start of the nature hike. She wants to take the calm she feels this morning up there, to start prepping herself for whatever softball showdown is coming with Cami. It's going to happen. Cami will make sure of it and probably Breanna will, too. From the start there's been that fierce, competitive vibe between them, separate from the fact that Breanna won't put up with mean girls. Playing softball against Cami is not the most important thing about camp. But it matters.

Thirty seconds later, she stands behind home plate, eyes squeezed shut, grinding the heels of her worn-out sneakers down into the dirt. The hard earth makes a good, grumbly noise, like it's swallowing the calm and beauty that she brought with her, so she can use it another time. She grinds harder. The sound gets louder. The ground starts to shake and rumble.

Her eyes pop open. A herd of deer bounds across the field, seven, eight, twelve of them. They trample the pitching rubber, leap through the outfield, send grass flying under their hooves. Pounding to the edge of the field, they jump over boulders and charge up the hillside, sending stones skittering.

All but one.

One brown doe stands at second base, head raised, ears flicking. She looks at Breanna, who stands, frozen, at home plate. Warm breath curls from the doe's dark nostrils. On one side of her chest, starting somewhere along her right leg and climbing halfway up her neck, she is covered with a black scar.

Breanna can't pull her eyes off that scar.

The doe sniffs the air and tosses her head. Breanna hardly dares to breathe. She doesn't want to scare the doe away. It feels like she could stand and stare at her forever. The two of them, together, on this silent field.

Clang. Clang. Clang.

The chow bell, the stupid chow bell, breaks the spell. The doe turns and runs and Breanna promises herself that she will find her again.

CHAPTER ELEVEN

TEAM BUILDING IS WEIRD.

Turns out that's what Breanna and all the kids from Team 17/18, plus two other teams, are doing after breakfast—team-building activities.

Back in the stubbly field where Breanna stood an hour ago, having that moment with the scarred doe, Marcos is trying to explain.

"This camp is all about what we can do when we work together and when we challenge ourselves," he says. "The way to win these team-building games is to constantly ask, *HOW can I help? WHO can I help? What can I CONTRIBUTE?*" Marcos' voice gets soft sometimes, in a way you can still hear, but then it bursts out, so loud and excited that Breanna jumps. She can't help but listen and get pumped, even though she doesn't want to. "You're on a team," he says softly, "and your team WINS when you TRUST each other.

When you LISTEN." Every time he says a word super loud, kids grin. He's got them, even her.

"Speak up when you have ideas," Marcos says. "Make suggestions to your partner. To your team. Who knows?" He stops and pulls at his skinny mustache. "You may have exactly what your team needs to win." He looks around. "This isn't a competition for the strongest or the most athletic. This is about being a team. Working together. The least likely kid may be the secret to your success." He looks straight at little Tess, which seems kind of rude. "Right, Tess?" he says.

She nods at him, seriously.

"You're the lucky ones," Marcos says, gazing slowly from one kid to the next. "Doing team building early sets the tone for the rest of your week at Camp Horizons. You'll have practice. You'll get it. It will help you with everything else."

Marcos talks too much.

Finally, Stacy steps up and starts dividing them into teams. She tells them to set themselves up along a row of volleyball nets that line one side of the field, partners sharing a position—and a bath towel. Breanna walks to the net where Stacy sends her, the cut grass smelling sweet beneath her feet. Cynthia, holding their towel, comes and stands by her. She doesn't say a word. Neither does Breanna.

Over at the next net, Pascale and Tess sit together in the grass, talking quietly. Tess seems like such a little kid. Whoever is in charge of this camp must know about Pascale, that she is a sweet pea, because they picked her, the kindest person, to be Tess's partner. Somebody in charge cared about that little bit of a kid. And maybe it's not the best thing for Pascale. Maybe she would have more fun with somebody else. But she'll be fine. And the thing is, with Pascale, Tess is going to be fine, too.

There's something sweet about the two of them, sitting there. Breanna tucks that image of them into the basket she keeps over her heart to store happy things she wants to hold on to.

Cami, trailed by Rachel the Minion, walks along the edge of the next net over, coming close to where Pascale and Tess sit. Heads together, talking softly, they don't see Cami coming. But Breanna does. She can see what's going to happen and she hurls herself toward them but she should have shouted because she can't get there fast enough as Cami, pretending that she doesn't know exactly what she's doing, sets her flip-flopped foot with her lime-green toenails down on top of Tess's fingers in the grass and stops walking, stops and shifts her weight forward, so it's all on top of Tess's hand and she twists that foot down and stays there, stays there, for two seconds, maybe three.

Tess is crying. Pascale jumps to her feet and glares at Cami. But then Pascale focuses on Tess, pulling her up and draping an arm around her shoulders before looking tenderly at the stepped-on hand.

Cami looks, too. "It's fine. I didn't mean to."

Breanna is there now, in front of Cami. "You did that on purpose," she says.

Cami rolls her eyes all the way up and scoots around Breanna. "It was an accident," Cami calls back, her silky-smooth voice cracking.

Breanna's dad's smooth-talking voice cracks like that, too, when he pretends to be sad or sorry. It is always a lie.

Breanna catches up to Cami striding away. She talks low, so only Cami can hear. "You and me are going have some trouble if you can't find it in your poison, lime-green heart to be a little bit kind to Tess here."

"Geez," Cami says. "What is wrong with you?" Cami glides away and Rachel the Minion hurries behind her. They take their place on the other side of Breanna's net. Cami is playing on the opposite side of Breanna in this team-building game, whatever it is. Good. Breanna can keep an eye on her. And she will.

Breanna is so angry that her heart pounds. She goes back to her place by Cynthia and picks up her end of the towel. She runs the corner of it between her thumb and first finger. It is old and worn, soft and nubbly, calming, which is nice, after what Cami just did. She feels her heart slow down.

She and Cynthia stand there, neither of them talking. They are so close and so silent that Breanna can hear Cynthia sucking on her teeth, *phhht, phhht, phhht.* They have talked twice since they got to camp, once at the chickadee spot and this morning in the cabin when Cynthia was barely awake. It's awkward. Usually Breanna would just start in, say something, like *Talk to me, Southpaw.* But she's been saying that to Cynthia, one way or another, for months, and it's gotten her nowhere. She doesn't know how to start this conversation.

She eyes Cynthia, looking for clues. Cynthia is busy. She's watching other kids, her eyes moving from one pair to another, from one end of the field to the other, like she's studying. Super focused, she stops on partners doing things together with their towels, lifting them on the count of three, slapping them in the air like they're hitting something, moving together from side to side, forward to back, towels almost taut between them. It's interesting to watch Cynthia watching.

Across the net, Cami, fully recovered, says, "When I say three, we lift fast." Cynthia's eyes turn to them. "One, two, three!" Cami shouts. Her half of the towel flies up. Rachel's is late by half a second and jerks out of her hands. "On three, dummy!" Cami shouts. Face bright red, Rachel grabs for the edge of her flailing towel. Cami is mean.

"They're right," Cynthia says. "Counting together is the thing to practice." Cynthia is talking to Breanna.

Okay.

Cynthia's eyes move from Cami and Rachel the Minion to Breanna, then back. "But also," she says, all normal, like they've been talking to each other this whole time, "Look at that guy James and his partner." Holy crap. It's James and Max on the other side of the net. How did Breanna not see them? She feels a little tingly and it's embarrassing, and even though it's amazing that Cynthia is suddenly talking to her, Breanna has a hard time paying attention.

"They drop a little lower on two," Cynthia says. Breanna drags her eyes off James and forces herself to listen. "That's good for height. And see? It's not just up on three." She lifts her side of the towel to explain. "It's up and forward, toward the net. Unless we're setting a shot or something. Maybe, if we can, we name the move before we count. Like *spike* or *over* or whatever we're trying to do. Does that make sense?"

It does not. Breanna cocks an eyebrow. "Hi, Cynthia," she says.

Color rushes into Cynthia's face. The freckles across her nose and cheeks swim in red. "Yeah. Sorry. I'm not sure who's even talking to me these days. And you know . . ."

"*I'm* talking to you!" Breanna interrupts. She's suddenly mad. After this whole long summer of being ignored, she's really mad. "You know *I* am! I've been trying to talk to you for months."

"You're right. I've been a jerk to you, too." Nervously, Cynthia moves the corner of the towel from one hand to the other. But her eyes stay steady on Breanna's face. "You know my mom won't let me play softball, right?"

"Of course I don't know that! You never told me that," Breanna says. "You never told me anything." This news about Cynthia's mother is not good.

"Softball is dangerous for hands." Cynthia looks down at her hands. Her fingers are narrow and long. "At least that's what my mom says. I've got to protect my hands for piano."

"Why?" Breanna snorts out a laugh. "Are you a piano prodigy or something?"

"No. Not even close. But my mom's still hoping."

"That sucks," Breanna says, shaking her head. She means it. That sounds really crappy. It also raises a new obstacle on the softball front.

Cynthia nods. "Tell me about it."

Around them, kids are starting to laugh, a little softly at first, but then hard. Stacy pushes a huge wheelbarrow toward them. It is piled so high you can only see Stacy's feet maneuvering behind it. Orbs of pink, blue, orange, yellow, and green jiggle as she jolts along the uneven grass.

Water balloons.

That's what they're playing volleyball with.

Now that's cool.

Stacy hands out balloons to pairs in serving position and piles up an arsenal beside every net. "The more you work together," Marcos shouts, "as partners and teams, the drier you'll be. Good luck!"

His words are pointless. Even though it's kind of following volleyball rules, it's a water balloon free-for-all.

Cynthia and Breanna try to name shots and count when the balloon plops into their towel. But it's hard to be strategic when you can't stop laughing. A balloon busts against Breanna's shoulder. Another smashes against James's chest. Cynthia takes a fat blue one down her back and gasps.

Across the net, Niraj and Trevor are next to serve. Cynthia grabs a fresh orange balloon from the side and tosses it gently underhand to Niraj. The wobbly water balloon lands exactly where she means it to go. What an arm on that girl!

Niraj and Trevor count to three and serve the balloon from their soaking-wet towel. It clears the net. Partners on Breanna's team send the balloon lurching up in something like a set and another pair sends it close to the net, not over, and fast, so fast, Cynthia and Breanna whip their towel up together and smack the balloon down hard. It clears the net.

But Max and James are there, right there on the other side, and James is humming, softly humming and Breanna can't think of anything but that lovely sound and James stops humming and says something to Max and they catch the balloon in their towel and step back and count and launch that balloon like their soaking towel is a catapult. Faster than you'd imagine a sloshy balloon could move, it flies over the net and James is humming again and Cynthia is talking to Breanna, whose brain is listening to James. *Splat!* The giant orange water balloon smashes right against her forehead.

The cold of the water shocks her as it drips down her hair, her face, her neck. She feels her lips turning blue. For a second, she can't breathe. It's like nobody is breathing. The game has stopped. Everybody is watching her.

James, frozen, stares at her. There is worry in his big brown eyes. Seeing him, worried and beautiful, she breathes. She sucks in a mouthful of air. Exhaling, she busts out laughing, so hard. James's worried eyes turn happy and he grins and his face says *this is great* and he, beautiful he, busts out laughing, too.

"You copacetic?" Stacy, the counselor, is standing next to Breanna, who didn't see her coming.

Breanna doesn't know what she means. But she looks at James, who is smiling at her. "I'm fine," she says.

"Okay," Stacy says. "Step out if you want to take ten."

Breanna shakes her head. She is not stopping.

The game is on. She and Cynthia have figured out their towel, and they are good. And it happens that getting smacked in the forehead with a freezing-cold water balloon is just what Breanna needs to supercharge her already-honed competitive instincts. She and Cynthia start sending water balloons over the net like self-guided missiles. They're unstoppable. On their serve, she lands one on Cami's shoulder. The next on Minion's knee. The next on James and Max's towel. That one comes soaring back and it's a great volley and she can feel James watching her but she keeps her eyes on the water balloon and she and Cynthia work together and laugh their heads off and it is so much fun that she forgets about everything.

CHAPTER TWELVE

AFTER VOLLEYBALL, THERE'S A LOAD OF OTHER TEAM-BUILDING games. It's always the same cohorts, but the exact team changes every time. Breanna's getting to know these kids. Not their names—too many new ones for that. But she's learning their smiles and laughs and whether they dive or duck when a ball comes their way. It's fun. Sometimes James is on her team. Sometimes he's on the other side. Sometimes, he's off with another group and she loses track of him. But she tries not to.

She and Cami end up on opposite teams every freakin' time. It's like camp itself is pitting them against each other. All through the dumb stuff—three-legged races and tent-raising races and newspaper tower-building races, six feet minimum, standing up on their own—there is Cami to compete against. It pushes Breanna to her competitive heights.

As for Cami, she might be good at softball, but she is not good at team building. Not once does Cami's team win. No matter what the game, no matter who else is on her team—Cami loses. It must be Cami's fault. Breanna can't tell exactly what she's doing to make her team lose every time. But Cami and her lime-green toenails are team-building poison.

It's fantastic.

"Okay, everybody," Stacy calls. "We're at our penultimate team-building game."

Breanna looks around to see if anybody understood that.

"Second to last," Cynthia whispers. "Or second most important."

Penultimate is nothing like *chow*, but Breanna would like to know why Stacy doesn't just use normal words like a normal person.

The penultimate team-building activity involves big blue tarps.

And it's impossible.

Teams of twelve, as many as can squeeze onto the blue tarp with hardly room to breathe, have to turn the tarp over—while standing on it. If anybody steps off, the team has to start over.

Impossible.

Breanna and Cynthia stand too close together on the tarp. Cynthia is watching what kids are doing on other tarps spread out across the playing field. It's like how she watched the other kids while they waited for water balloons, trying to figure things out in advance. It's not working this time, though. She's got nothing.

But Max. He's got something. He (and James) are on Breanna's team and Max is moving around from kid to kid on the tarp and talking quietly and sending them places where they start doing things. Pascale and Tess start feeding one of the corners of the tarp underneath itself. He sends other kids to stand, bunched up tight, on two other corners, including the one where Breanna is.

"Max," Breanna says when he comes up to her. "We're all going to die of claustrophobia if you send one more kid to this corner." He sends her and Cynthia to an empty corner, the one opposite Pascale and Tess. Their job is to feed that corner of the tarp underneath itself.

The tarp is getting smaller. Max keeps kids moving so Pascale and Tess and Breanna and Cynthia can keep feeding the tarp under itself. It's tight. It's hard.

"Stop," Max says. "Trade places with James, Cynthia. His arms are longer."

"Right," Cynthia says with a nod, like she gets this. Breanna does not.

But she is dang happy to be kneeling down, feeding tarp under tarp with James, so close to him that she can feel the heat rising from his arms.

Kids move from side to side. The tarp is crowded. Max, calm, keeps things moving. Smiling, he walks to Breanna and James. "I have high spatial intelligence," he says. "I can see exactly how this works in my head. We're going to win."

Breanna believes him, at least the part about his high spatial intelligence. But she's not sure they're going to win. His voice carries. Cami, on the next tarp over, has heard him. She is watching them and telling her team to do exactly what they do, point by point.

"Hurry," Breanna says to James.

"I'm hurrying," he says. But he's so cool—now and always—that Breanna isn't sure he knows what *hurry* means.

"Cami's copying," Breanna says. "We've got to beat her."

"Everybody's copying," James says.

Breanna looks around. He's right. Almost every tarp is falling into a pattern just like theirs. It's not fair. Max solved this—he should win this. "Hurry," Breanna says again. James laughs and his hands go faster. Hers do, too. They roll and reach and once they bump and an electric current runs up her arm.

The tarp is packed and tiny and Max keeps kids moving. He makes Breanna move, and then Tess, too. There's only room for one on the two disappearing corners. All around them, other tarps are getting smaller, Cami's fastest of all. If Cami breaks her losing streak on this game, Breanna is not going to be happy. Breanna watches, eyebrow cocked and angry, as Trevor and Niraj on Cami's tarp shuffle to a new spot. Niraj sees her. He looks up and smiles and waves and bumps into Trevor, who steps off.

Marcos blows a whistle. "Start over," he says.

Cami's team groans. Trevor's face turns scarlet, even his scalp under his tight curls.

Cami is mad. "That's not fair," she tells Marcos. "It was just one foot. It wasn't all the way off."

"We told you the rules," Marcos says.

"Dang it, Trevor," Cami says, once Marcos walks away. "We're going to lose now and it's your stupid fault. Way to go."

"Sorry," Trevor says, hanging his head. But in a second, he and Niraj are helping flip their tarp to start over and they are laughing.

Not Cami. Her leopard lip snarls. Her eyes narrow as she starts giving orders again. Cami is definitely mean.

The tarp is slipping beneath Breanna's feet and Max is pulling her to a new spot that grows behind Pascale, grows and grows. In those seconds that Breanna was distracted by Mean Girl Cami, Pascale, with her long arms, got hold of the corner that James was folding underneath and reaching out to her and she got it. She got it! Now she is pulling the whole thing through.

"Hurry!" Breanna shouts. She's so excited. Kids on a tarp two over are shouting. They're doing the same thing, pulling the tarp through, everybody leaping from one spot to the next. "Hurry! For Max!" Breanna says. *And to beat Cami,* she thinks. The tarp, new-side up, gets bigger and Max keeps everybody moving and Pascale keeps pulling and James is suddenly beside Breanna on the flattening, spreading-out tarp and they are killing it.

"Done!" Max shouts, pumping his arms over his head.

Marcos shrills his whistle.

They win. They win!

This one is exciting in a way the others weren't. All the kids on the tarp start hugging each other. James is coming straight for Breanna, and she panics, goes stupid and dodges left to hug a girl in a headscarf she doesn't even know. She could have hugged James and nobody would have noticed. She blew it. She's such a dope.

Everybody wants to hug Max and Pascale and there's a line in front of both of them. Cynthia, quiet, alone in the crowd, the way Breanna has seen before, waits in line in front of Pascale. Pascale turns to hug whoever is next and she sees Cynthia and there is a pause, a tiny pause, one you wouldn't notice if you didn't know something big might be happening, and then Pascale smiles her sweet pea smile and Cynthia's shoulders unscrunch from her ears and they hug. It's only for a second and they don't look at each other and Cynthia's face flushes beneath her freckles. But she is smiling as she walks away and Breanna knows that if she had half the guts that Cynthia's got, she wouldn't have dodged when James came to hug her.

Everybody's done, long done, except Cami's team. The kids lie in the grass and suck on popsicles and watch the confusion on that last tarp. Without Max to copy, they can't remember how to do it. Cami's giving orders, but it's chaos. And that Trevor. He steps off again, twice. It must be sabotage.

Finally, Stacy gets on their tarp and tells them what to do. They finish, last, by a lot. Breanna, grinning a great big grin, watches Cami's eyes move around the group of gathered kids who just saw her lose big time. Her eyes stop at Breanna and they are cold.

Breanna knows better. But she doesn't stop herself. She can't! She gives Cami two big thumbs-up. Cami's lip snarls and her eyes narrow and they flash at Breanna with what looks like—yeah, it has to be—hate.

CHAPTER THIRTEEN

"EVERYBODY REFRESHED?" STACY SHOUTS. "READY FOR MORE?" A few kids cheer. A very few. "We have one more activity. The ultimate team-building activity. First lunch, and then we start."

Breanna yawns, tired. She thinks of her smelly mattress in cabin 17. She'd like to be snoozing there right now.

Sucking on a grape popsicle, her second, thank you very much, she walks side by side with Pascale up to the main building. Five steps away, Cynthia, walking with Tess, nods her head while Tess talks. She doesn't know how it happened that Cynthia and Tess started talking, but it's like they are a group of four now. It's nice the way it gives Breanna a chance to talk to Pascale alone.

"Well," Pascale says softly. "It's like she's a really little kid. I feel like her big sister. Or her mom."

Breanna flicks her popsicle sticks into the trash can by the porch. "It's what you get, Pascale," Breanna says, "for being such a sweet pea." Pascale laughs at that.

In the cafeteria, Trevor plops himself down next to Breanna. "Hey Breanna," he says. "Is it time yet?"

Holy crap. He's asking about the prank. The prank! Hours have passed and she's been having a blast and she hasn't thought about the prank, not once.

This stupid camp is tricking her.

"Working on it," she lies.

"Cool!" Trevor says. "Whatever you need. I'm your man. Me and Niraj." He pops open his bag of potato chips, pulls one out, and plops it whole into his mouth. Niraj would never let her get away with an evasion like *working on it*. He's going to be bugging her soon, she knows. Besides, time is flying. It's already Tuesday afternoon. The Sky Ropes are Friday morning. Two and a half days. That's all she's got. She's got to think of something, fast.

Geez. She hates those ropes. Just the thought of them scares her so bad.

She grabs hold of the worn cuff of her sweatshirt and rubs it lightly between her fingers. It is soft, soft like the first nubbly blanket from her earliest memory, a blanket she rubbed in the closet in the room with the high-up window in the old house off McNichols. Her mom closed her in there and told her to be quiet, quiet. The touch of that blanket between her fingers calmed her. It's how she learned that texture soothed her.

Suddenly, her prank brain flames. She knows what she needs to do: attack the Sky Ropes, straight on.

She stands up and walks across the cafeteria to where Niraj sits talking to James. She feels her face burn hot; she can't help it around James. But she ignores it. With two fingers, she motions for Niraj to come talk to her, away from everybody. They stand at the big window, looking out over the wide, blue lake. It's smooth today, the sky and water sharing the same soft blue as far out as you can see.

"What's up?" Niraj says.

"Time for reconnaissance. Tonight. You and me and Trevor. Midnight. Front steps of this building."

"Yes!" Niraj says, pounding his fist in the air. "We'll be there."

After lunch, Stacy stands in the middle of the playing field. "It's time for our last team-builder," she says. "It's a doozy of an obstacle course relay race." Breanna could have guessed that much, seeing how Marcos is out in the field, setting up cones by some rows of tires.

"Cool!" Niraj says loud. Of course, he's happy. He's fast.

"Don't get cocky," Stacy says, smiling at him. "It's more rigorous than it looks." Past the tires, Marcos sets out tunnels, the toy kind, for kids. It looks like standard field-day stuff. "We'll divide you into teams," Stacy says. "Each partnership is part of a larger team and does the course together, as a pair." She looks around, waiting, building anticipation. "But here's the convolution." Breanna would like to know what exactly Stacy means by *convolution*. Stacy reaches her hand into a Beecham Public Library tote bag at her feet and pulls the *convolution* out. It is a yellow bandana. "The one doing the obstacles," she says, "wears a blindfold."

"No way!" Niraj says.

"Yes way," Stacy says, grinning at him.

The whole field of kids erupts into wild talking. Cynthia, quiet, looks carefully at the obstacle course Marcos is setting up.

"Pipe down! Let me wrap this up," Stacy shouts. Kids stop talking, but there's suddenly a whole lot of energy in this crowd. Breanna can feel it. "One of you is blindfolded," Stacy calls. "The other one walks along beside them, giving them directions and telling them what to do."

Kids bust out talking again. But Breanna laughs. She thinks of her friend Mitchell, who is off doing who knows what somewhere at camp. He's got one eye. He's going to kill at this game. Cynthia keeps staring at the obstacle course. She's doing that thing, carefully studying one obstacle at a time, figuring this out. Cynthia is a strategist. It's so cool.

Stacy blows her whistle. Everybody keeps talking. "Muzzle it," she shouts. Kids go quiet. *Muzzle it.* Breanna's going to remember that one. Stacy and Marcos organize teams and send kids to their courses. "The task is achievable," Stacy shouts, once everyone is where they need to be. "Give your partner crystalline directions. Stay with them. Coach them every step. But don't touch them." Her voice is hoarse, but she shouts louder. "This part is important. You can only use words. If you touch your partner, curtains! You start over." She grins and yells at the top of her lungs. "Here's the secret: Go slow!"

Like that's going to happen.

The second Stacy shouts, "Go!" the first set of blindfolded kids dashes onto the course and starts falling all over themselves. Niraj plows down two cones before Trevor catches up with him. Cami goes hard left instead of straight. Even coordinated Pascale trips and falls at the tires. There's blood or mud or both on one knee when she stands up. Little Tess wrings her hands.

It's chaos out there!

But Cynthia, standing in line, waiting with Breanna, watches it all, calm and focused.

Breanna elbows her. "I don't follow directions very well," she says.

"No kidding," Cynthia laughs, only half paying attention. Then she says, "Mostly I follow them too well. You know?"

Breanna knows.

Stacy waves in the partners ahead of them. Cynthia pulls her eyes off the course and faces Breanna. "Can you be accurate? Can you tell me exactly what to do?"

Breanna nods.

"I mean it," Cynthia says. "One thing at a time. What direction. Where to step. How many times. Can you do that?"

"Yeah," Breanna says. Cynthia is intense.

Out on the course, somebody yells. It's Max, faceplanted in the grass. James pulls him up—touches him—and they have to start over.

"Okay," Cynthia nods. "If you can be precise at every step, we can totally do this." Her face is glowing. She is into it.

"Red Team on deck," Stacy shouts. That's them. "Get ready." Cynthia adjusts the red blindfold around her eyes and Breanna pulls it tight. Marcos, jogging from one course to the next, runs through and double checks. "Red Team, GO!" Stacy slashes her arm through the air.

Cynthia doesn't move. She waits for Breanna to tell her what to do even on step one. "Start walking, one, two, three," Breanna says. "Step left one baby step. Now straight four. Three more. Stop. You're at the cones." Cynthia doesn't guess. She doesn't do a thing without Breanna telling her. She is smiling. "Left two. Forward, six. Yeah, yeah, like that."

They're doing amazing. Moving the slowest, in a way, but also not messing up. Nobody else is managing that. "Stop," Breanna says. "You're at the tires. Pick up your foot and feel slow where to put it down."

Cynthia picks up her left foot and edges it forward until it pokes the tire. Gliding her toe across the surface, she finds the middle and sets it down. She lifts her right foot up just as carefully, then waddles both feet to the front and starts over on the next one.

Cynthia is a ninja. A careful, instruction-following, obstacle-course-killing ninja.

They're at the tunnel, which most kids dive for and miss. "Stop." Breanna says. "Kneel down. Put your hands out." Cynthia does that. Her hands find the tunnel. She feels all around the opening, puts in one hand, then the other, one knee, then the other. She moves slow, catching her balance every time. These tunnels aren't tied down, and kids have gone rolling straight into other people's courses. Not Cynthia. She creeps, and when it lolls one way or the other, she stops and waits and goes on only when it's still. She doesn't roll anywhere.

She climbs out the other end, and Breanna is right there, super excited. "Quarter turn right," Breanna says, and she must sound as excited as she feels, because Cynthia breaks into a huge smile and red spreads beneath the freckles on her face. "Walk, one, two, three, four!" Breanna says. "That's it! That's it! We did it!"

Cynthia peels off her blindfold and she is laughing and Breanna is laughing and they high-five and hug and look at each other and laugh some more. It's a great feeling. They passed kids who were halfway along when they started. They've given their whole relay team a boost, so that all of a sudden, their team, which had been one of the worst, is definitely in this thing.

Cami, standing behind the finish line, shouts at a boy on her team rolling sideways in the tube, "You've got to be kidding me! What is wrong with you?"

Breanna wants to catch Cami's eye and give her another thumbs-up, so bad. But she stops herself. As she and Cynthia walk past, Cynthia whispers, "The real question is what is wrong with *her*. She's the worst."

Amen!

Cynthia keeps walking away from the obstacle course. "I don't care what *you* do now," she says. "But I can't watch this. We did so well and now our team could blow it. It's too stressful."

"That's cool," Breanna says, surprised again by how much Cynthia cares. This super competitiveness is great for a Gonzo Gazelle. Cynthia's team value is only getting higher. "I'll do what you do," Breanna says, following Cynthia to the edge of the meadow, where the tall grass smells like honey and sage.

Those are Gran's smells. Breanna misses Gran, the way she used to guide Breanna's hands, cutting circles from rolled-out dough, how she used to laugh and kiss Breanna on the top of the head. Breanna inhales as deep as she possibly can.

Out where the meadow turns to trees, she sees Michael Plotz, that boy who was cussing on the bus, liplocked with Lorie Quinn, that girl he was cussing at. Apparently, he's not such a bad kisser after all.

Her mind slips suddenly to James but she shuts it down.

Breanna and Cynthia sit down in the tall, sweet-smelling grass. Lying back, Breanna lets the sun hit her full in the face. She thinks about how Cynthia is a strategist, a good one. What they just did on that obstacle course showed straight-up smarts and teamwork, the secret weapons of the Gonzo Gazelles. Cynthia's going to fit right in. Breanna glances at her, the escaped curls of brown hair along her forehead rising in the breeze. After all these months of working so hard to connect, it's suddenly easy. Softball feels like it's going to happen, for sure. Even with piano hands.

"Breanna, look!" Cynthia lies in the grass, one arm up, one long finger extended. A dragonfly, iridescent blue, its wings whirring, circles and nearly lands and circles and nearly lands and circles and lands on the tip of Cynthia's pointed finger. Its big eyes bulge. Its lacy wings shimmer. The bright sun glints off its narrow body.

Breanna sits up and edges closer, hardly daring to breathe. The dragonfly walks a few steps. Cynthia laughs, her hand trembles, and the dragonfly lifts off, darting around them. It's amazing.

Breanna has been this close to a dragonfly once before, a red one. She remembers, even though she was a really little kid.

There was this empty lot two doors down from her cousins' house, in Mexicantown, in Detroit. There'd been a house there once, but it was abandoned, like things were then, even in Mexicantown, where folks stayed put, if they could. The windows of the abandoned house got broken. The porch collapsed. Then somebody torched it, and it was just an empty, blacked-out basement where all around, the grass grew tall.

It was the best playground. The stuff she found with her cousins down there! A full-on toilet, its white tank cracked down the middle. Rusty box springs that weren't as bouncy as you'd think. A fancy doorknob with a key sticking out. Crazy things everywhere. Creatures, too, fat grasshoppers, chipmunks, pheasants.

But once, on a summer morning, she was sitting in grass like this, listening to her cousins talk about a funny new girl working at La Gloria Bakery and wondering what they could afford to buy there for lunch. A shiny red dragonfly whizzed over Breanna's nose, catching the sun like treasure. She jumped up and tried to grab it with her fat little hands. She chased it till she wore herself out. Her cousins laughed, and then they all went to La Gloria.

It's a sweet memory that she keeps in that basket over her heart. She was always plodding after her cousins, guys, a lot older than her. And they let her. They were good to her. They still are when she gets to see them. It's good to remember that there were happy times in Detroit, before her dad turned into . . . into whatever it is he became.

He'd been good before that. He'd been the one who taught her to swing a bat, to aim a ball, who took her to her first Tigers game, holding her on his shoulders in the seventh-inning stretch, swaying with the crowd as they sang:

Take me out to the ball game,
Take me out with the crowd;
Buy me some peanuts and Cracker Jack,
I don't care if I never get back.

A cloud passes over the sun, and even though it's warm here in the grass, Breanna shivers. Yeah. There were happy times.

But they don't count.

Not after all the crap he pulled before the court said he couldn't come within five hundred feet of her or her mom. Still, he shows up at her ball games sometimes, standing beside his green Chevy truck way out past the bleachers. She can always see him. Those times, it takes all the concentration she can find in the world to block him out and lock down that high-up window in the old house off McNichols. "Fly, baby! Fly!"

"Gather 'round!" Stacy's voice brings Breanna back to now, where grass tickles at her neck and there is no dragonfly in sight.

Why did she do that? Why did she let her brain wander off like that—*again*? She knows better than to think about her dad and let him into her head. But there's something about camp. It's not like regular life where she knows how to manage. Camp is surprising in ways that make her let down her guard—Cynthia, James, the dragonfly. She was ready for camp to suck, and it does. But there are good things, too, really good things, and they are catching her off guard and mixing her up and making it harder to keep everything under control.

Marcos announces the winners of the obstacle course. It's not Breanna's team.

"Crud," Cynthia mutters beside her. She really cared. But it's not Cami's team, either, and that's enough to feel like a win to Breanna.

They walk back toward the main building, the sweet-smelling grass in the meadow crunching beneath their feet. Along the marsh, spotted frogs watch them from lily pads.

"I can't believe we've wasted the whole day playing pointless games," Cami complains. Her silky-smooth voice sidles, the way voices like that do, so that everyone can hear. Cami is looking up a high, high hill. Breanna doesn't mean to, should know better, but her eyes track up, following Cami's gaze, up, up, up, until way up there, on top of the highest of all the high hills out east of camp, she sees a circle of trees and poles and wire cables glinting in the sun. The Sky Ropes, again. Tiny from here, like prison towers for evil fairies. "Other kids are already on the Sky Ropes," Cami's saying. "That's the only reason I came. And we don't get to do them till Friday. This camp sucks."

The Sky Ropes. Crap. Crap. Crap. Breanna's gut clenches. The fun of the afternoon drains away.

Suddenly it's just Breanna and the Sky Ropes and Cami's silky-smooth voice, complaining in the background.

Those ropes. Those evil ropes.

Breanna wants to take them out.

CHAPTER
FOURTEEN

OF COURSE, CAMI WON'T STOP TALKING ABOUT THE SKY ROPES.

The girls are all back in cabin 17, changing out of their sweaty, muddy clothes. Breanna runs cold water hard in the bathroom sink, splashing it on her face over and over, to wash away sweat and dirt and sticky sunscreen. But mostly to drown out Cami, who won't shut up. They've got a little bit of extra time before dinner. It's the only real free time, Stacy explains, that they get all week. Pascale pulls her regulation green garbage out from underneath her bed and grabs some playing cards. "Let's play Scum," she says.

"I don't know how," Tess says.

"We'll teach you," Cynthia says. "It's easy. And it's funny."

"I'm out," Breanna says. "I need a nap."

She climbs up in her bed while two girls she doesn't know sit down with Pascale and Cynthia and Tess on the splintery wood floor to play Scum. She'd like to join them. But this is a chance to think. She wants a prank that takes out the Sky Ropes and she needs to think of it now.

She lies down on the bunk and rubs the slippery edge of her blue sleeping bag between her fingers. Her prank brain revs. It thinks of toilet paper.

It's not original, that's for sure. But if she and her friends could stockpile a serious supply of toilet paper, they could disable the Sky Ropes for at least Friday morning when Breanna is supposed go up. It would take a lot of toilet paper. They'd have to carry it a long way. But Mitchell and Scott would have done the ropes by then, and they'd know how to get there and they could tell her how to deploy the toilet paper for maximum effect. The thought of being under those ropes even just to throw toilet paper over them makes Breanna's gut clench. But it's not the worst idea.

She thinks of the pictures of the ropes from the pamphlets she buried in her yard. Once you're up high, most of the things you climb on—obstacles—are made of rope. Rope can be cut. Rope can be unknotted. With enough kids helping, they could sabotage the course. Breanna tries to imagine her and her friends up on those ropes in the dark. They wouldn't have the safety vests or cables that were also in the pictures. Up there in the trees, they would be undoing the very obstacles that held them up. It would be easy to fall. They could die. No. Absolutely no to that idea.

Her prank brain is going strong. It flashes her another idea: a chainsaw. A freakin' chainsaw. This is what she's looking for. She needs to cut the Sky Ropes down. Of course! That would be the most outrageous, truest prank in the world. And for sure, no one would ever forget it.

There has to be a maintenance shed somewhere. There has to be a chainsaw inside. She's going to find it. That's what she and Niraj and Trevor will be in search of tonight. She knew she'd figure out what they'd be up to before midnight.

She loves this idea. Loves, loves, loves this idea. She's never used a chainsaw, never held one, never even seen one up close. But she has watched Guardian Trees working along Birk Street, where she lives, shearing off the high-up branches of dying silver maples before chainsawing them to the ground. She can almost smell the sweet, free-floating sawdust and feel it sifting yellow through her hair. This is going to be great.

Later, in the cafeteria at dinner, Cami is still talking about the Sky Ropes and all kinds of other unnatural, high places she's been.

Plates clatter. Forks scrape. Hundreds of kids shout to be heard in their conversations. Still Cami's silky-smooth words carry to Breanna from four tables over. She sits next to James, her chair pulled up close to him. "I did these serious high ropes in Costa Rica," she says, loud enough for everyone to hear. "We ziplined through the jungle, so high up in the air that I screamed the whole time." She laughs. "So awesome." She touches James's arm. He smiles and nods, but all the time, he's beating out the rhythm of some song in his head against the table edge, bangs swishing over his brown eyes.

Breanna is staring. She's not even thinking about it. Cami catches her and narrows her eyes in that familiar glare. They are locked in a staring contest.

Breanna's not about to look away. But she wasn't ready. She was sitting there eating lasagna, basking in her prank plans, admiring James, and feeling annoyed about Cami.

Cami has caught her off guard, defenses down.

Now Cami is in her head. She's poking around. Breanna can feel it, like she's peering into the darkest, most secret places that no one is allowed to see.

Cami's lip lifts in that leopard snarl. She's found something. Breanna thinks of the lockbox she keeps under her heart, where all the bad stuff from her whole life lives in permanent lockdown. Everything that has ever made her afraid is trapped and chained in there, so it can never make her afraid again. What if Cami got in *there* somehow?

What if she saw Breanna's terror of the Sky Ropes? It's right there, on top. It feels like she did, the way Cami is looking at her. And what if she saw that high-up window in the old house off McNichols? What if she saw Breanna's dad?

No.

No way did Cami get in there. Breanna's too good. Too careful. Lockdown is lockdown.

Cami's just trying to play her. Breanna can see it in the way her glaring eyes don't look sure, the way the snarling lip dips down for one second, not confident. Cami wants Breanna to think she knows something. But Cami doesn't know anything. She doesn't.

And maybe all that Cami has seen is that little basket over Breanna's heart where she keeps everything good, that dragonfly and how cool it was to do the obstacle course with Cynthia and Max figuring out that blue tarp game and James laughing with her during volleyball, that especially. The basket was right there. Maybe that's what Cami saw, all the stuff that makes Breanna's life amazing, even if she can't afford to play travel softball.

Breanna's got to end this. She tears her eyes away from Cami and rubs the soft cotton of her sweatshirt cuff. She closes her eyes and breathes and the rest of the room comes back into focus so that it's not just Breanna and Cami, locked together in battle. There is James and Niraj and Cynthia at Cami's table. Here, at her table, is Trevor and Pascale and Max. The sun is low out the big window. The lake is deep blue and quiet. Its liquid calm reaches her.

Other conversations find her, not just the silky smoothness of Cami's voice. Unfortunately, lots of kids are talking about the Sky Ropes. She breathes deep again. She can handle it. The cohort at the next table over has gone up already, so of course they can't stop talking about it.

"Did you do the spider web?" a girl with bright green glasses asks. "That was hard!"

"Great view," a skinny guy with a big Adam's apple says. "I could see clear to Cadillac Stadium." The whole table laughs. But it isn't funny. Cadillac Stadium must be three hundred miles away, back in Beecham. Breanna stares down at her plate, imagining the way a chainsaw might vibrate in her hands as she cut through a pole holding the Sky Ropes up.

Almost too soft to hear, Tamar, a quiet girl Breanna knows from Sternmore Academy, says, "I won't be doing that again. Nothing like that at all. That was awful."

Breanna would kill for some contraband noise-canceling headphones.

Her eyes find Cynthia, who sits at Cami and James's table. Her head is down, her lips pressed tight, her face a blank mask. There is a sense of space around her, like she is her own small island. But it seems okay. Like it's what she wants, not what is happening to her. She seems calm and in control—exactly how Breanna wants to feel and doesn't. But Cynthia's also watching, eyes darting from one person to the next, taking it all in, everything, everyone. Niraj, Trevor, Cami, Rachel, James, Pascale. Breanna sees Pascale catch Cynthia's eye and they both smile.

Cynthia is a hawk studying a field full of prey. No. That's not right. She's not a predator.

She's just. Just . . . what?

In fifth grade, Breanna called Cynthia *Miss America*, because she acted perfect. Then *Southpaw*, for her famous left-handed throw. Before that, since second grade in Mrs. Codger's room, where seven-year-olds had to learn the words to explain that evil teacher, Breanna had called Cynthia *Control Freak*.

But that had been wrong, too.

Cynthia folds her arms across her chest while Cami says something very loud about a giant waterslide in Cancun. Cynthia's eyes dart across to Cami, but she doesn't frown like Pascale or roll her eyes like Breanna. No. Cami doesn't get to Cynthia at all. It seems like nothing does.

Cynthia is a fortress.

That's it. *Fortress Cynthia!*

Scanning the room, Cynthia catches Breanna's eye. Her lips turn up in a tiny smile, like they did with Pascale, and Breanna knows that there is a friendly crack, for her, in the fortress, too. She feels a little jolt of joy and tucks the feeling into the basket over her heart.

Fortress Cynthia is her friend.

Some counselor named Roger turns on the microphone. Roger's big arms are tan, his hair sun-bleached, his teeth perfectly straight. "How's your day been, campers?"

A few kids mumble in response.

"What's that?" he asks. "I can't hear you!"

More kids call out, "Good." "Okay."

"I want to hear that your day's been great!" He's one of those. Roger shouts into the microphone and the echo burrs in Breanna's ears. "On the count of three. One, two, three."

"Great!" kids shout.

"One more time!"

"Great!!!" The whole room floods with noise and the microphone screeches and if that guy asks for one more shout, Breanna's going to snap that mic in two with her own bare hands. But he doesn't ask. Instead, he launches into what's next. It's free time, Camp Horizons–style.

There's lots of stuff to choose from: swimming, soccer, board games, nature walks, drum circles, softball. Softball. But the complicated part is that the whole cohort has to agree on what to do—softball—and do it together. First, each table—there are two per cohort—has to agree and then they send an emissary to the other cohort table to negotiate.

"Group consensus," Roger says, mic squawking.

Without even meaning to, Breanna looks at Cami, who is already staring at her. They're on it, both of them.

Softball.

They're going to make this happen.

"Softball," Breanna says to her table. "Softball." "Softball." "Softball." Pascale shakes her head, a look of amused disgust on her face. She knows how things are going to go down.

"How about games," Max says from the other side of Trevor. "You know, board games, inside, sitting down."

Breanna angles a steep eyebrow at him. "Did you even hear what I said?" she asks. She knows she's coming on strong, but she thinks Max can take it.

"Indeed, I did." Max meets her eyes. "Board games, anyone?" The kids at the table laugh nervously. "Softball it is," Max says.

They send their emissary, Rachel the Minion, to Cami's table. Beautiful James comes to them. "I'm a double agent," he says, looking straight at Breanna and smiling his beautiful smile. "My table chose softball." He glances back. "Well, Cami chose softball. But I'm thinking soccer. How about I take that back as the request from this table?"

Breanna snorts. "Softball, dude. We're all about softball here."

James looks at the other kids, but they're all looking down, except Pascale who shakes her head. *Abandon hope*, she's telling James.

Seconds tick by.

"Softball. Okay." James, laughing, puts his hands in the air and shakes his head so that his bangs swish. He is really cute.

Breanna watches James talking to his table, and questions nag at her brain. Did she act just like Cami in making everybody play softball? Do the kids in her cohort think she and Cami are alike? Does James? They're not. She needs to make sure she shows them in the way she plays tonight.

Suddenly Max is beside Breanna, talking at full speed about baseball stats. It's probably interesting. But two tables over, Cami—eyes narrowed in that glare, lip curled up in that snarl—stares again at Breanna. Everything about her, from her stiff, straight shoulders, to the lift of her chin, to the way she stands up without taking her eyes off Breanna, shouts that she is done losing for today.

CHAPTER FIFTEEN

MAX HURRIES ALONG BESIDE BREANNA, STILL TALKING ABOUT baseball stats a mile a minute. They tramp down the trail, across the boardwalk, toward the field. Halfway there, Breanna remembers her glove.

Her glove!

She needs it. It's back in cabin 17, stuffed in the garbage bag under her bed. If she'd have known they were going to play ball tonight, she'd have carried it with her all day, if she'd had to, through every bit of team building.

She always plays with that glove. It's soft and worn from all the balls it's caught, stained black with sweat in spots. It's perfect, the way it fits her hand, the way the fingers mold to hers exactly. Not having her glove is like trying to play with somebody else's hands.

She's in the middle of this pack of kids pushing along the narrow boardwalk being carried along to the softball field. Already she can see the hard dirt infield, the chain-link backstop, the pitcher's rubber.

Doesn't matter. She's running for her glove.

Against the hard tide of kids, Breanna pushes her way back. Once she's on the grass, she sprints, past the main building, through the wooded trails, all the way up to cabin 17. She grabs her mitt from under the bed and slides it on. Cool and soft against her hand, it smells like leather and sweat and summer nights. She wastes precious seconds just feeling it there, comfortable and right.

Then, full out, she sprints again, back to the softball field. The sun hangs low, turning a long line of gauzy clouds over the lake bright pink and orange and purple. She can judge the night sky from her evenings at Sugar Maple Park with her friends this summer. It will be dark soon. They don't have much time.

Breathless, she reaches the field, sure that she'll be joining a game that's already started. But kids are hanging around doing nothing. SheThor, that cool naturalist and camp nurse, stands at home plate, a big equipment bag over her shoulder. Cami, taller, looms beside her. They are deep in a conversation that seems to be holding everything up. Breanna needs to hear this.

"Nobody said slow-pitch when we chose games." Cami's voice is silky smooth, but the edge that's always in it is harder tonight. "That's not fair," she says. "We thought it was fast-pitch. That's a better game. It's what we came to play."

Unmoved, SheThor shrugs. "Sorry for your confusion," she says. "We play slow-pitch at Camp Horizons." Opening the equipment bag, she empties bats and gloves and a catcher's mask out onto the dirt. "This is a place where we work together. It's all about the team here. Slow-pitch is a team game." She cocks her head at Cami. "Not a pitcher's game."

"Roger should have told us." Cami looks out along the huge mown field, where other cohorts are gathering for their games. "I'd be playing soccer right now, not wasting my time on slow-pitch if I'd have known."

Yeah right. Breanna almost laughs out loud. She saw the look in Cami's eyes, the straight-out *I'm coming for you* glare she sent Breanna when they were picking games. It was going to be softball, no matter what.

Watching Cami, feeling her own keen competitive drive rising, Breanna regrets, for a second, the way she flashed Cami those two thumbs-up when her team had to start over on the blue tarp. Things between them were intense enough. She didn't need to make it worse. Pascale wouldn't have done that.

But dang. She wants to beat Cami tonight!

"Sorry," SheThor says. "Slow-pitch."

Heading back to her team, Cami kicks at the hard-packed dirt. A thin layer of dust coats her new white sneakers.

"Let's go!" SheThor shouts. "Who wants to be captains?"

Faster than fast, Cami's arm shoots up. Breanna's, too. Nobody else raises their hands. Really, who would dare? But it's almost embarrassing, the way Breanna, whose goals in life are to win, to be tough and funny, but also kind, not like her dad, is acting just like Cami right now, mean Cami. When it comes to competition, they're the same. But they're not the same in any other way. She needs everybody to see that.

SheThor scans the kids milling around home plate. "Nobody else?" she asks. "Just these two?" She shoves a thumb at Breanna and Cami. "You might come to regret this." A few kids laugh, but nobody else steps up. "Okay. We've got Cami and Breanna as captains." She shakes her head. "Flip a quarter to see who picks first."

It's Cami, of course. She chooses James and gives him a big, non-snarly smile.

Dang. Breanna was going to pick him first. Earlier tonight, walking to the field with Max talking at her ear, she had imagined James shooting her a fast, long throw from right field and her tagging a runner—Cami—out at home. They would high-five, with both hands, then hold on, hold on, for a second, or four.

She's staring at James. It's her turn to pick and she's staring at James. *Get a grip!*

Without a thought, she picks Cynthia. Of course she does. She's been waiting months to have Fortress Cynthia on her softball team. Face blank, Cynthia takes her place next to Breanna. Cami takes Rachel the Minion. Breanna takes Pascale. She knows Pascale's game inside and out, taught her everything she knows.

"Pick Tess," Pascale whispers to Breanna. Tess, that little peanut, Pascale's camp partner. "Don't let her be last, like every other game of her life."

Breanna shakes her head and picks Niraj. They've played a lot of ball together. She knows he can play when he concentrates, and she'll expect him to concentrate.

"I mean it, Breanna. Pick Tess." Pascale does not give up. "I'll make up the difference. Just do it."

Breanna makes a bad decision. "Tess," she says. Dang Sweet Pea. But it's almost worth it, the way some bright light turns on in little Tess's face.

"I've already got our name picked out," Tess announces, running over to join the line of Breanna's team. "We're the Wildebeests." Nobody argues because nobody cares for one night of softball. But the Wildebeests? Please.

Cami keeps picking kids who look like athletes, though most of them are new to Breanna and probably to Cami, too. It's a lot of guesswork, kids from five different schools, only a handful familiar. James keeps whispering to Cami and pointing at Max. Cami never picks him. Breanna doesn't either. She took Tess. That was enough. She gets Max anyway the last pick of the last round. Head down, Max drags his feet along the hard-packed dirt as he joins Breanna's team.

The sun, blazing orange against the dark gray sky, touches the lake by the time Cami throws the first pitch. It's to Niraj, fast Niraj, who can get himself to base in a hurry. It only takes a few pitches for Breanna to see that Cami is really good. Control, precision, variety—inside, outside, deep, close in. She's got mad skills that matter, even for slow-pitch. Lots of fast-pitch pitchers can't switch to slow-pitch. The skills are totally different. Breanna can, though, and clearly, Cami can, too. Still Niraj makes a wild, desperate reach for an outside pitch and connects and his legs churn fast down the baseline and he sprints through first before Rachel the Minion can catch the sleek throw from James in right field.

"Safe," SheThor shouts. She's the umpire. It's good they have an umpire, seeing how pumped up and fierce Breanna feels right now. She wants to crush Cami, grind her under the flaking heel of her worn-out sneakers. Cami feels the same. Breanna's sure she does.

Pascale, another speedster, gets a base hit, too. Breanna, reliable heavy hitter, third in the lineup, needs to bring them home. She watches Cami signal the outfield to move in. In! Just to play mind games. Just to be mean.

It works. Breanna's palms are sweating. Standing in the batter's box, waiting for Cami to stop rolling her shoulders and shaking out her arms, Breanna decides to do a little mind game of her own. "They let you pitch for the Leopards?" she calls. Cami narrows her eyes into that glare. "Bench warmer?" Breanna taunts. "Farm team?"

With a sudden windmilling windup, Cami throws a hard, fast pitch that burns across home plate and flames into the catcher's glove.

Breanna could feel the heat on that ball.

"Ball one," SheThor shouts. She turns to Cami. "That was an illegal pitch and you know it. Do it again and you're off the mound." SheThor folds her arms across her chest and her biceps bulge. She is not a person to mess with. She looks over at Breanna, checking to see if Breanna is rattled.

She is. Very. But she's not going to show it. She meets SheThor's look with a confident nod.

"Follow the rules, Cami," SheThor says. "I'm serious." The thing is, in slow-pitch, the pitcher has to throw the ball up high, high enough to give it an arc. A legal pitch arcs between six to twelve feet up, which means it's never all that fast. Cami's pitch didn't arc at all. It was deadly straight and fiery fast. Illegal but impressive!

Cami tosses the ball back and forth in her hands. She stands on the pitcher's rubber, staring Breanna down.

Breanna's palms are still sweating. Her heart is thumping so loud she thinks Cami might hear it. She sticks out her arm, signaling that she needs a break. She steps away from the plate and wipes one hand, then the other, off on her sweatpants. She looks at Niraj on second, at Pascale on first and takes a long, slow breath. She can do this. She's done this a million times. She steps back into position.

Cami pitches immediately, the ball arcing high and spinning. Breanna watches it. It's coming down. It's falling in her sweet spot and she twists back slightly and pivots forward with all her power and her wrists break and her bat swings and the ball drops to the ground behind home plate.

"Strike one!" SheThor shouts.

That was an incredible pitch—a legal one. It tricked Breanna. She thought it was coming straight down, but it spun away, into the strike zone at exactly the right second. She blew it. Her face burns hot and red.

Stepping away from the plate, she takes a few warm-up swings, just trying to calm herself down. Back in the batter's box, her heart pounds in her ears. Cami's next pitch is lower, but not too low. It's faster. It's dropping fast. It's close. It's good. She swings as the ball moves outside.

"Strike two," SheThor calls. "Helluva pitch," she mutters.

It's true. Cami is good.

Breanna digs her heels into the hard-packed dirt. She grits her teeth and angles her fiercest eyebrow at Cami, who is taking her sweet time. On the rubber, she scratches her elbow, the back of her knee, the top of her head under her black Leopards cap. Breanna's hands are slick with sweat.

Cami pitches without warning. She throws high, twelve feet high, and the ball drops straight down, no curve, no spin, but Breanna can't be sure and it's dropping down fast and it's coming down straight and it isn't breaking and she swings.

"Strike three. You're out."

She missed! She swung too late. The ball dropped straight. It was an easy pitch. And she missed.

She stands at home plate, bat limp in her hand, too shocked to move. She makes the big hits. She doesn't strike out, almost never. How could she have let this happen?

"Batter up," SheThor calls.

Breanna drops the bat and walks to the dugout, disgusted with herself. If she can't hit Cami's pitches, how are the less-experienced Wildebeests going to manage?

But Trevor hits a double, and James overthrows so Niraj makes it home safe. James is not as good as Breanna thought he'd be. At least there's that.

But of course, Tess and Max strike out, like her. And though it's getting dark as the Wildebeests take the field, that doesn't explain how Trevor fails to catch every hit to left field, easy catches, like he's never played ball in his life. By the time SheThor calls the game for dark, Cami's team is up three to one, no outs in the bottom of the first.

Cami moves down the bench, high-fiving each of her teammates. "Let's give a cheer," she shouts. "We're the Roar. Hear us roar!" *The Roar?* That name is worse than *Wildebeests*.

Cami's team circles. "We're the Roar. Hear us roar!" they chant, three times before they shut up.

Leaving the field with her team, Cami shouts, "Thanks, Wildebeests. Good game!" Such a team player. Now that she's winning.

"Yeah?" Pascale shouts. "You think this is over? We'll finish this tomorrow."

Pascale! Oh, geez.

"I can't wait," Cami calls back in her silky-smooth voice. Bright beneath a tall light along the boardwalk, she flashes two thumbs-up.

Breanna wants to slug her.

Cami picked a stronger team. Duh. Breanna has Tess *and* Max. But Trevor looked like an actually coordinated human being who could catch a softball, but he's not and he can't. And Niraj, who's usually decent, was sleepwalking at second base. This is bad. Her team is bad. Cami is going to stomp her. She already has. And— thanks to Pascale—she's going to do it again tomorrow.

Breanna is nothing if not a come-from-behind kind of player. She loves her Rec and Ed Gonzo Gazelles because they're stealthy. They surprise stronger, more athletic teams with their teamwork. But this feels different. The gap between the two teams is huge. Too huge. The Wildebeests—a stupid name her stupid team deserves— are so much worse than the Roar. And Cami herself is the best player Breanna has ever faced. She pitches like she's Major League.

She fields. She hits. She's like a College All-Star. There's no way the Wildebeests can stop that. It makes Breanna sick.

And still, this day, this endless, complicated day, isn't over. There's a campfire session down at the lake.

It's too much.

Walking back in the dark, glove still on her hand, Breanna lags behind, further and further, till she's kind of straggling on her own and she's just about to make a run for it, back to cabin 17 to be alone and get some thinking time in before she sneaks out in a few hours. That would be good.

But here is SheThor, circling back, herding Breanna like an ankle-biting dog, marching her through the marsh, past the main building, down the long wooden stairs to the water, on to the next thing, like it or not.

CHAPTER SIXTEEN

BREANNA WALKS SLOW DOWN THE STAIRS TO LAKE OJIBWE, SheThor close behind her. It's not that she's trying to take off, not anymore. It's not even that she wants to be alone to think, which she does. It's just that, as the dark lake opens up in front of her, it's beautiful, almost too beautiful to handle. She has to stop and stare.

Above her, the sky, already shifted from deep purple to black, shimmers with more stars than Breanna has ever seen. Ten million as big as your pinky nail, another ten million as small as a pin, they hang in swirls and tangles that reach and whirl up into some wide and endless covering, like the sky is the great, grand ceiling of the world and this is a special-occasion place she's being allowed into for the very first time.

"I never get over it," SheThor says. Breanna jumps. She'd for-gotten that SheThor was there. "I never get used to how gorgeous this place is."

Out over the lake, a bright moon shimmers silver across dark water. Perfectly still on the stairs, Breanna hears soft waves lap against the shore. "Yeah," she whispers. "Gorgeous."

Tucked back against the hill, the red-gold glow of campfires stretches out along the sand. Their sweet smell fills the air. "You're at the fourth one to the left," SheThor says. "I checked."

"Okay," Breanna says.

And it is okay, she finds, walking to that bright fire, joining a bunch of kids she knows better than she did this morning, all of them here, under the beautiful stars.

Seeing her coming, Cynthia pats the old log she's sitting on. Breanna edges through a few kids standing behind the logs that roughly circle the fire. Pascale and Tess sit in the sand in front of them. Pascale's legs are stretched out long, her head is thrown back, and she is staring up at the beautiful sky, looking so happy.

"Everybody's afraid." Marcos is talking, standing in the middle of the circle, the campfire casting half his body in light. "I'm afraid every day. Little things, like where to plug in my phone because my battery is at seven percent. Big things, because scary stuff could happen to my family. Real things. Bad things. Today or tomorrow."

They're talking about fear, of course. Breanna does not need this right now.

"I can't fix all the things I'm afraid of," Marcos says. "Sure, some I can. There's almost always a plug to charge my phone."

.

A few kids laugh. Not Breanna. This talk of being afraid is bad for her. Thinking about fear is bad for her. She rubs her fingers against the log beneath her, feeling how the surface is rough, here, and over here, but smooth in most places, worn down by lots of butts. Touching this fallen tree calms down her brain, which, with Marcos talking about fear, was starting to go someplace she didn't want it to.

"The other stuff?" Marcos says. "The stuff I can't change? I just admit my fear is there. I say, 'Oh, you again. Hello.'" He raises up his palms and shrugs. "On bad days, do you want to know what I do?"

No. Thanks for asking.

"I picture my fears, my worries, as a parrot."

Across the fire, James smiles. James. He must have been right there, with the fire like gold on his skin, this whole time. How could Breanna have missed him?

"Yeah," Marcos says. "A parrot named Eduardo. Loud and squawky with his feathers all messed up, resting on my shoulder. On the worst days, I swear I feel that sucker digging his claws into my skin."

That gets a big laugh.

Ha. Ha. Ha.

In the sand, Tess, leans back against Breanna's shins. It's weird, but it feels good, a buffer between Breanna and Marcos and his fear parrot, Eduardo.

The fire pops. The embers glow black and red.

Breanna concentrates hard on blocking out what Marcos is saying. She's heard enough. She's sick of fear. What he's saying is too easy. Fear as a parrot you let rest on your shoulder? No way. More like a Dementor coming to suck everything good out of your life and memory and that little basket over your heart. The best strategy, the only strategy—she knows—is to lock fear down.

She's got it figured out. That big metal lockbox under her heart is wrapped around with seven chains and done up with a padlock as big as your face. She's been slipping stuff into it for years, sneaking it in fast, when nobody's looking, and slamming down the lid. Most everything in there is from the bad days, when her dad was at his worst, pounding on the door because he couldn't get his key in the lock, late, late, at night, in that tall old house off McNichols, her mom saying it was all a game, making her a nest of soft cotton blankets on the closet floor and whispering, "Don't make a peep, baby bird." Breanna rubbing the softest blanket between her thumb and first finger and calming down. Her mom, in the morning, pouring Cheerios into Breanna's bowl, shushing her when she asked about her puffy black eye and her red and purple cheeks, while her dad smoked on the other side of the table, the tip of his cigarette glowing in the morning dark, no lights on, the way he wanted it and that cigarette, its smell, its sizzle when he calmly reached over to snub it out on Breanna's little shoulder.

There it is.

Breanna sits up straight. Her knees knock into Tess's back, and Tess gives a little yelp.

The whole problem with this stupid camp!

This camp is bad. It treats fear like a game, asking her to challenge herself to do phony things she's afraid of, when she's got a whole world of fear from her real life sitting just below her heart and it isn't made-up. All this talk about fear, plus all this nature, and its sneaky way of making her let down her guard, plus the

Sky Ropes looming over everything. It's getting to her, making her sloppy. She's letting things jimmy at the padlock and rattle the chains. Stuff she never, ever, ever thinks about is pushing out and sneaking through and making her think about her dad.

Her dad!

No.

Not him.

His place is the lockbox. Only there. What happened with him is over and she's handled it and it's stored safe in her lockbox that nothing is coming out of and nothing new is going in to.

She won't let this stupid camp throw her off her game. She won't.

"I've got fear muscles now." Marcos is still talking. "Admitting I'm afraid helps me be braver. I know that doesn't make sense. But it's true."

It is not.

"Doing something even though I'm afraid makes me stronger."

It does not.

"And so I practice, and I get braver and stronger in the face of fear. That's what I mean by building up your fear muscles."

Please. Shut. Up.

And he actually does. But it's Stacy's turn now. Fine. Let her do her best, the glitter-loving lightweight. She's not getting through.

"The whole point of the physical challenges at Camp Horizons," Stacy says, "is to build your confidence by pushing the boundaries of what you think you can do. We present you with safe but difficult things and invite you to do them—the Sky Ropes being the most obvious example." She pauses and looks up at the dark sky. "But lots of things here are scary. We acknowledge that. We are trying to give you know-how to help you deal with the reasons you don't want to try things. The biggest impediment is always fear. Right?" She looks around at the group. Kids are listening. Breanna is listening, even though she doesn't mean to be.

"For some of you, the Sky Ropes will be easy-peasy," Stacy says. "Lucky you. For others, standing under them and looking up will terrify you. If that's you and you guide your partner through them, which will be your job when the time comes, you'll have done something courageous, no question."

Across the circle, James pokes at the fire with a long stick. Smoke billows up and he half disappears. Still Breanna sees him nodding slowly. He is buying this fancy speech about phony hard things. He may be beautiful, but that doesn't make him smart.

"Here's what we're asking you to do," Stacy says. "If you feel afraid, acknowledge it. Say, 'Hello, Fear!' Try to do one thing, just one thing, that really scares you." She swipes hair out of her face. "The truth is, camp life is full of scary. The cafeteria. All these new kids. Feeling all alone in the crowd. Is that you?" She looks around the circle.

In front of her, little Tess vigorously nods. Pascale, fingers glowing in the firelight, reaches up and rests a hand on her shoulder.

"Find one person. Say *hi*."

Tess nods harder. How embarrassing for her.

"The cabin, sleeping away from home, maybe for the first time. The night noises. The dark. Is that you?"

Nobody responds. Really, who is going to admit to that? But everybody's listening, leaning toward Stacy in the middle of the circle. "Tell your camp partner. Maybe say, 'I can't sleep.' 'I miss my mom.' 'I'm scared.'"

Suddenly Stacy ducks as something dark and swift swoops low over the circle. "Eek!" Stacy says. "Bats. That's mine. Hellacious bats. I'm terrified, even though I know they won't hurt me." Two more swish close and Stacy gasps. But she's still there. Still up there talking.

Breanna knows what it means to hold on and keep going in the face of scary things. She respects that Stacy is doing that, up there in front of them. Respects it for real.

"Let's open it up to the group," Stacy says. "Does anybody want to confess something they're afraid of?"

What a question! Does Stacy really think that anybody's going to answer that, expose themselves to all these kids?

But Tess's hand is already up in the air. Breanna wants to lean over and say, *Don't do it, Peanut. Don't let anybody see you sweat.* But it's too late. Stacy calls on her.

"I'm afraid that nobody will like me," Tess says. "I'm afraid that I'll be bullied again. Like in my last school." Pascale's arm slips around Tess's shoulders.

"Oh, Tess." It's Cami. She's standing behind James, her face in shadow. "You know we only tease you because you're cute and little. We don't mean anything by it." Breanna hears the edge in Cami's silky-smooth voice.

"Cami," Stacy says. "I'm glad you have kind feelings toward Tess." Yeah, right. "But here's the thing: Tess answering my question was very brave. And it isn't actually supportive if, in response, you tell her that she shouldn't feel what she feels."

Whoa, Stacy! Straight-up calling Cami out. *That* is not light-weight, not lightweight at all.

Firelight just reaching her narrowed eyes, Cami folds her arms against her chest and slumps deeper into shadow.

And somehow, after that, the conversation takes off.

James says, "My brother joined the Marines last month. I'm proud. But I'm scared, too."

Pascale says, "I worry about my sister leaving for college. I'll be the only kid at home. My parents will ask *me* all the questions."

Max says, "I'm scared of making my softball team lose." Amen to that.

It goes on like this forever. These kids are a bunch of scaredy-cats.

Breanna can't help but notice that Cynthia doesn't say a word. She sits, perfectly straight on the hard, uncomfortable log, sucking, *phhht, phhht, phhht,* on her teeth. Fortress Cynthia. Breanna would love to know what she's thinking right now.

Later, much later, after roasting marshmallows in the embers, after walking back to the cabin, flashlights searching the woods for El Chupacabra, after getting things just so for sneaking out fast, after lights-out, Breanna feels Cynthia's heel poking at her through the mattress.

Blinds pulled, the cabin is pitch dark. Outside, peepers croak. Crickets click. Skunk spray hangs in the air. "You awake?" Cynthia whispers.

"Yeah." Breanna says.

"What did you think of that talk down on the beach? It was kind of intense." Cynthia is asking Breanna exactly what she wanted to ask Cynthia.

"Ummm. Snooze fest," Breanna says. She's not ready to tell Cynthia what she really thought, how it made her feel off balance and scared.

"I didn't like it," Cynthia says.

That's interesting. Breanna didn't like it either, but she can't make herself say so. They lie in the dark, quiet. But Breanna feels like talking. She angles her elbow up on her soft, smiley-face pillow. "You didn't raise your hand to answer Stacy's question," she says.

"No."

"So? Would you tell me? What you're afraid of?"

There is a long silence. Finally, so quietly that Breanna can barely hear, Cynthia talks. "Lots of things," she says. "Everything. I think I'm afraid of everything."

Breanna didn't expect that, not from Fortress Cynthia. She sits up in the dark and looks down the row of bunks to make sure that there's no sign of life from Cami's bed, the one closest to the door and farthest away. There isn't.

She wants to hear more. She wants to hear it all. But she doesn't want to seem too interested, in case that spooks Cynthia. She lets seconds go by. Softly, she says, "What do you mean?"

"Everything. I'm serious." She is not speaking in her Fortress voice. "My parents have this idea that I'm some kind of genius and I'm not dumb but I'm not special and I can just see how everything I do is less than they want. I disappoint them all the time. It's scary and it makes me sad and it's going to get worse, because the big ones are still coming, you know, like not being able to keep up with the real piano prodigies and not getting into Harvard and not being a PhD brainiac, like them. There's all that." She stops and takes a deep breath. "But what I'm most afraid of right now is that I'll never have friends again, after what I did last year."

Breanna stares into the dark, stunned and kind of thrilled at how Cynthia just told her all this real-deal stuff. Cynthia trusts her. Breanna wants to say something back that shows she trusts Cynthia, too. That's what Pascale would do. But Breanna has no idea what to say. She could tell Cynthia that she's brilliant and can go to college anywhere she wants, but she doesn't know if that's true. Or that people are going to forget about what happened last school year, and maybe they will but maybe they won't. Or that she, Fearless Breanna Woodruff, is afraid of stuff, too.

Right. And then Cynthia will say, *Of what?*

And what's Breanna going to do then? Tell her? Say Cami's pitching? Heights? The Sky Ropes? Or totally go for it and say what she's only said to her mom and once to funny Mrs. Diehl, the counselor she talked to for one whole year at the pediatrician's office, *You know what I'm scared of? I'm scared of my dad.* She can taste those bitter words. They're right there, on the tip of her tongue. But they won't be said. Even if she wants to say them. Which she probably does not.

It seems like a long time before she finally thinks of something that feels okay to say. "I'm your friend," she speaks into the dark. "You have me. You know that, right?"

"Well, you texted me enough this summer." Cynthia laughs and it's loud enough that Breanna checks the row of sleeping girls again.

"Even if you don't like me, you think I've got a pitching arm, and that seems close enough."

"Truth," Breanna says, a smile spreading across her face.

In the quiet dark, Breanna leans down and rolls the window blind open. She wants to see the fat moon through the oak tree again tonight.

Ah! It's there, its silvered light seeping through the branches. Tess mumbles and rustles in her sleeping bag. Pascale breathes deeply, out and in.

"Are you asleep yet?" Breanna whispers to Cynthia.

"No."

"I'll tell you a secret."

"Okay," Cynthia says, her voice slow and heavy.

"I think James is beautiful." Geez! She can't believe she said that! What a stupid thing to say. She didn't mean to do that.

But Cynthia doesn't say a word. Breanna hears her heavy, even breathing. She's asleep. Maybe she didn't even hear.

CHAPTER SEVENTEEN

THE CABIN IS SILENT. ALL AROUND HER, GIRLS BREATHE HEAVILY.
Sleeping, Pascale mutters what sounds like *grapefruit*.

Lying in the dark, waiting, Breanna uses one of the three flash-lights she brought from home to look at the watch on her wrist.

It's an old watch, for little kids, with Hello Kitty hands point-ing the time, that Jorge, her cousin she loves best, gave her for her seventh birthday. She's kept it ever since, because it was from Jorge. She doesn't wear it anymore, of course. But she couldn't bring her phone, and sneak-outs require precise time-tracking, so she needed the watch for moments like now.

Hello Kitty's little hand points to eleven, her big hand to ten. It's 11:50. Time to go.

The moon is high and bright. The oaks and pines that line the trail through the cabins sigh in the wind. Breanna's flashlight shines a bright beam over the soft, pine-needled ground. She feels the hair on the back of her neck prickle as the hulking shadow of a raccoon rises along the side of a cabin. She shivers and smiles. She loves that feeling.

Niraj and Trevor are already there, waiting on the front steps of the main building. She knew that they would be here already, that, totally into this, they would come early.

"What are we doing?" Niraj asks, his hands running up and down his half-bare arms. He's only got his T-shirt on and it's cold.

"We're going to find the gardening shed," Breanna says. "Or maybe the tool shed. We've got to break in."

"Wow!" Trevor says. "This is radical."

"Okay. What are we looking for?" Niraj asks, calm and ready, like the professional prankster he is.

"Chainsaw," Breanna tries to say it cool.

"Chainsaw?" Trevor asks, sounding like he wasn't expecting that.

"Yep," Breanna says.

"What are we going to do with a chainsaw?" Trevor asks. "Dude, have you ever used a chainsaw? Do you know how they work, because I don't, and my guess is that they aren't that easy to use and that lots of things can go wrong and are you sure about this?"

"No," Breanna says. She's not going to lie to these guys. "But if they have one and I can get my hands on it, then I'll figure it out." They are walking now, along the grass in front of the main building, through the dark, each of them sending one of Breanna's flashlights beaming out ahead.

"Where's the shed we're going to?" Trevor asks.

"I don't know." Breanna doesn't lie about that, either. "Have either of you seen some place that might store tools or equipment or, you know, a chainsaw?"

"You know what?" Trevor says slowly. "I did. The first day, when we came in on the bus. By that CAMP HORIZONS sign over the road, there was a building, like a big shed." They've stopped while Trevor delivers this valuable news. His flashlight beam keeps going, shining everywhere, road, bushes, sneakers, sky. "There was a truck parked in front that said CAMP HORIZONS on the side and in the bed was a wheelbarrow and stuff that looked like rakes and shovels and all that kind of yardwork stuff, you know?"

"That sounds like exactly the place," Breanna says.

"That sign over the road was a long way back." Niraj says it with a sigh. But he starts walking again. Their flashlight beams guide them across the pitted parking lot and down the bumpy road they came in on. The moon hangs high and round and bright. Past its glow, the stars twist up into the deep dark. High-up wind rocks the tips of the pines and carries that sweet pine smell down to Breanna, walking in this beautiful night.

At 12:33, Breanna looks at her Hello Kitty watch. It's so late. They've walked a long time after this already tiring day.

Two minutes later, Trevor says, "It's right here."

And it is. A big shed, just like Trevor said. Breanna runs her flashlight over a long, low building covered in rusted white aluminum siding. She tracks the beam across three windows that run down one side. Walking to the other side, she finds two windows and a door with a dull yellow porchlight, weak in the dark.

In front, off the road, a gravel driveway leads to a dented gray garage door.

"Way to go, Trevor," Breanna says, shining her light on him. He has totally earned her respect, coming through on the shed like this. He grins wide.

"Now what?" Niraj says.

Breanna lights him up and he shields his eyes. "You know what," she says.

"Yeah, I do." He laughs. "I do. I do."

Together they walk to the barely lit door. Breanna tests the round doorknob. Locked. They move from one window to the next, checking the latches. Locked. Locked. She is not deterred. There are three more windows and a garage door still to check.

"I know," Trevor says. "Let's put a rock through one of these windows." Bright in the beam of Breanna's flashlight, he's holding a stone that fills his big palm. She can't tell if he's joking, but she's pretty sure he'd throw it if she said to.

She rolls her eyes, but he can't see in the dark. "No," she says. "A good prank takes discipline."

"Yeah," Niraj agrees. "That's one of the reasons Breanna is the best. Discipline."

Niraj might not say that if he knew she wanted to chainsaw the Sky Ropes down. But she appreciates the support. Trevor's stone thuds down to the grass.

They check the three windows along the other side. Locked. Locked. Locked. Niraj runs his flashlight over the gray garage door as Breanna searches for a handle to try. She finds one, on the far side, rusted and worn. She grabs it and yanks with all her might. The unlocked door flies up.

"Dude," Trevor says. Shining his flashlight inside, he illuminates a truck.

Breanna shines her beam inside, too. She sees the truck that fills most of the front part of the shed. Backed in, facing out, it is dark green, the bumper crumpled, the left headlight broken and drooping. Along the grill a crust of rust crackles up to meet the Chevy bow tie centered in the middle. Breanna knows this truck.

It is her dad's truck.

He is here. Somewhere, close by, in the dark, he is here.

Unable to move, she stands, staring at the truck. Her eyes won't blink. Her feet won't turn away. Her hand won't hold her flashlight. It clatters to the gravel and the light goes out. The world goes blank. No moon. No stars. No friends.

Just her. The green truck. And her dad.

She needs to shout. She needs to scream, *We've got to get out of here!* But her mouth won't open and her throat is tight and that high-up window in the old house off McNichols is leaking out of her lockbox.

She hears herself make some strange sort of choked noise. Niraj, edging past the green truck, must hear it, because he suddenly swivels his flashlight around and shines it right in her face. Seeing her, he freezes. "What's wrong? Is something wrong?"

Breanna feels dizzy. "I need to sit down," she says, dropping hard to the gravel of the driveway. Her legs won't hold her. Her head is sloshing. The ground beneath her moves in waves, like she is in Lake Huron, on a rare vacation with her mom and the clouds roll in and the waves start to foam and her mom yells from the bluff, "The wind just shifted. Get out now," and she knows she needs to hurry but her legs won't work.

She is paralyzed, collapsed on this driveway that moves in waves, staring at a green truck, almost invisible in the dark shed. Niraj is beside her now. He stands over her, his flashlight beam bathing the top of her head. "Breanna," he says quietly. "Is this the prank? Are you pranking Trevor and me?" Breanna can't see his face, but his voice sounds unsure. She shakes her head no.

The flashlight beam spreads wide as Niraj settles on the ground beside her. She feels sad that Niraj would think that she would prank him like this.

"Breanna," he says, his voice gentle. "Breanna, what's happening? You're scaring me. I've got a water bottle. Do you want some water? Are you dehydrated? I fainted once when I was dehydrated." He hands her the water bottle he carries everywhere.

It is metal, cold, and smooth in her hand. She runs her fingers over it and feels the misty damp of invisible condensation along the surface. Touching it helps. Her heart slows down. Breathing deep, she unscrews the lid. She takes a long drink and feels the water cold against her teeth and tongue and throat.

Niraj pats her three times on the back. It's awkward. But he is trying to help her, she knows that. She pulls the bottle away from her lips and lets the cold water splatter down her chin and fall onto her sweatshirt. She needs to feel that cold against her skin. Feeling that—feeling something—might stop the motion of the waves beneath her, might push down the memories busting free of her lockbox.

Trevor wobbles out of the shed. His flashlight, clamped between his teeth, lights up three super-size packs of toilet paper mounded in his arms. He says something—Breanna can't tell what because of the flashlight in his mouth—then stops, eyeing her and Niraj sitting together on the gravel. The toilet paper thuds to the ground as he pulls the flashlight from his mouth. "No chainsaw," he says. "But so much other cool stuff. Weed whackers. A riding mower. Giant tree loppers. We could do something crazy with this stuff, right?"

Trevor, in that second where he stood, flashlight in mouth, toilet paper in arms, corkscrew hair shining in the light from Niraj's flashlight, looked funny. He still does, kicking at the huge packs of toilet paper he dropped to the ground. Funny. Just what Breanna needs right now. She laughs once and the cold waves of gravel beneath her go quiet. Just that fast, her brain starts getting right and she knows that the truck in the shed is just a truck. A green Chevy truck, not her dad's. She feels jangly, for sure, her legs as mushy as microwaved burritos. But whatever just happened is over.

Trevor said there was no chainsaw. She remembers and floods with relief.

A chainsaw?

What was she thinking?

How many millions of things could go wrong with that? People could get seriously hurt. This is the least disciplined idea she's ever had. And she was into it. She was!

Her brain is jumping from horror to comedy and she's starting to shake, deep down, with laughter that she would like to hide. She should probably answer Trevor, who stands looking at them, but she's thinking about everything that could go wrong with a bunch of kids and a chainsaw and she cannot believe herself right now.

Niraj, dependable talker that he is, steps in to save the moment. "We didn't find a chainsaw either," he says. "We looked for it and it wasn't there and that's what we needed to know and we've been waiting for you to finish."

"Right." Trevor says. He picks up one of the toilet paper packages on the ground and holds it up high. "So much toilet paper. Loot chest, dude." He grins in the bright light of Niraj's flashlight.

Loot chest, dude. Trevor is so funny. Breanna, still sitting on the cold ground, quietly rumbles with laughter. It's 1:00 in the morning. She's brought Niraj and Trevor out in the dark in the middle of nowhere in search of a chainsaw and Trevor has found a mountain of toilet paper instead. She laughs harder and it's not quiet and she can't stop and she is doubled over on the ground and holding her belly and tears are running down her face and she is laughing and she can't stop.

Niraj watches her. He's close enough in the dark that she can see a few teeth show in a quiet smile. He gets to his feet and dusts off his butt. "This is so great," he says. "We know where to get all the toilet paper we want if we need it. Way to go, Trevor." He's making this make sense to Trevor when it actually doesn't make sense at all. He's protecting her. He is the best. He holds out a hand for Breanna and pulls her up. "Right, Breanna? We don't need toilet paper tonight, do we?"

"Right," she says, wiping her face off with the sleeve of her sweatshirt, her laughing spell finally past. "Tonight was reconnaissance. That's all. Let's stash it back in there for now. Maybe we'll decide to use it later." Trevor and Niraj carry the toilet paper back inside. Breanna can hear the quiet murmur of their voices, then their laughing.

Niraj has done her a solid tonight. He's given her cover in front of Trevor. It's bad enough that Niraj saw what he saw. But he's a true friend. Trevor, she doesn't know. It would have been way too humiliating if he had seen how she dropped at the sight of that truck.

Trevor bounces as they walk back to camp, his flashlight skittering everywhere, his voice trailing off as he rushes ahead or drops behind, chasing moonlight and shadows and El Chupacabra.

Niraj, who would usually be bouncing himself, walks close to Breanna's elbow. It feels like if she hesitates at all, he's going to grab her arm and steady her. She doesn't like that. She doesn't need him to look after her. But she knows he's being kind and that he is worried.

The walk back is long. Her flashlight won't work. She feels tired.

After about ten, slow minutes, Niraj quietly asks, "What happened back there?"

She doesn't know what to say. But he has been so good to her tonight that she wants to tell him something. "Niraj," she says. "It was the truck. It's just dumb."

"What do you mean?"

She swallows hard. Not even funny Mrs. Diehl, the counselor at the pediatrician's office, knows that Breanna is scared of green trucks. It's barely something Breanna can admit to herself. She doesn't know how she can explain this to Niraj, who, more than anybody else, believes in Fearless Breanna Woodruff.

She decides to try. "My dad," she says. In the moonlight, she sees Niraj's wide eyes settle on her face. "My dad drives a green

Chevy truck. Like the one in the shed." They walk on, their feet launching pebbles out into the dark.

For once in his life, Niraj doesn't talk. Breanna swallows again, pushing back a bitter taste in her mouth. "He wasn't—he isn't— nice," she says, reaching for the cuff of her sweatshirt and rubbing it gently between her thumb and first finger. "He was great when I was really little. And then he wasn't. He was mean. I moved to Beecham because it wasn't safe at home."

They take a few more steps. Niraj is still silent, and Breanna has said all that she can. She has never told a friend anywhere near this much about what has happened to her.

Niraj takes a deep breath. "I'm really glad you weren't pranking me," he says. "I would have been mad at you for getting me out of bed in the middle of the night to prank me."

Niraj is talking to her like normal. What just happened and what she just said haven't changed the way he sees her at all. In fact, somehow, things feel better, clearer. She can't quite believe it, but she is straight-up grateful. "I'm sorry it was a waste," Breanna says.

"A waste?" he says. "What do you mean? We broke into a shed. We found the toilet paper motherlode. You spilled your guts to me— and I won't tell. I get that. It's been a great night, Breanna. The best!"

Tears prickle in Breanna's eyes. She wants to hug Niraj, but that would be weird. "No, Niraj," she says. "You're the best. I mean it." And she does.

He grins. His teeth are wide and white under the moon. "One thing I need to know, though," he says. "Were you really looking for a chainsaw?"

"Yeah," Breanna says, "I was." She laughs and her voice echoes out into the dark.

"What the heck?" Niraj says. "What did you want a chainsaw for?"

"For chopping down the Sky Ropes."

Niraj busts out laughing so hard in the middle of the dark road that he can't walk. He throws back his head and the night comes alive with his laughter, the trees rocking and the clouds pausing and the stars, ten million stars, dropping closer, just to hear. His flashlight shakes in his hand, its light bouncing everywhere. "You mean that! I know you mean that. *G-O-A-T. G-O-A-T!*"

Breanna feels her face burn with pleasure. It's so much fun when he tells her she's the best. It's so much fun to sneak out and do bad stuff with him, even if it doesn't get them anywhere.

They can't stop laughing about sawing down the Sky Ropes all the way back to the main building. "Cutting down Sky Ropes," Niraj says. "Now that would be life-changing, just like they say the Sky Ropes should be."

Not for the first time in her life, Breanna pictures the Stillwagon Juvenile Hall of Detention off Platt Road in Beecham. Really, what was she thinking?

Back at camp, they linger on the front steps of the main building. "This was a blast," Niraj says.

"Totally," Trevor says.

"I'm glad there was no chainsaw," Niraj says.

"Same," Breanna says. "Same." And then they bump fists and head back to their cabins to get a few hours of sleep before morning.

DAY THREE

WEDNESDAY

CHAPTER EIGHTEEN

NEXT MORNING, BREANNA IS THE FIRST ONE AWAKE. SHE COULD USE more sleep, but her brain races with what happened last night. That was crazy.

Then she remembers the doe. She'd forgotten about that strange moment alone on the softball field staring at that beautiful, scarred doe. But thinking of it now, sunlight pouring in through her open window, the air in the cabin cool and fresh, she can't imagine how she forgot about it for one second.

The creature fills her brain. She thinks of the warmth from the doe's nostrils curling white in the morning chill, of the soft sleekness of her tawny brown coat, of the huge scar stretching across her legs, chest, and neck. Oh, she was beautiful.

Breanna wants to find her.

She pulls her soft old University of Michigan sweatshirt over her head. She slips on her sneakers and tiptoes across the splintery wood floor. It doesn't squeak, only sighs softly, like a slow release of breath, like it's being quiet on purpose, helping her, so that, for a few minutes of glorious freedom, she can sneak out and find her doe.

Running lightly down the trails, she breathes in the crisp air. No tall walking birds block her way. She asked Stacy about them yesterday. "Sandhill cranes," Stacy had called them. She'd said they were "mostly harmless," and laughed like that was funny. Breanna didn't get it.

There is Scott, standing on the porch of the main building again, waiting for breakfast. One fat white goose waddles around the corner toward him, and she feels that flicker of an idea that came yesterday. She slows down, focusing her brain to see if she can fan it into something visible.

And then she's got it. Those geese. Those fat, funny geese. They could be Niraj's raccoons, for his prank idea! *1, 2, 4.* A second goose wanders on to the porch and pulls at Scott's shoelace, untying it. What a tame baby. But still—an animal who doesn't belong inside a building. It could work.

She pictures kids coming into the cafeteria and finding counselors chasing geese. It will make them laugh. They'll talk about it and wonder who did it and she'll make sure the blame falls on her and not Niraj. Hey! It might be good enough to get her sent home. Really, this late in the game, that might be just right. She feels an unexpected prick of sadness at the idea of going home. There are things she likes about this camp, likes a lot.

But not the Sky Ropes. That's what the prank is really about, fighting the Sky Ropes. She can't attack them straight on. She learned that last night. But something that helps her skip the Sky Ropes completely and makes kids talk about that girl who got sent home for her funny prank? That seems pretty great right now.

She picks up speed again, her reliable prank brain starting to organize. She'll talk to Niraj in the cafeteria. They'll pull it together today and be ready by tomorrow morning. This will work.

She feels sure of herself, maybe for the first time since Monday night, telling everyone about El Chupacabra. That was a moment where she took charge. Now she's doing it again, not in the undisciplined way of last night, but in the realistic way she knows how to do. This is how camp is supposed to feel.

The feeling lasts five seconds. Because, just past the end of the boardwalk, a giant boulder waves wildly. "Breanna!" it calls.

"Who's there?" she says, the idea flashing through her brain that it's James, come to meet her here, in secret. *Stop it. Stop it.*

A kid pops up from behind the rock. Not James. Max, James's camp partner, the worst softball player of all the not-too-great Wildebeests. "Come here," he shouts, then crouches back down behind the rock.

What the crap?

Breanna walks to the boulder and crouches down with Max. "You stalking me?" she says, mad that he's shown up when she wants to find her doe. Madder that he isn't James.

"Yes. Basically." Max's uncombed hair stands straight up on the back of his head. "I have to talk to you. It's urgent." He pulls a phone from his back pocket—a contraband phone.

"Hey, you're not supposed to have this." Breanna grabs it out of his hand. "Have you got a signal?"

"Look at the screen," Max says, not even trying to take the phone back.

She looks. Max has got a signal, enough for his phone to show an open page. It's a page full of baseball stats, the sort of thing Breanna could look at all day long. It's so normal—not what she expected to find on Max's phone. "Baseball fan?" she asks.

"Playing the game is a one out of ten. Watching is a four. But running the numbers?" Max's face breaks into a big grin. "That's the best. Eleven out of ten, eleven being a prime."

"Man, you're weird," Breanna shakes her head at him. She loves baseball stats, too, but more than playing the game? No way! "Why did you stalk me out here? Why are you showing me this?"

"You know the book *Moneyball*?"

"The movie." Breanna nods. "It's old." She wonders where the crap this is going.

"They won with stats, right? That one guy?"

"Jonah Hill?"

"I don't know his name," Max frowns. "But the stats guy."

"Yeah. So what?"

"Because that's me. I'm the stats guy." Max grabs at his phone, but Breanna doesn't let it go. He points at the screen. "Look. I've got it all down."

Breanna looks closely. It's not a baseball stats site, which is what she'd thought. It's something Max has made, a spreadsheet he created on his phone, hidden under the covers in the dark.

Everything that happened in last night's game is here, in its own neat box. Every strike, ball, hit, RBI, error, out. Breanna can see exactly what the Roar did right. What the Roar did wrong. The Wildebeests, too. That part is painful.

"Holy crap," Breanna says. This! This is a map. The start of a map that leads to beating the Roar—or at least to having a chance. "This is every at-bat?" Breanna asks.

"Yep," Max says. "Every one."

"Can you do this again tonight?" Breanna says. "Any other time we play?" Max is a genius. Moneyball Max.

"Well, that's the deal," Max says, dropping his eyes. "See, I don't want to play. I'm a liability." He points at a line on the screen. "Look at my numbers. They don't lie." And it's true. Every time Max goes near a ball, bad things happen. Keeping him off the field is classic addition by subtraction—they're a better team without him. "Let me watch. Just watch," he says. "I'll get everything down."

"I'd be cool with that." Breanna scrolls up and down and over, looking at Max's killer chart. "This is exactly what I need." She shakes her head, amazed. "But how are we going to slip this past SheThor—Grace? You not batting? That's an automatic out. And Cami?" She lowers the phone and looks at Max. "She'll throw a fit if you're not in the rotation or on the field. She wants you out there, helping us lose."

"I've thought about that," Max says. Of course he has. "I need to injure myself. Fall, twist my ankle, sprain my wrist. I'm such a klutz, it probably won't even be on purpose."

"If you can pull that off and get SheThor to buy it, then we're golden." Breanna puts up her fist to bump Max's. This is crazy good. All of a sudden, she's got a secret weapon—stealth information that can build better teamwork. The Wildebeests can be like the Gonzo Gazelles, sneaking up on the Roar and giving them a great big surprise. "I'll trip you myself," she says, "if you think that will help."

Max laughs. He reaches up and takes his phone from Breanna's hand. Pulling up a new screen, he shows it to her. "According to my countdown clock," he says, "we have 372 seconds before the bell for breakfast rings. We should go."

"Go without me," Breanna says. "I need a minute." She really wants to find that doe. And just like that, she's running again.

The mown fields open up ahead of her. A single doe grazes. Breanna slows down. She doesn't want to spook the deer, even though it's not her doe. There is no black scar spidering across her chest.

She searches the small herd quietly grazing in the field. All of them are the same light brown, with the same white along their bellies. One deer, facing away, raises its head and looks back, right at her. The others do the same, their bodies tense and ready to run. But that one who looked first doesn't tense. She chews calmly, gazing over her shoulder at Breanna.

It is her doe. Tendrils of scar reach around her neck. Breanna can see them.

Slowly, the doe turns and faces Breanna, who creeps forward, sneakers crunching in the dry grass. A deer nearby bolts and, like yesterday, the rest follow. But not Breanna's doe. She watches them go and they don't go far, stopping, looking back, dropping their heads to graze again.

Standing strong and square before her, the doe looks at Breanna, who has walked so close that they stand eye to eye. Breanna stares at the black web of the scar. At the center of the doe's chest, the marks are thick and twisty, ragged and uneven, like they have grown up over a deep, wide hole. Black, hairless tentacles reach down her right shoulder and thigh on one side and halfway up her neck on the other.

Something hurt her bad—a gun, a bear, an angry buck. Something blasted through fur and skin and muscle and sinew and nearly killed her, that's for sure. But here she is, head high, ears alert to every sound, standing quietly with Breanna. She is beautiful, more beautiful than all the others.

Just a few feet apart, Breanna and the doe watch each other. They are so close that she could touch the deer's muzzle. But she doesn't—it wouldn't be right. The doe stares at her. A ring of gold in the deepest dark of the doe's iris glows in the morning sun.

Breanna feels the deer see her, really see her. Somehow, she has let the doe in. Like she did last night, telling Niraj about her dad.

It scares her.

She feels the doe studying her chest and she knows that the doe is considering the sweet little basket, where Breanna has already tucked in the doe herself. She is also examining the lockbox Breanna keeps below her heart, padlocked and chained around with seven chains. This deer is seeing everything, even the little round scars on Breanna's arms and legs, always hidden with sleeves and sweatpants.

The doe sees it all and with it the complex web of emotional scar tissue that covers it up, just like the twisted black scar running up and down the doe's chest.

Watching white curls of air rise from the doe's nostrils, Breanna is aware that she is holding her own breath, actually breathless.

She did not know that she could be seen like this.

Her hands, hanging at her sides, begin to tremble. Her legs begin to shake. Tears run down her cheeks and she can't stop them. She can't hide from this doe what she is always hiding from everybody, including herself—memories, scars, pain, fear.

The doe snorts and paws the ground. Breanna is sure that she will turn away and run now, done with Breanna, having seen that she is weak and scared.

But no. Slowly, the doe raises her eyes to Breanna's face. "Nobody broke us," the doe says. "Even when they tried." She lowers her head, like she is bowing, her eyes with the ring of gold steady on Breanna. "Show your scars," she says. "Lead on."

The words are hard. Breanna wants to tell her *no*. But before she can, the doe gives her one more steady look, then turns and runs. The others follow and the ground beneath Breanna's feet shakes with the pounding of their hooves.

Crying, shoulders shaking, Breanna watches them go. She reaches under her collar and runs her finger over the thick, round scar on her right shoulder. It's one of the places where her dad, coming off a high, crushed out his lit cigarette against her skin. It's not her worst memory. It's not that high-up window in the old house off McNichols. But it is bad.

And the doe saw! That doe with her own magnificent scar. She saw. Breanna felt it. And the doe said *Show your scars*. Breanna knows she means not just the real scars, but her invisible scars, too, all the hard and secret things she's always locking down. And standing with the doe, the doe seeing her and not running, she felt the weight of the lockbox under her heart. She still does. And it is heavy. She doesn't want to carry it around but she doesn't know how to put it down or what to do with all those memories that she doesn't want in her life and she is crying so hard that she's afraid the kids who must be coming down for breakfast will hear her clear over at the main building.

Nearby, somebody says, "You big dope." Somebody's here. Quickly, Breanna gulps back sobs and swipes her sleeve across her hot, wet face.

"You're not supposed to disappear like that." The voice is Cynthia's. She's coming through the marsh, flip-flops smacking against the boardwalk. "I've been looking everywhere for you."

Deer disappear up over the hill, their sharp hooves sending a final cascade of dirt and pebbles tumbling down. Breanna wipes her face off one more time and turns toward Cynthia. "Sorry," she says. "I wanted to see the deer. They were here yesterday, too."

Cynthia looks hard at Breanna. It must be obvious that Breanna's been bawling. Cynthia must have heard and seen. But she doesn't say a word. They stand together on the boardwalk, leaning over the handrail, running their fingers over the prickly surface of dry cattails.

One thing about Cynthia: She knows how to keep her mouth shut.

CHAPTER NINETEEN

THERE'S ENOUGH BACON AT BREAKFAST FOR THIRDS. ALSO pancakes and scrambled eggs, grainy compared to her mom's creamy ones, but good enough.

At the table this morning are cabins 17 and 18, top bunks. Niraj, the person in the world she most needs to talk to, sits beside her. James, across the table, softly drums his hands along the edge. He smiles when she looks over and her face turns hot. She knows it's red. She's embarrassed by that, but she smiles back for a second.

It helps that she has work to do.

"I know how to pull off your prank," she says quietly to Niraj. "The raccoon one, but without raccoons. Can you figure out how to get a meeting together today? The whole gang?"

"Hey," he says, looking at her closely. "Are you okay? I mean, I feel worried about you. Sneaking out to that shed was great, but . . . you know."

"Yeah," Breanna nods her head. She appreciates him asking her straight up like this. "I'm fine. It was a freaky thing. It's over."

"Okay," he says, but he's studying her, like he's making sure it checks out. She hopes he believes her. For now, it feels true. It seems like he sees that, because his face breaks into a huge Niraj smile. "I knew you'd figure out how to make my prank work. For sure I knew."

Niraj's enthusiasm feels good. "The schedule is so tight here," Breanna says. "Do you think we can pull off a daytime planning meeting?"

"That's tricky," Niraj says. Breanna can tell that he's thinking hard. She's relieved. Her reliable prank brain came up with an idea, but it's not stepping up for the rest. This camp is bad for her prank brain.

"We don't have much free time," Niraj says. "But . . . But. There's like half an hour before dinner where things are kind of loose, you know?"

Breanna nods.

"That's the right time. Scott and Mitchell I have to tell now, before their cohorts take off. I'll find them." Already, his eyes scan the room, looking for them. "I'm thinking we meet behind this building tonight at five thirty. It's private back there, mostly." Breanna is intrigued that he knows that. "I'll bring Trevor. Okay?"

He's figured everything out, that fast, which is exactly what Niraj, concentrating, can do. "Yep," Breanna says, nodding her head.

"Yep to all of it. I'll tell Pascale. Cynthia, too." Niraj frowns at Cynthia's name. "She's solid, Niraj. Trust me."

"Okay," he says. "I trust her if you trust her."

"I do," Breanna smiles at the words. She really does trust Cynthia. She counts her as a friend and a valuable Wildebeest teammate and in her gut—she's pretty sure—as a Gonzo Gazelle, someday soon.

Niraj is on his feet and weaving through the maze of tables and chairs and loud kids and clattering dishes to where Mitchell sits, just in front of the window, the big blue lake glittering behind him. Breanna lets herself stare at it, breathing in the shimmer where the angled rays of morning sun catch the water and shine it bright.

Stacy, that glitter-loving counselor, wanders into Breanna's line of vision. She is walking around the cafeteria, saying a chirpy good morning to everybody. It should be annoying, but it's not, not exactly. Stacy doesn't act like somebody in charge, even though she knows how to take charge when she needs to. Kids, seeing her coming, chew with their mouths wide open and lick syrup off their plates and roll up their pancakes and pretend to smoke them. Stacy laughs and asks the plate-lickers if they missed a spot. That seems pretty good for somebody who says *chow* and likes rainbow pens. Stacy is growing on her.

Pascale, sitting beside James, calls across the table, "Where did you take off to this morning? Cynthia didn't know."

Breanna shrugs. Nobody needs to know about Max, or the doe. Especially the doe.

"Have you looked at the schedule?" Pascale says.

Breanna shakes her head. She knows there's a schedule. She knows she was given one in the camp folder she got in the parking lot of Vincent Chin Middle School. But that folder is sticking halfway out from underneath her bunk. She hasn't opened it once and she's never going to. "Enlighten me, Pascale," she says.

"'Ropes Pre-Instruction.'" Pascale holds up a piece of paper that says WEDNESDAY on top. She points to a line. But Breanna doesn't look. She already heard. "Ropes Pre-Instruction."

Holy crap. It's starting for real—the official Sky Ropes part of camp. If only she had gotten herself kicked out already. The bacon in her belly rumbles. Her fingers go cold. The heat in her body drains down her legs and out her feet and she feels icy.

Nobody can see. Nobody knows. But she feels exposed anyway.

Team 17/18 and one other cohort circle their chairs around in a corner of the big cafeteria after all the other chairs are stowed. Breanna stations herself near the window, so she can feel the sunshine coming in from outside and watch the lake spark blue. That will keep her as calm as anything can right now.

The big room is echoey with this smaller crowd in it. Breanna sits with Pascale on one side and Cynthia on the other. Between them, she feels as safe as she can be, which is not very.

She grabs at the elasticized cuff of her sweatshirt and rubs it gently between her thumb and fingers. She thinks about the ribbed grain of the cloth, about how her fingers move up and down across tiny ridges, about how, when she brushes it with just a little force, it stretches in the same direction as her finger, then bounces back when she lets go. It helps. It does.

Marcos, slicked-back hair still damp, is the first counselor to stand up and start talking. "Don't worry!" he says, looking around the circle. "Nothing's changed. No ropes today." He pauses long enough for a few kids to laugh nervously. "The Sky Ropes are complicated," he says, his face serious. "Roger, here," he points to the hulky, muscle-bound, too-tan guy they met yesterday, "is the ropes guru." Roger grins his great big straight-toothed smile. "He'll explain how the Sky Ropes work and what they're like. We want you to have a clear picture, to know what to expect before you're face-to-face with the ropes."

Breanna grips the hard plastic sides of her chair. If she holds tight enough, she can feel a tingle in the tips of her fingers, nearly numb with cold. "After Roger," Marcos says, "Stacy is going to talk to you about helpful ways to think about the ropes and talk about them and how to know what's right for you. Okay?" He scans the circle, one kid at a time. "Okay," he nods. "Let's hear from Roger."

Breanna watches Marcos walk to a chair on her left. She concentrates on Marcos, how he has a mole beside the strip of beard on his chin, how his combed-back hair brushes the back of his T-shirt collar, how his brown eyes move from one kid to another, even when he's not up front. If she concentrates on Marcos hard enough, maybe she can block out whatever ropes-guru Roger is up there saying.

It doesn't work. Roger's deep voice keeps breaking through. He talks about safety harnesses. He talks about safety cables. Breanna knows about those things from the pamphlets but hearing about them in person terrifies her. "Line on," he's saying.

Without warning, the whole circle repeats, "Line on." Like creepy trained parrots—a pandemonium of parrots, which is what a bunch of them are called. These kids are like Eduardo, that fear parrot, sitting on Marcos's shoulder.

Stop it, Breanna wants to shout. *Don't listen to Roger. We don't have to do this. Challenge by choice! Challenge by choice.* But she doesn't have the heart to speak up. All she can do is make her brain think about other stuff—everything, anything but the Sky Ropes.

Roger is nobody. Roger is a gas cloud from the Crab Nebula. Mrs. Fairis taught them about the Crab Nebula last year, at Sternmore Academy. Astronomy was a cool unit. They came to school one morning at 4:00 a.m. and looked through telescopes on the playground. It was a star party. It was freezing, but there were tables set up with portable stoves and they cooked pancakes and drank hot chocolate, and she tucked that morning into the basket over her heart.

Everybody but Breanna says, "Line off." She doesn't know why they're saying it. She doesn't know what it means. Goose bumps rise along her icy arms. She's freezing. Her stomach hurts. She shouldn't have eaten that third slice of bacon. There were two kinds of syrup at the star party, maple and boysenberry. Who'd ever heard of boysenberry syrup? Marcos should stop looking at her. Marcos is a tool.

Suddenly Cami, across the circle, is talking—and looking straight at Breanna. "How many times do we get to do Sky Ropes?" Cami asks. "Do we have to wait till Friday?" Cold pumps through Breanna's body. Cami stares at her. Breanna remembers how Cami got inside her head and heart yesterday and looked around before Breanna could shove her out.

She knows something. What she's saying right now is meant for Breanna because she knows—it feels like she knows—that Breanna is afraid.

"I'll take that question," Stacy says, standing up from a chair on Breanna's right. "Remember how I said that the ropes would be easy for some people?" She looks around the circle. "Cami might be one of those lucky people. I've heard her stories. She's got experience with rope courses and other kinds of extreme activities. And that's superb!"

Stacy is looking at Cami, very seriously, and Cami is looking back at her, a leopard snarl catching up one side of her lip. "But that's not true for most of us," Stacy says. "So don't think that being excited to do the ropes more than once—gracious—even once, is normal. Normal doesn't matter. What matters is what makes sense for you." She studies the circle of kids. Most are looking down, staring at their hands or the floor or a smashed fly in front of their right shoe. Seconds go by before James looks up and nods, his face a little pale. He might be scared. James, scared. Breanna finds the possibility comforting.

"To answer Cami's question," Stacy says, "there might be time, on Friday afternoon, after all the teams have gone up, for people to do the ropes a second time. It depends on the schedule and staffing."

"I want to do the Sky Ropes fifty times," Cami says. Nobody is looking at her. Max, sitting next to James, looks ready to puke.

"I know you've all heard a lot about the Sky Ropes," Stacy says. "But remember that you are in charge of your experience. What is our approach to activities here?"

"Challenge by choice," Cynthia says firmly.

"Yes," Stacy says. "Challenge by choice. You do what makes sense for you. That's a lot of responsibility. It means you have to try to figure out what's right for you and trust what you think, even if it's different than what the people around you are thinking and doing. That's really hard." Staring around the circle, she makes eye contact with anyone who's looking up. Quickly, to avoid her, Breanna gazes out the window at the sparking, blue lake. "So let's say you decide not to do the Sky Ropes," Stacy asks. "What happens then?"

"Everyone will make fun of me," Tess says. She is sitting on the other side of Pascale, who rests a hand on her arm. Tess! Breanna can't believe the stuff that she just says, right out loud. It seems clueless—but honest, too. Yeah, that little peanut is honest. That takes guts. Breanna has to give her that.

"That's the fear," Stacy says, "isn't it? That people will make fun of us or think less of us."

Around the circle, many kids nod their heads. Stacy's read the room—she's no dummy.

"Okay," Stacy says. "That's right out in the open, where it belongs. First, if your friends don't want to do the Sky Ropes, don't make fun of them. It's their concern only. Second, if you don't want to do them, be ready with safe words. 'The Sky Ropes aren't right for me.' That's what we recommend. No explanation necessary, no details necessary. 'The Sky Ropes aren't right for me.' If someone is saying that to you, hear them. Trust them. Give them the respect of letting them *choose their challenge*."

She looks around. The room is silent. Everyone is watching her, even Breanna. "Let's say those words together," Stacy says. "Just in case."

"The Sky Ropes aren't right for me."

"Again."

"The Sky Ropes aren't right for me."

Breanna says it along with almost everyone in the circle. It feels big to say it, together, with all these other kids. Some of them are scared, just like her. She can taste a tang of fear in the air, and it's more than just hers, she's sure.

From the corner of her eye, she watches Cami, who doesn't join the group in saying the words. In fact, her arms are folded across her chest, and her lip is lifted in that snarl, and she rolls her eyes every time everyone else says it. She isn't scared of the Sky Ropes, obviously, but more than that, she doesn't respect anybody who is. Her body language says that loud and clear. At least the other kids aren't acting like her, not even Rachel the Minion, who practices the words along with everybody else.

Those words. They give Breanna hope. She feels the blood in her body slightly thaw and start pumping again. Feeling is returning to her fingers and her toes. *The Sky Ropes aren't right for me. The Sky Ropes aren't right for me.* She tries to etch the words into her soul so that she can believe them enough to trust them and maybe, maybe say them when she needs to.

But should she? Can she be Fearless Breanna Woodruff and say those words? Stacy says she can. So bad, she wants to believe she can, that those words might, for real, be safe words, with actual power to protect her.

Except—what if they don't work? What if what they actually do is destroy the reputation she has worked so hard to build since the day she moved to Beecham? That reputation is everything. She can't lose it.

Those words are risky.

They could save her.

They could grind her to nothing.

She does not know which.

CHAPTER
TWENTY

ROPES PRE-INSTRUCTION IS BAD ENOUGH, BUT INSTEAD OF ENDING
on the safe words, like she should, Stacy invites them all to walk out
the front door together. They stand on the porch and Stacy points
up. Up. UP.

To the Sky Ropes.

Sure, Breanna knows they're there. She feels their shadow all
the time. But following Stacy's pointing finger, up, up, up, not being
able to stop herself from looking all the way up to those towers
with cables glinting in the sun, Breanna feels something terrible.
Fear, yeah. Dread, yeah. But something else, now, too.

There's this creepy feeling you get when someone—a stranger
or your dad in his green Chevy truck, who by law isn't supposed
to come near you—is watching you. Maybe you can see them and
maybe you can't. But you feel their eyes on you and you know

they're watching. That's what it feels like looking up that high, high hill to the Sky Ropes.

The Sky Ropes are watching her.

It's not that they have eyes. Not exactly.

But they have something. Some way of seeing. Some way of knowing. They are tuned in and electric and following her.

She is so scared of those stupid ropes. She acknowledges it, just like Marcos said. But what good does that do? It doesn't make her feel any less scared.

Around her, other kids' eyes track up the hill to where Stacy points. They elbow each other and grin. Tess whispers to Pascale, who bends low to hear. Trevor and Niraj pump the air with their fists. Max and James step off the porch, talking quietly as they look up the hill. Cami and Minion high-five, though Minion looks a little green around the face. Cynthia, alone, leans back against the pale-yellow building, arms folded across her chest, looking up. She is doing her strategizing thing—Breanna knows what that looks like now—to the Sky Ropes. Breanna would like to borrow her calm in the face of those ropes.

It seems like they can all actually imagine themselves up there, doing the Sky Ropes. Breanna can't. She just can't.

Stacy sends them off to their cabins to change into swimsuits for watersports. Cynthia, jogging up from behind, pokes Breanna's arm. They walk together, slowly, letting everybody else go on ahead.

"That was intense," Cynthia says. "Those ropes are scary." She shakes her head. "I know I was talking last night about all the stuff I'm scared about in the future, like not getting into the right school, but the Sky Ropes! They are here-and-now scary."

Breanna laughs.

They walk up the hill together, silent for several steps. "You're scared of the ropes, too," Cynthia says, her voice slow and thoughtful. "You hide it. But you're my friend now. I can tell."

For a second, Breanna can't breathe. She wants to shout *I'm not afraid! No friend of mine would call me scared.* But what comes out instead, before she can think right, is "Yep."

Oh no! Now she's done it.

She's confessed to Cynthia. She didn't mean to. But now Cynthia knows that she's afraid of the Sky Ropes and Niraj knows that she's afraid of green trucks—and her dad. These are secrets, things she keeps buried in her lockbox. No one is supposed to know. This feels like a disaster.

"Well then," Cynthia says, taking a giant step in front of Breanna and turning to walk backward. Her face blazes with fierce, steady determination. "No ropes," she says. "You and me. No ropes." She puts up her fist. "Solidarity, okay?"

"What?"

"Solidarity."

Solidarity. Cynthia is with her. That's what that word must mean. They are a team against the Sky Ropes. This is not what Breanna expected. She accidentally confessed and suddenly she is not alone.

She puts up her fist and bumps and feels freakin' relief.

In the cabin, Cynthia slathers on sunscreen, something Breanna forgot to pack. Cynthia hands her the bottle before she even asks. Pascale, standing at the bunk beside them, takes it next, sharing Cynthia's sunscreen without even thinking.

It's all so normal, friends being friends. Breanna loves it. She went a long, lonely time without friends. She'll never forget what that felt like. What she feels now, the easiness in this group and Cynthia's *solidarity*, is what she craved all those years without even knowing it. Pascale hands the bottle of sunscreen to Tess.

Rubbing in the last white bits of sunscreen on her neck, Tess makes an announcement. "Those Sky Ropes are too high," she says. "I'm not doing them." Chin jutted out, like she's ready for an argument, she looks around at Pascale, Breanna, and Cynthia. "My mom said that coming to camp would be hard, and I chose to come. So *that's* my challenge by choice." She plunks herself down on her bunk. "I'm already done."

"You're brave, Tess," Pascale says, resting her hand on Tess's shoulder. In her head, Breanna agrees. "Choosing not to do the Sky Ropes is brave."

What a sweet pea thing to say, Breanna thinks. But then it flashes into her brain that it might actually be true, that it takes courage *not* to go up the Sky Ropes. Without warning, she feels a catch in her throat, like she might cry. It's so stupid. She pushes the feeling back, glad that the cabin is busy and full and no one is paying her any attention.

In minutes, they all spill outside and head down to the waterfront. This activity is optional—Breanna just has to show up.

She can sit in the sun or take a nap on the beach or draw in wet sand with a stick if she wants.

Except it turns out that water sports are cool!

They swim. They cannonball off a platform out in the lake. Twice, with such a sly bump of her hip that he never sees it coming, she pushes James off. Twice! The way he throws his head back and laughs when he surfaces the water makes Breanna laugh, too. He's fun.

They canoe, something Breanna is not good at. But Marcos makes it okay. As they glide their canoes down a river that feeds the big lake, he gives some basic instructions, reminding everyone how canoeing works. Cynthia, in the back of their two-person canoe, is a strong paddler. Soon, they are pulling together and maneuvering sweetly and there's that feeling of teamwork that Breanna loves.

"No water fights," Marcos says. "That's the rule. Absolutely NO splashing other canoes." But then, super fast, he grabs a bucket from under his feet, scoops up water and dumps it over Stacy's head, behind him in the same boat.

"Scofflaw!" she shouts and, with a powerful sweep of her arm, sends a wall of water at his face.

Every canoe has a bucket. It's great!

At first it's all water fights and paddling fast to get away from Niraj and Trevor and Pascale and Tess, who are close by. They are all soaking wet and shouting. Then things quiet down, and that's great, too. Breanna and Cynthia slip through lily pads, one smooth canoe in a long line of canoes.

Without warning, Breanna's brain runs along the riverbank and bounds up the stairs and shoots past the main building and takes off up, up up the hill, to the Sky Ropes. Even in the peace of the river, she feels their electric vision.

Her eyes follow where her brain leads, and up on the highest hill, she can make out shapes, no bigger than ants, moving across the ropes. Those are kids up there, doing the Sky Ropes! Her whole body gets tight. She has to force her eyes away, because every shadow along the hill looks like a little ant classmate falling down, down, down off the ropes.

"Stop it," Cynthia says. "Stop looking. You're making it worse."

Breanna nods. It's true. But it is hard not to look.

Just then, James and Max glide up silently beside them.

"Hey," James says, smiling his beautiful smile. Breanna feels hot red heat rise on her face. Suddenly, as fast and sly as *she'd* been on the platform, James douses her with a bucket of cold river water.

She splutters. She yells. What a sneak attack! Laughing, James and Max dig in their oars and glide away. Cynthia and Breanna paddle hard after them, determined to take their revenge. By the time Stacy blows a whistle to announce the end of watersports, the four of them are completely soaked. The water beaded on her skin and dripping from her T-shirt makes Breanna feel saturated with happiness.

On the stairs, walking back up to the main building, James catches up with Breanna. "Hey," he says. "That was great." His wet sneakers squelch.

Breanna grins at him. "We trounced you in that canoe," she says. "You're a big old loser."

"No, you didn't. You're more drenched than I am."

"Am not."

"Are so."

They give each other a hard time. She thinks again of her cousin Jorge. James is taller, louder, younger than Jorge was when Breanna had a crush on him. But still, James reminds her of Jorge. The swishy bangs are part of it. But it's something else, too, something gentle in his brown eyes, something kind that's just part of who he is. It was true of Jorge, who used to read her *Curious George Rides a Bike* over and over, however many times she asked. It seems true of James, the way he's good to Max, who other kids bully, the way James gets this worried look on his face when he thinks someone (she) might not be okay, even when they're goofing around, the way he can be teased and tease back without it ever getting mean.

She likes this guy. She hates to admit it. She doesn't have time for it. But she likes him.

Climbing the stairs with James, Breanna is aware of the dripping T-shirt clinging to her belly and of water cascading down her sturdy legs, uncovered for a change. Maybe she should feel embarrassed around so many skinny girls in bathing suits, but she doesn't. She just doesn't. Besides, beautiful James started a water fight with *her*. Beautiful James is talking to *her*.

Cami, the stripes of her swimsuit the same lime green as her toenails, comes leaping up from behind. She ignores Breanna. Lightly, she shoulder-checks James. "Where were you? I looked for you on the river and couldn't find you."

"I was there," he smiles. But it's not the kind of smile he gave Breanna. It's lower voltage. For sure.

"We're having a team meeting before dinner," Cami says, her smooth voice extra silky. "Going over the Roar's lineup, talking strategy." Her voice gets that hard edge. "Not that we need it, right?"

"We're playing softball?" James asks. "Again?"

"Of course," Cami answers. "Breanna's friend Pascale set it up last night." Cami, two steps ahead now, looks back at Breanna. As they walk, her eyes scan Breanna up and down, finally resting on Breanna's solid gut poking through her wet T-shirt. Breanna follows Cami's gaze, so Cami knows that she knows exactly what Cami is doing—sizing her up, judging her, trying to make her ashamed of the strong body her mom has taught her to be proud of.

Breanna knows this cruel game. She learned it when they moved to Beecham. Somehow, folks in Beecham thought her chubby little-kid body was their business and made a point of talking to her mom—and her—about it.

Nope. This is one way Cami cannot get to her. She's practiced this one.

Finally, Cami looks Breanna in the face, her lip lifting in that snarl. "See you on the softball field," she says.

Breanna angles an angry eyebrow at her.

And maybe it's on purpose, and maybe it's that Cami is still watching Breanna's face, the two of them in another serious staring contest, but whyever it happens, Cami walks straight into Max. He stumbles over a rock on the edge of the path and his ankle wobbles and bends too far and he goes down hard into the bushes.

He's holding his ankle. He's got fresh scratches on his arms and face. But when he looks up and sees Breanna, he flashes her a victory grin.

Bless that mean girl!

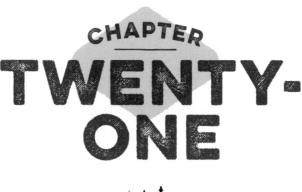

CHAPTER TWENTY-ONE

STACY RUSHES UP THE STAIRS AND PULLS MAX TO HIS FEET. "I NEED two strong people to help Max to the infirmary," she says. Without a thought, Breanna shoots her hand in the air. Stacy points to James. "You're his camp partner," she says. "You're one." She looks at Breanna, shamelessly waving her hand now. "And Breanna. You're two. Thank you!"

James and Breanna each put an arm around Max. Even though Breanna's arm isn't exactly touching James's arm, she can feel heat from his skin prickling along hers. It's nice.

They get Max to the infirmary, in the main building, across from the cafeteria, where SheThor, the cool camp nurse, hangs out. All the way there, Max doesn't put any weight on his right leg. He seems hurt, actually hurt. But maybe, and this is what Breanna hopes, he's just good at acting.

"Hey," Max says, hopping along. "We've got to talk strategy for tonight." Breanna cocks her head at James and lifts an eyebrow. "Oh, right," Max says. "Enemy camp."

They laugh. Cynthia laughs, too. Breanna didn't know that she had followed them, but here she is, coming up behind. It's cozy, the four of them, on their own, together. Camp is slippery like that. Bad things, like Sky Ropes pre-instruction, followed by perfect things, like a water fight in the river and heat rising off James's skin and being with just her friends right now.

As much as she loves the good stuff—and she does—she can't let herself be tricked into thinking it's okay here. It's not. She's got to be on guard. She's got to hold tight to her lockbox, which seems penetrable here in a way it's never been before. And she's got to find a way to be Fearless Breanna Woodruff in the face of the Sky Ropes. Even at moments like this, when camp feels amazing, she can't lose sight of that, most of all. Because if she's not Fearless Breanna Woodruff, then she's nothing.

What she's got is Niraj's goose prank. It's not much. Just thinking about it now, a wild desire erupts in her prank brain to go back to the chainsaw. She stops it. She knows it's just the ropes, messing with her. She glances at James as they heft Max up the steps of the main building. She could tell James about the goose prank. Maybe he'd join. Then she'd know some important things about who he really is.

SheThor opens the infirmary door. The windowless room they step into is tiny for five people. There is an old metal desk, its plasticky wood top curling up at three edges. There are two plastic chairs, one with broken slats in the back. There is an old phone, the big kind connected to an answering machine. A phone connected to the outside world. Good to know.

An open door joins the tiny room to a long, skinny room next door. That one is filled with light from windows, open to a soft breeze. Eight neatly made single beds run along the windowed walls. There is old wood paneling on the two inside walls and speckled linoleum on the floor. It's old here. But it's kind of cool, like a place you could really rest, if you needed to.

James and Breanna lower Max into one of the white plastic chairs. SheThor sits down in front of him. With Max's leg in her lap, she squeezes her thumb and fingers along his ankle.

"Does this hurt?" she asks. He shakes his head. "How about this?" He shakes his head again. Her fingers move around and over and up and down, "Here? Here?"

"There," Max says with a little jump. "Definitely there." He's hurt. He wasn't faking that jump. Talk about taking one for the team!

"Can one of you Good Samaritans make yourselves useful?" SheThor looks at Breanna, Cynthia, and James, who lean against the dull brown paneling that lines her office. Well, Cynthia isn't leaning. She's crouched forward, intently watching the slow progress of SheThor's fingers along Max's ankle.

"Okay," James says.

"Sure," Breanna says. They answer at the same time, their voices blending into one. Breanna feels her face burn hot.

SheThor sends them both off to the back entrance of the kitchen. Softly, James hums "Brown-Eyed Girl." She knows the song. Her cousins used to sing it at night, when they played a guitar around bonfires at the vacant lot down the street from their house in Mexicantown. She thinks of the words, "You, my brown-eyed girl." Breanna has brown eyes. Maybe James is trying to tell her something.

Stop it! She can't let herself do that, get silly over a song hummed by this boy who always has music in his head. She can't lose focus on what's important here at camp.

At the kitchen, Eric, head cook, whose brown hair is rolled up in a bun on top of his head, plods to the freezer to get them an ice pack. James hums. The back door to the kitchen is open and Breanna sees one of the geese, fat and white, brazenly setting a webbed, orange foot on the speckled, stained kitchen linoleum. Gutsy goose! For all she knows, those geese might march into the cafeteria on their own. This prank might be too easy.

But it'll be funny. She'll take funny.

They walk back to the infirmary. The ice pack is slippery in Breanna's fingers, sweaty from being this close to James in the narrow hallway. She stops. "James," she says. He stops, too. "My friends and I are planning a prank. We're meeting up behind this building today at five thirty to work out the details." She knows her face is red, but she keeps going. "Want to come?"

"Hey!" he says. "You're a big old rule-breaker."

"You aren't?" Breanna cocks an eyebrow at him, showing him her bright red face. "I'm disappointed."

James throws his head back and laughs and it is beautiful. "I'll come," he says. "For sure." She can't hold back the great big grin that stretches across her whole face.

In the infirmary, SheThor wraps an Ace bandage around Max's ankle. Taking the ice pack from Breanna, she shows them all where to place it on his leg and explains how long and how often. "You're all here. You're all responsible for this young man's recovery," she says. "He needs to stay off this foot for at least a day, maybe more. It's got to be iced on schedule to keep the swelling down. Can you all help with that?"

They nod.

SheThor disappears into the other room. Max and Breanna high-five. They did it! Max is officially off the team.

SheThor brings back crutches. "Take it easy," she says. "Stay off the leg. Keep it elevated. For tonight, stay close to the main building. You'll get tired using crutches. If there's softball tonight, you're sidelined."

Max nods, smiling too hard, but SheThor doesn't seem to notice.

"We'll check in before breakfast in the morning," she says. "Okay?"

"Okay," Max says.

"The rest of you know your jobs?"

"Sure." "Yeah." They nod their agreement, happy to help, a little team of conspirators (even if they don't all know it), setting in motion the Wildebeests's come-from-behind, surprise victory.

CHAPTER TWENTY-TWO

NIRAJ GOT IT RIGHT. THERE IS, IN FACT, A LITTLE DOWNTIME BEFORE dinner.

By 5:20, Cynthia and Breanna join Trevor and Niraj, who wait behind the main building, near the back kitchen door.

"Hi! Hi!" Niraj says. "I'm so ready for this." In his right hand he holds narrow pieces of white posterboard with string attached to the top, his signs that say *1, 2, 4*. Breanna is glad that they're going to use them.

They stand in a strip of grass between the back door to the kitchen and a thick patch of bushes. *Viburnum*, Breanna thinks, remembering the description SheThor gave on the nature hike. She reaches out and pulls off a velvety leaf and runs it between her fingers. It's not that she needs to calm down right now. It just feels nice.

By 5:25, Pascale joins them. "Tess fell asleep. I nearly did, too," she says. "But I made it. This better be worth skipping the first chance I got for a nap."

"You know it will be," Breanna says. Pascale doesn't look convinced. Cynthia is watching, not talking, a quiet smile on her face that Breanna hasn't seen before. It looks happy and curious and like Cynthia might actually be ready for whatever is about to go down.

By 5:28, according to Breanna's Hello Kitty watch—which she hopes nobody notices—Scott and Mitchell come jogging up.

"What are we doing, Breanna?" Mitchell asks.

"Prank time!" She smiles, trying to catch them all up in her enthusiasm. She's excited. It's not the level of prank she hoped for, but it's not nothing, either. She looks over Mitchell's shoulder, watching for James. Two of the fat white geese wander around the corner of the building. One pecks at the grass near her feet, so tame. Everybody's here but James. She needs to give him a little more time. "Hey, Eyeball," she says to Mitchell. "Did you do team building yet?"

"Yeah. Today."

"How did you do on the blindfolded obstacle course? I mean, with one eye." This might be a rude thing to ask, but it's done.

Mitchell laughs quietly. "We were the worst," he said. "I promise you one eye did not help me." A goose pulls at the hem of his jeans. "My camp partner's a nice guy, but he just got here from Syria, and this camp makes him think that American schools are nuts. It's pretty fun though. We laugh a lot."

Silent, they stand, awkward in a rough circle, waiting for Breanna, who is holding out for James, to start things.

Cynthia touches Scott on the shoulder. "Nice to see you," she says. Breanna knows Cynthia means it. Scott was kind to her after she let him be in trouble for what she did.

Scott smiles and nods.

Behind him, Breanna sees James, coming around the back of the building.

James! He came!

"Hi," he says, and he's looking only at her. "I had to get Max settled in the cafeteria early. But he's good now. He says to tell you he's saved you a seat."

"Cool!" Breanna says. About Max saving her a seat. But mostly, about James showing up.

"Okay, everyone." She takes a deep breath and dives in. "Niraj thought of a great prank. It's simple, but it'll be funny. We need funny at this camp that's obsessed with fear." Quickly, she explains about Niraj's signs. He holds them up proudly. "Raccoons are dangerous," Breanna says. "Pascale says so. But look at these geese." She points at the two that are right here. "They're tame, as you can see. Early tomorrow morning, we catch them. We hide one. We put Niraj's signs around the necks of the other three and drop them into the cafeteria before breakfast. Chaos ensues!" In her head, she can just picture Stacy, running after the penultimate goose.

Pascale, arms folded across her chest, looks at Breanna in her Pascale way, maybe amused, maybe disgusted. "Geese?" she asks. Breanna can tell from the way she says it that she does not like the idea of geese, either.

"Sure. Look how nice they are." She points at a third goose, rocking from one orange foot to the other, in front of the back kitchen door. "This will be easy-peasy." That's something Stacy would say. It doesn't feel very convincing, but she grins, trying to pull them all in. "Fat, tame geese running around the cafeteria."

"Epic," Niraj says.

"Totally," Trevor says.

"Hmmmm." Cynthia clears her throat. James is staring at Breanna, his mouth not open or closed, but kind of stuck in between. Pascale is shaking her head and quietly laughing. Scott catches Pascale's eye and laughs, too. Amusement was not what Breanna expected. Hesitation, maybe. Enthusiasm, definitely. But not this.

"Breanna," Mitchell says. "Have you ever been around geese?" He angles his head at her and he looks like he might laugh out loud. "Like at a farm or a petting zoo?"

"Sure," Breanna says. "The hissy Canadian geese at Sugar Maple Park. But not tame ones, like these. They're nice."

"Well," Mitchell says. "I hate to say this, but geese are scary, even tame ones. As soon as we come for them, they'll charge us. They'll smack us with their wings and their weaponized-snake necks. They'll bite us. Geese are not a good idea."

"Come on, Mitchell," Breanna says. "Those geese are fat and slow and they're pets. They can't hurt us."

"Mitchell's right," Scott says. "Geese are mean." The whole group goes quiet. Scott has spoken. If he actually says something, it matters.

"Aw, man!" It's Niraj. "Will they give me rabies, Pascale?"

She shakes her head.

"Then I'm in. This is a Breanna-level prank that I thought up myself. I'm doing it."

"Same here," Trevor says.

Breanna points at her own chest. "One," she says. "Two." She points at Niraj, who gives a strong, clear nod. She moves around the circle. Scott shakes his head. Mitchell puts up both hands in a *not me* kind of pose. "Three," she points at Trevor, who flashes a thumbs-up. Pascale folds her arms across her chest and gives Breanna a look that says *absolutely not*.

"Four," Cynthia says when Breanna gets to her. "I'm doing this. I'll deal with a crazy goose. I've never snuck out anywhere, I've never done a prank." She's got a wide, happy grin on her face that Breanna can't quite believe. She didn't see this coming. "I'm not going to miss this chance."

"No way!" Pascale says, laughing. "You? Who *are* you?" She has to cover her mouth because she is laughing so hard. "Okay," she says when she's gotten her laughing under control. "I'm doing this. I want to see Cynthia breaking out and doing a prank." She looks at Breanna and shakes her head, and it's clear that she can't believe that Cynthia is in.

"Five!" Breanna says, so excited. She gets to James. *Come on, James. Come on,* she thinks. He's the one she wants to join in the most. Cynthia and Pascale joining in is amazing. But getting James to do this? *That* would be epic.

James stares at the ground. With his left foot, he taps out some song that only he can hear. Seconds pass. "Yeah," he says, lifting his eyes to Breanna's. "I don't want to miss this, either. Six."

"Yes!" Breanna shouts. It's a go. They've got enough kids, including Mitchell and Scott, who changed their minds after everybody else joined in. And they've got James. It couldn't be better!

CHAPTER TWENTY-THREE

JUST AS THE CHOW BELL RINGS, THEY AGREE THAT THE PRANK WILL
begin at 5:30 tomorrow morning.

A few minutes later, in the cafeteria, Max pats the empty chair
beside him, inviting Breanna to sit. "Crutches are armpit murder,"
he says, glaring at his crutches leaning against the table. But then,
he's on to softball. "Let's start with James." He looks at her hard.
"Since your brain is already there."

Face burning red, Breanna pulls her eyes off James, who sits at
a table halfway across the room. She must be so obvious.

"James is good," Max says. "But he's not careful. He's playing
for fun. He's not out for blood the way you and Cami are."

Whoa. Max sees that? Maybe everybody does. It keeps worry-
ing at Breanna that the other kids see her as a super-competitive
mean girl, just like Cami. Breanna wants to win, and she fights hard,

but she works hard not to be mean. She is all about the team and the people on it, including Tess, that little peanut, who can't play to save her life, and Max, who is much more valuable with a sprained ankle. That's what she wants people to see. Mean is Cami. Mean is her dad. She is not like them and everybody needs to know that.

Max is still talking. "At bat, James is strong when he connects," he says. Breanna pulls her brain back from its spiral into worry. "He'll hit a solid double, at least, every chance he gets."

Breanna nods.

"Shut him down. Make your pitches wild, unpredictable, so he never knows what's coming. Strike him out, or pitch him short, so he reaches out and pops one up. Easy catch for you." Max stops to eat a baby carrot. "Got that?"

"Yeah," Breanna says. She stabs her fork into her mac and cheese, hard and brown along the edge.

"Cami's got a big stick, too," Max says. "She's nervous and quicker to swing, but super powerful. You've got to neutralize her." Mouth full, Breanna nods her agreement. "I mean it," Max says. "No low pitches to Cami. Keep them high and slow and too stupid to swing at. Walk her every time if you can."

Breanna swallows a half-chewed noodle. "That's no fun," she says. "What's the point of pitching if I can't strike out Mean Girl?"

"She's better than you," Max says, his face serious. "No one-on-one combat out there. You'll lose, and the Wildebeests with you."

"No she's not!" Breanna says. She has to say it. But Max is right—Cami is better.

Across the table, Niraj is talking and talking to Rachel the Minion. She is making a show of not listening, looking away, rolling her eyes, ignoring his questions and dumb jokes, which Breanna can hear herself. Niraj is the best. He doesn't deserve to be treated like that.

"Niraj," Breanna calls across to him, interrupting Max's analysis. "Got your atomic arm limbered up for tonight?"

Niraj looks confused. He and Breanna both know he has no such thing. He practiced his fielding all summer, with her and Pascale, Scott, and Mitchell. He improved, yes, but his arm's not great. Not atomic, for sure. After a pause, Niraj laughs. "Yep, I do," he says, curling up his right arm and flexing. "Yep. Yep. Me and my atomic arm."

There's actually a little bit of bicep to see. Breanna grins. "Our secret weapon," she announces to the whole table.

Rachel the Minion rolls her eyes, like she doesn't think Niraj is worthy of all this good attention. But at least Niraj isn't talking to her anymore. And if the Roar thinks that they need to shut down Niraj? That wouldn't be the worst thing.

"Are we playing again tonight?" Niraj calls across the table.

"Oh yeah," Breanna says. "We're playing." She sounds just like Cami. She hates that. But they are playing tonight. Pascale said so and it's important. And maybe they'll play tomorrow and the day after, too, as many nights as it takes for the Wildebeests, with Max as their secret weapon, to beat the Roar.

Detailed and thorough, Max talks softball through the rest of dinner. He works through every player on Cami's team, one by one. He tells Breanna who gets a pitch inside, who gets it outside, who gets it short, who gets it flat. They rearrange their outfield and some of the infield. Cynthia they move to shortstop. Whether she likes it or not, she's smart and she's fast and she can hit her target—they need her where it counts.

Breanna listens hard, tries to hold and organize this amazing intel in her head so she can use it in the game when she needs it. She wishes her brain were working better, but it's not quite right here at camp.

She is slurping up a brownish-yellow lump that's probably butterscotch pudding when Max says, "I've got to head out."

"Okay," Breanna says. "Thanks. This is great. We'll miss you tonight."

"Oh, I'll be there," Max smiles. "I'm going up now."

"What?" Breanna says. Max isn't supposed to go anywhere but the cabin tonight. SheThor was clear about that.

"I'm going to find a spot, deep in a bush or behind a rock, where I can see you and you can't see me." He hitches the crutches into his armpits. "Grace won't know. I'll hide too well. But I've got to watch tonight and get fresh stats. That's my job."

Breanna knows she shouldn't go along with this, seeing how Max is really hurt and how she told SheThor she'd help take care of him. But she doesn't argue.

"You're a genius, Max," is all she says. She feels ready. She feels almost strong, which isn't normal at this place.

She cannot wait for tonight's game.

CHAPTER
TWENTY-FOUR

BREANNA STANDS ON THE PITCHER'S RUBBER, TOSSING THE BALL against her glove, soft and snug on her hand. There was only a small skirmish about free time after dinner. Pascale had called for another game last night and most kids remembered that. Or maybe they knew Breanna and Cami wouldn't budge. Or maybe they wanted to play. Breanna hopes it's that.

The sun, low over the lake, glows soft and red. A breeze picks up the hair that has come loose from the ponytail pulled through her Detroit Tigers cap. She can smell the sweet, damp rot of the marsh, and she breathes it in. Eyes closed, ball and glove curled against her chest, she focuses her brain like a laser.

Cami steps up to bat first again tonight. Breanna straightens up. She's about to throw when Cami sticks out her arm and yells, "Wait!" Stepping out of the batter's box, Cami hits the ground three times with the tip of her bat, then holds her bat in front of her, pushes her butt back, and shifts her hips back and forth. She did this last night, too, this stupid batting dance. What a diva.

SheThor finally says something to Cami that Breanna can't hear and Cami steps back up to the plate. Fine. Cami can dither all she wants. She won't get under Breanna's skin. Four dull balls are coming for Cami. Breanna's ready.

She takes a deep breath, pulls back her pitching arm, and lobs the ball. It's supposed to arc high and drop slow, slow, over the plate. But it doesn't. It arcs low and drops fast. It's a perfect pitch.

Smack! Cami's bat connects.

Helpless, Breanna watches the ball singe over her head, past Niraj between first and second, hard into left field, where Trevor lets it bounce twice. At least he scoops it up and sails it to third.

But Cami is already there.

A triple! A freakin' triple on the first pitch.

Dang it. Breanna meant to walk her. Cami rattled her, walking away from the batter's box the way she did. It was a dirty trick. SheThor should have stopped her.

James is warming up. Pascale, crouched down behind home plate, pulls off her catcher's mask and makes eye contact with Breanna. Slowly, Pascale drops her head and lowers both hands down past her knees. Her signal is clear, and it's not about pitching. It's personal. "Bring it down," she's saying. "Stay cool."

Stay cool. Stay cool. Breanna repeats the words in her head. James is a big hitter. She signals the fielders to back up. She should have done that for Cami. She's not thinking right. She's got to focus. But it's James, standing in front of her, bat back, hip cocked, eyes brown and gentle. She knows she's got to throw him off, confuse him, like Max said. But it is hard to focus.

Stay cool.

Stance loose, James waits in the batter's box. He's crowding the plate. She can use that. But just as she's about to send him a pitch way inside, the corners of his mouth turn up in a sweet grin.

Her brain disconnects. Her arm throws anyway. It's hardly a pitch. More like the ball escaping from her fingers in his general direction, with just enough velocity to roll across the plate.

"Ball one," SheThor shouts.

No kidding.

Pascale lowers her hands in that *stay cool* signal again.

Yeah. Yeah. Stay cool.

Breanna is trying. She's trying to keep James off balance, make him guess, make him reach, so he can't connect with power. But what she really wants to do is to stop Cami, on third and poised to run, from getting home. Honestly, she's got to stop them both. Ball and glove against her chest, Breanna closes her eyes and tries to think. She runs her fingers over the roughed-up surface of the yellow softball in her right hand and lets it calm her.

She knows what to do—strike James out with one of her trickiest pitches. She starts with her best one. It arcs up the full twelve feet, just like it's supposed to. But it keeps going. It's too high. Everybody, including SheThor, can see that. James lets the ball drop to the dirt.

"Ball two," SheThor calls.

This is bad. Breanna needs to make a statement, right here, right now, and shut the Roar down. She'll try something else, a trick pitch that makes James swing, one where he connects, but barely, so the ball rolls off the tip of the bat and Pascale catches it easy and steps back to tag a flying Cami out at home. That will take care of them both.

Max won't approve, but it's the right play.

James is barely in position when Breanna sends up her pitch, high and slow, with a sweet, unexpected drop outside. James swings.

Crack. He connects hard.

The pitch wasn't tricky at all. It was perfect for someone with arms as long as James, exactly what she wasn't supposed to throw. James flies past first, then second, while Trevor runs back and back, trying to catch the ball soaring past him. He's getting burned, bad.

Breanna can't bear to watch. She hears SheThor shout, "Safe!" Cami has run home.

James gets a triple. Instead of a walk to first.

Two at bats. Two triples.

This is not the way tonight was supposed to go.

Breanna sucks.

It gets worse. Rachel hits a single. James jogs home. By the time Cynthia, bless her, catches a pop fly and Niraj tags out a runner on second, finally ending the Roar's endless at bat, the Wildebeests are down by eight. Eight.

It's a blowout. And it's Breanna's fault. Her brain isn't right. She's let Cami get to her. James, too. She's let this whole stupid camp throw her off her game.

Cami, on the other hand, is proving she deserves her spot on the Lanton Leopards. Her pitching arm is stunning, pitches soaring high, coming down tricky behind the plate, dropping to the inside corner once, the outside corner next, not as deep as you think, and if you do manage to connect, the ball rolls off the bat and the catcher or the shortstop has got it in a flash.

The Wildebeests chant, "We want a pitcher, not a belly-itcher." They demand justice from SheThor when she calls a strike that maybe was a ball. But really. Cami is masterful. The best pitcher Breanna's ever played against. And even in slow-pitch, that's enough to cream the Wildebeests tonight.

Finally, finally, SheThor calls it on account of dark. Breanna's never been so happy for a game to end. Cami leads her team in a loud chorus of "Two, four, six, eight. Who do we appreciate? The Wildebeests!"

The score is too shameful to admit, and it's her fault.

Everybody is walking away from the field, on their way to the next thing, because here at camp, there's always a next thing. Breanna lags behind, till it's just her, waiting for Max to limp from the shadows.

"You were the worst," Max says, fighting his way out from underneath a big bush. Fresh scratches on his arms glow red in the dim light. "What were you doing?"

"Thanks a lot," Breanna says. But she knows it's fair.

Slowly, at the pace of Max on crutches, they walk over the boardwalk. "I did learn more stuff," Max says. "They got cocky and showed me their weak spots, and they've got them. We'll go through it all, you and me. If you'll listen to me this time, we might be able to come back."

"Okay. Okay. I'll do what you say," Breanna says. "But it's hard at this stupid place. Everything about it makes me lose my cool."

Above her, stars, far away and cold, blink on. Her eyes follow the hillsides, until she's staring at the spot where the Sky Ropes must be. "This place. I swear."

"You, too?" Max says. He's followed her eyes. He knows exactly what she's talking about. "Aren't they horrible? I detest the Sky Ropes."

"Yep," she says, before realizing that she has now told one more person that she is scared of the Sky Ropes. But Max doesn't care. He only wants to talk softball. And even though Breanna has just played the worst game of her life, the conversation helps. She knows there's always tomorrow. Softball tomorrow. Max said it, and it's got to happen. She'll make sure.

They're at the main building and Max is about to take off for his cabin, where Grace thinks he's been all this time. Breanna is as ready as she can be to head down to the campfire on the beach.

"At least it's challenge by choice," Max says, suddenly shifting the conversation to the Sky Ropes. "Personally, I have insufficient data for assessing the risks. On that basis, besides terror, my choice is no."

"Solidarity," Breanna says, putting out her fist to bump.

"Solidarity," Max says, bumping. "Yes!"

Now there are four people not doing the Sky Ropes—Cynthia, Tess, Max, Breanna. Four that she knows about.

Maybe instead of pulling a prank, she needs to start an anti–Sky Ropes movement. All the way down to the water, the possibility is tantalizing.

CHAPTER
TWENTY-
FIVE

ON THE BEACH, WHERE TEAM 17/18 IS JOINED BY ANOTHER COHORT
around a bonfire blazing gold in the dark, a movement seems unlikely.

Tonight, those kids from the other cohort have already done the
Sky Ropes, and this is their big chance to tell everyone about it. Listening to them talk reminds Breanna of going to church with her
cousins, when she was a little kid. It's like these kids are testifying.

"Scary, but worth it," a short, high-voiced guy says.

"Fricking cool," a kid with a Guardians cap on backward says.

"Awesome," a girl named Jung-ah, who Breanna knows from Rec
and Ed softball, says. Her voice is full of feeling. "I can't believe I
did it."

It seems like every kid from those two cabins did the ropes.
Breanna finds kids in the group who look like chickens, scrawny
little ones, prissy ones, ones dressed in black who look like they

couldn't get excited about something if they had to. As soon as she picks out a kid who looks like the type to skip the Sky Ropes, that's who stands up next and says, "Greatest thing I've ever done. Amen." They don't really say *amen*, but they might as well.

She has to admit, it's powerful, hearing these kids explain what doing the Sky Ropes meant to them. It makes her question herself. If it was so good for them, maybe it would be that good for her. If they could feel good about mounting the high-up platform and doing one obstacle only, the easiest one, maybe she could, too. Maybe it would be all right, a challenge she could choose.

No. No. No!

She cannot do this. She cannot buy into this big camp lie that doing the Sky Ropes means something. It's something somebody made up to be hard for kids who don't know what hard is.

That's not her.

She knows. She knows.

A memory, that high-up window in the old house off McNichols, flashes into her brain. It's happening again. Her dad is leaking out again. With all her power, she pushes him down and squeezes the lockbox shut.

The Sky Ropes are not right for her. That's the truth.

She has got to be strong enough to stand by it, no matter what these kids say. The trick is how to make it so nobody cares. The prank is key. Softball, too. They could save her whole reputation. She needs to think hard and practically about both of them. And she needs to stop thinking about James. He sits over to her left, elbow on his knee, face on his palm, staring intently into the fire. Enough wasting energy on a guy she doesn't actually know.

Arrow-straight, sitting beside Breanna, Cynthia also gazes into the dancing orange and yellow flames. Breanna can feel the intensity of her concentration. It's rising off her in waves. Breanna worries that she might be hearing something that is changing her mind, that even Fortress Cynthia might be overrun by all this talk, manipulated into doing the Sky Ropes.

She and Cynthia need to talk.

Solidarity feels in danger.

She is glad, at least, that Max isn't here, being mesmerized by the bright, blazing fire and the awed voices of those kids who've been up on the Sky Ropes already. He won't get this data input. He'll still be the voice of reason.

Breanna searches the faces of the other cohort, one by one. There are three kids who say nothing. Only three. She wants to catch them after and find out why they didn't talk. But as the night draws to a close and Stacy douses the bonfire, those kids dissolve into the night, following their counselors down the beach.

Maybe tomorrow she'll recognize a face in the cafeteria. She can talk to them there. They have to have something different to say than all those other kids around the fire tonight. They have to.

Together, Cynthia and Breanna walk up the long, wooden stairs. The night is cool. The velvet sky is streaked with stars out over Lake Ojibwe as far as you can see. Smooth, steady waves lap the shore. Cynthia is quiet, except for the *phhht, phhht, phhht* sound she makes, sucking on her teeth.

"What are you thinking about?" Breanna asks.

Cynthia walks a few steps up the hill toward cabin 17. "I don't know," she says. "Those kids made me think. That's all."

"Not me." It's Tess. She and Pascale have come up behind them on the left. "I'm not doing the Sky Ropes. I don't care one bit what all those kids have to say."

Tess is the greatest. Breanna kind of loves her.

It's dark in the cabin. Breanna lies awake, listening to somebody snoring, watching a girl halfway down the line of bunks reading under the covers with a flashlight.

She's sick of camp and how she is here, soft and careless and unfocused. She's off balance. It's like the ground beneath her feet isn't solid. She keeps thinking about her dad. She's gone years, years, hardly thinking of him at all. But now, at camp, she's doing it a lot. It's like every time she thinks of the Sky Ropes, she thinks of her dad. This camp is messing with her head in a bad, bad way.

She reaches down and opens the blind. Pale moonlight streams in. Pascale, outside the covers on the next bunk, turns to look.

"How's it gone with Peanut today?" Breanna asks softly.

"It's been great," Pascale says. "We had a blast in watersports. How about you?"

Breanna thinks for a second, not wanting her friend to see how unsteady she feels. "It was okay," she says. "Canoeing was great. But I'm getting tired of all these stupid conversations about fear."

She looks over to gauge Pascale's reaction, but there isn't one. She rests on her elbow, smiling at Breanna in the soft dark.

"I wish it would just stop," Breanna says.

"Hmmm," Pascale says. "There *is* a lot of talk about fear, for sure. But you know, I think it's interesting."

"Not me," Cynthia says from the bunk below. "I agree with Breanna." Cynthia's sleeping bag rustles as she rolls to her side. "It stresses me out, thinking about all the things I'm afraid of. What do they want? A list? Because I've got one, and it's getting longer by the second."

"See? That's interesting," Pascale says. "What's on your list, Cynthia?" Pascale's whisper rises with excitement.

"I'm scared of everything," Cynthia says. "I already told Breanna."

Breanna feels sweet warmth move through her body. Cynthia just claimed her, here, in front of Pascale. Cynthia has given Breanna a place, even if she and Pascale are turning into BFFs again. Breanna didn't know it would matter to her to be included in that friendship. But now that she has been, she knows that it does.

"And after the last two days," Cynthia says, "I can add missing the ball when somebody throws it to me. Nobody told me that baseball was a really scary game. So many things you can do wrong!"

"Softball," Breanna says. "Slow-pitch softball."

"See?" Cynthia says. "Even the name is something to mess up."

"I'm scared of Cami." This time, it's Tess, wide awake, too.

They all go silent. Breanna glances down the long row of bunks, just to be sure that Cami is asleep. There's no movement, no sign of life, from her or anybody else in the whole cabin. The girl who had been reading under the covers snores lightly. It's just the four of them, talking in the dark.

"I get that," Pascale says. She drops her face over the edge of the bunk to look at Tess while she talks. "Cami's tricky. She walks this line where she seems normal. But then these cruel things come flashing out and you're not even sure she meant them or that she knows."

"Oh, Pascale," Cynthia says. "You're being way too nice to Cami. That cruel stuff is always there. Some flashes are just sharper than others."

"It's true," Breanna says, glad that Cynthia sees Cami as clearly as she does. "And for sure she knows what she's doing. Think about how she stepped on Tess's hand yesterday."

"Yeah," Tess says. "She made it seem like she didn't see me. But that's not possible." In the dark, Pascale nods her head. "Cami's been mean since the day I started school," Tess says. "That was third grade, when the doctors decided I was big enough. But Pascale is right about Cami being tricky. Cami was mean in ways that I couldn't explain. It's like nobody else ever saw or heard a thing." In the moonlight, Breanna sees a line of tears run down the side of Tess's cheek. "She's worse than the kids who were mean out in the open, who stole my snow hat or called me 'midget.' She's sneaky."

"Amen!" Breanna says, a little too loud. She lowers her voice. "Is that why you don't like me calling you Peanut? Because kids called you names for being so little?"

"Yeah," Tess says. "But Breanna, it's okay if you say it. You're the opposite of Cami. And you call Pascale Sweet Pea and you're her friend. So, if you call me Peanut, then we're friends, right?"

Tess knows that Breanna isn't mean like Cami. If Tess knows, other kids must know, too. What a freakin' relief. "Right, Peanut," she says, warmth flooding her heart. "We're friends. Especially if you aren't going to do the Sky Ropes."

Suddenly Tess sits up in bed. Her bare feet don't reach the splintery floor. "What do you mean?" She's staring up at Breanna. "Aren't you going to do them, either?"

Tactical error!

Breanna does not want to have this conversation with Tess, or even with Pascale. Already too many people know that she's afraid of the Sky Ropes. Telling more kids, even her friends, is not smart. She takes a slow, deep breath, to think.

"I just mean," she says, backpedaling fast and seizing on what Pascale said earlier in the day, "that it's gutsy for anybody to say no to the Sky Ropes when there's all this pressure to do them. What I mean is . . . I respect you for choosing not to do them."

Tess, sitting in the band of moonlight, smiles. "Thank you," she says. "I respect you, too. Pascale told me that you aren't afraid of anything."

That's more like it!

Breanna is aware that Cynthia could say something now. She could tell Pascale and Tess that Breanna is afraid of the Sky Ropes and isn't going to do them, either. But Cynthia doesn't say a word.

The girls are silent. Maybe they have fallen asleep, but they aren't breathing heavy, like the sleeping girls in the other beds. Breanna is thinking hard. The thing is, there was something beautiful in telling Niraj about being afraid of her dad and telling Cynthia the truth after Sky Ropes pre-instruction and not denying it to Max when he saw that she was scared. Admitting that she was afraid and having her friends be okay—more than okay—with that was different than any other moments in Breanna's life. She felt exposed, out-in-the-open exposed. But with a few words, each of them made her feel like being scared wasn't the biggest deal in the world. They made Breanna feel normal and maybe a little bit safe.

Tonight, in the dark, Breanna has done the opposite. She hasn't lied. But she hasn't corrected the absolutely untrue version of herself that Pascale has shared with Tess. Breanna's not ready to dive in and tell the truth, not tonight, after that disaster of a ball game and that terrible bonfire, listening to kids describe the wonder of the Sky Ropes. But maybe, if anybody's still awake, maybe Breanna could say something *closer* to the truth.

Into the dark, not knowing if anyone will hear, Breanna says softly, "Pascale exaggerated. I'm not as brave as she says I am." She laughs a little. "But that's what sweet peas do."

She hears Cynthia's bag rustle. She sees Tess, who had lain back down and crawled under the covers, turn her way. Pascale, too. They're all awake and listening. "I'll tell you a story," Breanna says. "It's about something that scared me when I was a kid, even though it wasn't supposed to. I mean, it was cool. But it scared me."

"Tell us!" Tess whispers, bringing her hands together under her mouth.

"Once, in after-care, in Detroit," Breanna says, a memory filling her mind so vividly it's like she's there right now, "we did a field trip. It was the start of first grade, a few months before I moved to Beecham. We went to Heidelberg Street. Have you heard of that?"

"Of course," Cynthia says. "The Heidelberg Project. It's world-famous. I've seen it."

But Pascale shakes her head and Tess says, "No."

"It's this place, this street, where this guy named Tyree Guyton lived. He couldn't get a job when he came back from the army, and Detroit, well, you know. Detroit went through some bad times. And he saw how life was rough for the people all around him and for him, too, and he gathered all these things up, like stuff thrown out of apartments when people got evicted and stuff left in houses that people abandoned, and he took it to his street and started making art with it."

Breanna lies flat on her back, studying the shadowy peaks of the eaves. She doesn't like this memory, but it's not one she keeps in her lockbox. It feels okay to share it now. "He painted these big, bright polka-dots all over his house. He put up this plastic Superman flying out of a window. And there were lots of houses on his street that were empty, like they were in Detroit, you know. It's better now," she says. "So he stapled stuffed animals all over one abandoned house. He put vinyl records all over another. Painted clocks on another. His street got famous, like it was a statement about Detroit and all the rotten, cruel, unfair things that had happened there and how people managed to make something out of it anyway."

"It sounds kind of weird," Pascale says.

"For sure," Breanna answers. "I mean, his neighbors still lived there, and people came to look at it from all over the world. One of the neighbors put up a sign saying it wasn't a zoo." Below, Cynthia's sleeping bag swishes. "Some people felt like he was making Detroit worse, making it a joke or a junkyard. So they started burning down the houses. That was all a long time ago, before I ever saw it. But when I was almost six, we went on this field trip to see what was still there, and we got to meet Mr. Guyton. He was really nice. We got to pick out stuffed animals that were in a big pile and choose a place to put them."

"That sounds fun," Tess says.

"It was fun. In a way. But one boy found a teddy bear with its head almost torn off. He put it on the hood of a pedal car that was half buried in the dirt." Breanna stops and takes a deep breath. She probably shouldn't say what she's going to say, but it seems like the right thing to do if she wants to tell her friends something true about herself. Not her whole self. That's too much. But something that says *I'm not exactly fearless.* "The thing that scared me was the mannequin. It was sitting at the wheel of the pedal car, cut in two at her stomach to fit. A naked, white lady mannequin. After that kid put the bear on the hood, it looked like some naked lady hit the bear and knocked its head off."

"Ooooof," Pascale says. "That's dark."

"I still have nightmares about that bear," Breanna says softly, giving away more than she means to. "No. The mannequin. Mostly the mannequin."

"That's not real," Tess says. "You shouldn't have told us that. Now I won't be able to sleep."

"Totally real," Cynthia says. "It's world-famous. Tyree Guyton's stuff is in the Detroit Institute of Arts. University of Michigan

Museum of Art, too. Ha!" she laughs. "Now you know what I do on Saturdays. Besides practice piano."

They all laugh quietly at that. Poor Cynthia!

Breanna lets out a long, slow breath. It felt good to tell that story. She's never exactly admitted that Heidelberg Street scared her. Even though it was art, even though it was a field trip, even though there were good things about it that she'll never forget, like Mr. Guyton—it scared her.

The full moon, half hidden now behind ratty clouds, casts Pascale in shifting lines of light and dark. Her eyes are bright, though, studying Breanna. "That's a weird story," Pascale says. "But at least you're afraid of something. I like knowing that."

Breanna laughs. If Pascale only knew.

"I didn't sleep last night," Tess says. Breanna knows that's not true. "I didn't bring a pillow. This mattress is too thin." She thrashes around in her bed. "And now I'm scared. I won't be able to sleep tonight, either."

Right now, Breanna's head is resting on a pillow, the round, yellow smiley-face pillow that she got with the giant claw at Quality 16 Theaters. She grabs it out from under her head. "Hey Tess," she says, reaching it down. "Use this. I don't need it."

"Oh!" Tess says. "Really?"

"Really."

"Oh, thank you!" She shuffles around some more, tucking the pillow under her head, curling up in her sleeping bag and getting comfy.

Over a big T-shirt, Breanna is wearing her soft old University of Michigan sweatshirt. It's easy to pull it off and wad it up under her head. She's comfortable enough without a pillow.

She's no princess.

In a drowsy voice, Pascale says, "Let's all go to Heidelberg Street together, okay? I'll drive on the day I turn sixteen."

They're going to be friends when they turn sixteen!

And tomorrow they're pulling a prank.

DAY
FOUR

THURSDAY

CHAPTER TWENTY-SIX

IT SEEMS LIKE FIFTEEN SECONDS PASS BEFORE CYNTHIA SHAKES Breanna awake.

"It's time," Cynthia says. "Come on." Cynthia has a watch with a vibrating alarm, so it was her job to wake them up for their 5:30 prank.

In the dark, quiet cabin, Pascale ties her sneakers while Breanna fishes her good gray sweatshirt out of her garbage bag. Cynthia is already dressed.

Breanna passes out the flashlights and they sneak out into the chilly morning. Silently, hands hiding the beams of their lights, they slip past the girls' counselors' cabin, the closest one to the main building.

Niraj and Trevor, Scott and Mitchell, and James wait, noiseless, five feet away from the back kitchen door. Crowded up against thick bushes, they are nothing but shadows. Halfway between the guys and the building, the four fat white geese lie curled up in the grass, beaks tucked under wings, asleep. Asleep! This is too easy.

Seeing the girls, Niraj waves and starts talking, very quietly. "How exactly do we catch these things, Breanna?" Even though his voice is soft, it alerts the geese. They get up, one by one. "Trevor wants to know."

"I do," Trevor says. "I don't get how this is going to work."

The geese peck at the grass, but they are watching, especially the biggest one, who side-eyes Breanna.

"Right," Breanna says, realizing she has no idea how to catch a goose.

But Niraj interrupts. "What I'm thinking," he says, "is that I should run up and grab the biggest one right around the middle." Pointing at the big goose, he reaches down and sets his three signs—*1, 2, 4*—underneath a bush. He steps forward. The big goose turns to him. It lifts its wings and stretches its snake neck and hisses, loud!

Niraj steps back. "That goose is scary," he says.

"Yeah," Pascale says. "I've been thinking about these geese." Thank goodness Pascale has been thinking. "Maybe what we do is bend down quick and grab their legs and flip them upside down and hold them as far away from our bodies as possible." She shrugs, like she's not certain. "I watched a YouTube video once on commercial farming of turkeys for a science fair project."

Cynthia nods her head, like she, too, has seen this random thing.

"In the video, this huge tom turkey flew over the fence, and a girl, Tess's size, really, just grabbed that thing around the ankles and threw it back." She stops for a second. "I don't know. Maybe it works for geese."

"That might work," Mitchell says. "Yeah. Yeah. Maybe we do it in teams, so one person distracts and the other one grabs. How does that sound?"

"That make sense," Breanna says, so grateful for her friends. "Go for their legs. Okay, everybody, let's team up and do this."

James is suddenly beside her. "You and I can take the one on the left," he says, pointing to the goose closest to them. "You go straight and keep its attention and I'll go to the side and get the feet." James just made himself her prank partner. That is very cool.

Just then, Niraj and Trevor leap together for the big goose. The other geese scatter, wings flapping, necks stretching, beaks honking. The calm one that James picked out is charging straight for Breanna, hissing, hissing, and Breanna jumps out of its path and James dives for its legs and it flies into the air and he misses and his face skids across the lawn. When he sits up, his beautiful face is covered in oozy green that is definitely *not* grass.

"Ewww," he says, wiping his face with his hand. He looks at his hand. "Ewww! Ewww!" He wipes his hand in the grass and his hand gets oozier. It's so gross. Breanna doesn't know how to help but she wants to. She peels off her sweatshirt and hands it to him. "Here," she says. "Wipe it off. Whatever it is." She knows what it is.

"Thanks," James says. He looks disgusted—who wouldn't be? But he is smiling. She watches as he wipes big green streaks onto her sweatshirt.

"All yours," he says, cleaning his green-streaked hands off last of all. Laughing, he holds it out to her.

She doesn't actually want it back, but she takes it and holds it gingerly, in two fingers. "Gross," she says quietly, laughing, too.

All this time, the big goose has been chasing Niraj. He runs in a crooked circle beside the main building and the big goose flaps behind him and flies at his head and it looks to Breanna like it's pulling out his hair.

"Ow!" Niraj says. "Ow!" "Ow!" Niraj keeps running and the goose keeps flapping and Trevor catches up to the goose and tries to grab at its legs but the goose's big wings beat wildly and they smack Trevor in the face and Trevor grabs his nose and they disappear down a small hill, three crazy shadows in the earliest rays of morning sun.

"Ow!" Niraj shouts. "Ow! Ow!"

The third goose is in trouble. Pascale and Cynthia and Scott and Mitchell have circled it and slowly advance. It hisses. It darts. It flaps. It charges at one of them and then another but can't pick a steady target. Spying Mitchell's toes in flip-flops, the goose darts forward and bites down hard. "Ouch, you little sucker," Mitchell says, hopping up and down. "That hurt."

In a second, Pascale shoots down and grabs the goose around its skinny orange legs. She holds it, hissing and flapping, upside down. Her long arms keep the goose's wings and snake-neck from smacking her, but it's all she can do to hold on.

"What in tarnation is going on here?" Eric, head cook, has come around the corner of the main building. The sun rising over the hills behind him gives enough light that Breanna can see his face. He looks mad. They're done for.

Fists crammed into jeans pockets, he glowers at Breanna, like he knows she's responsible. To her left, Pascale drops the goose she fought so hard to catch. It flaps away, honking and hissing. Breanna turns from Eric and gives James her hand to pull him up. They both wipe their hands on their T-shirts after touching and it cracks them up, even though that seems like the wrong thing to do in front of angry Eric.

Niraj and Trevor are nowhere to be seen. But the goose who'd been chasing them has followed Eric back. It waddles defiantly up to the kitchen door, hissing all around.

Eric watches it all, grimacing. "Leave my geese alone," he says, unlocking the kitchen door.

Suddenly Breanna realizes she never thought about that lock. She wonders how exactly she thought they were going to get the geese inside. Eric showing up earlier than they expected hasn't ruined the prank; it has saved her from full-on humiliation in front of her friends. Because she didn't think through the details. Her reliable prank brain was not reliable. Not this time. It's this camp, the Sky Ropes, this whole place, messing with her head.

Eric stops before he walks through the kitchen door. "The geese won," he says, shaking his head, slowly. "They always do."

His eyes drop down to a calm goose pulling the grass at his feet. "Y'all shower before you come down to breakfast," he says, and then he disappears inside, the lock clicking behind him.

Not talking, heads down, Niraj and Trevor trudge back to rejoin the group. The prank is a bust. There will be no geese in the cafeteria when the other campers come down for breakfast.

Niraj's signs—*1, 2, 4*—lie crumpled, stepped on, and streaked with green goo. "Sorry, everybody," Breanna says. "That didn't go according to plan." She is disappointed. But she is relieved, too. Not only did Eric save her from herself, but he and the geese saved her from being sent home today, and there is a part of her, the part that likes this stupid place, that is glad about that.

Nobody seems mad, not even Niraj and Trevor, even though the big goose bloodied Trevor's nose and pulled out a visible patch of Niraj's hair. Now that it's over, the two of them seem to find it hilarious. Breanna loves those guys.

Their high spirits are contagious. Everybody—Mitchell, Scott, Pascale, Cynthia, James—is laughing as they walk together to the front of the building. And Breanna is laughing with them.

"That big goose was fast!" Niraj says, rubbing the top of his head. "I mean, I'm a runner and I was running flat out and that thing was flying right behind me. I couldn't get away!"

"Dude," Trevor says. "Geese are mean." He wipes at the blood under his nose.

Mitchell clears his throat.

Don't you dare say I told you so, Breanna thinks.

He doesn't. He doesn't need to. They all know. They laugh harder.

They stand on the porch of the main building. The rising sun splashes pink and orange into the morning gray out over the hills. Wispy clouds thread yellow through the sky. Breanna knows they've got to take off for their cabins and clean up. Eric said so. And she, at least, wants to. But even though the prank went bad, this is a moment she doesn't want to end. It's fun and it feels so . . . so . . . comfortable.

Maybe too comfortable. Without thinking, she asks for help. "We need a new prank," she says. "It's Thursday. We're almost done here. Anybody got ideas?" She feels embarrassed as soon as she says it. She's the prank queen. Thinking up pranks is her job.

"Toilet paper," Trevor says. "We know where it's stashed."

"Yeah," Breanna says, but without much heart. Trevor's right, of course. They could sneak out tonight and toilet-paper those ropes. But it means actually going to the Sky Ropes, looking at them, touching them. Breanna honestly doesn't think she can manage that.

"Chainsaw," Niraj says, smiling wide.

"No." Pascale is suddenly serious. "I don't know what you mean, but no."

"There's no chainsaw," Breanna says. "We've checked."

Pascale looks horrified.

"Breanna's going to come up with something," Niraj says. "It'll be epic. We all know it will be."

Scott nods, clearly agreeing.

"I believe that," James says. He stands two steps down from her on the porch, his gentle brown eyes gazing at her through his swishy bangs. She feels her face burn hot. She likes him. She really likes him. He looks down at his green-streaked arms. "I'm heading back to the cabin," he says. "This stuff is gross."

That makes everybody laugh one more time.

Walking back to cabin 17, Cynthia is smiling hard. That's not like her.

"What's up with you?" Breanna asks.

She shakes her head. "I know things didn't work out the way you wanted," she says. "But that was so much fun." Her legs and arms are pocked with red from wings and beaks and snaky necks. She's going to be covered in bruises. "Thanks for letting me do that with you," she says. "I loved it."

"Breanna makes stuff happen." Pascale knocks lightly into Breanna, bumping her against Cynthia. And then they link arms, bruised, poop-stained arms, and climb the trail together and it feels wonderful.

CHAPTER TWENTY-SEVEN

STANDING UNDER A STREAM OF WARM WATER IN THE SHOWER, green goo swirling down the drain, Breanna can't figure out why she feels so dang happy. The prank failed. She failed. But it was great!

Pascale caught a goose by its feet and James laughed when he fell in poop and Niraj found a story—that bird chasing him and pulling out his hair—that he will tell for months.

There are so many things Breanna loves about camp: being Cynthia's partner, having Pascale in the next bunk, feeling the cold feet of the chickadee on her wrist, telling everyone about El Chupacabra, Niraj giving her cover, Cynthia being a softball beast, finding that doe, Max being her secret weapon, James being in her cohort, James existing in the world. So much! A whole pileup of amazing things. She's glad her mom made her come. She is. Sometimes it really is perfect here.

Softly humming "Brown-Eyed Girl," she brushes out her wet hair in the mirror over the sink. Cami steps up to the sink next door to stroke on black mascara. Their eyes meet in Cami's mirror and lock. Breanna sees Cami clearly, her eyes narrowed, her lip lifted in that leopard snarl. But she sees herself, too, the clean green sweatshirt she just pulled on, the dripping hair, the startled eyes, the nose she got from her dad. That nose. It's in the mirror with her and Cami. It's like he's right here with them. Like they're all mixed up in some strange, confusing way that Breanna can't escape even at the best moments.

Suddenly all the hard things about camp rush back into Breanna's head: Cami, the Sky Ropes, her dad leaking out of her lockbox. This is exactly how camp is messing with her—one minute she's carried away by good stuff and the next she's swamped, swamped by bad stuff that isn't under control.

Standing at the sink, staring at Cami, she feels wrecked inside. What happened this morning isn't good. It's a disaster. It's Thursday and she's got no prank. The Sky Ropes are tomorrow. Tomorrow! What is she going to do?

All she's got are Stacy's safe words—*The Sky Ropes aren't right for me*. It feels like the weakest thing in the world. And Cami, eyes narrowed at her in the mirror, knows. She knows. If Breanna can't figure out some decent plan to get out of the Sky Ropes, Cami, this mean girl, is going to do some damage. Breanna can tell.

CHAPTER TWENTY-EIGHT

ALL ANYBODY WANTS TO TALK ABOUT AT BREAKFAST IS SOFTBALL.
Everybody's into it now. There's going to be another game tonight
and Breanna isn't even trying to make it happen. The Wildebeests
are mad; they're determined to make a comeback. And the Roar is
looking to bury them. It's tense.

Breanna loves competition. But this is feeling personal, even
overwhelming. It's not what she needs right now when she's got
bigger things to worry about.

Slow, frowning, Max picks his way through the packed cafeteria
on crutches to the chair beside Breanna. Before she can even say
hey, he starts in.

"First thing about tonight is you've got to be cool. Can you be
cool?"

"Yeah," she says. But she's not sure. "How's your ankle?" she asks. She'd rather talk about that.

"A little sore," Max says. "But James is really strict about keeping it iced, so that helps."

Breanna told SheThor she would help with the ice, too, but she hasn't thought about it once since yesterday in the infirmary. Another fail.

She does her best to listen to Max as he goes through strategy for tonight's game. But it's hard to concentrate. The Sky Ropes are tomorrow and she's not ready and she doesn't know what to do and Max goes on and on. Finally, he seems done.

But then, Pascale elbows her in the side. "Check this out," she says, holding up the creased, worn schedule she carries around in her back pocket. She reads from the part marked *Thursday*. "'Mystery Activity.' What do you think that means?"

What does that mean? Breanna's gut clenches. She doesn't want Pascale to see how off-balance she feels. "Whoa," Breanna says, trying hard to sound like her usual annoyed self. "So next up is an activity so bad that they won't tell us what it is till we're trapped into doing it? How is that challenge by choice?"

"It gets worse," Pascale says. "There's an asterisk by it and down at the bottom, the asterisk says, 'Please don't share this activity with campers who haven't done it. Let everyone have the experience of surprise!'" She looks at Breanna and shakes her head. "That means almost every kid in this room has done this 'Mystery Activity' and not one of them has told us about it."

"What a bunch of chumps," Breanna says. She searches the room for Scott or Mitchell; they probably know. She's going to find them and she's going to make them tell her.

But it's too late. Scott and Mitchell and their cohorts are already leaving.

Whatever the Mystery Activity is, Breanna is going in blind, which is the last thing she needs

At first, it's easy. They walk, back out the road the bus brought them in on four days ago. Stacy walks fast, in the lead, laughing with Niraj and Trevor. Knowing them, they're telling her all about the geese. Probably she could get them in trouble for what they did this morning. But Breanna doesn't think she will. Stacy has surprised her. She is the real deal. Breanna trusts her. She does.

In the middle of the group, Pascale and Cynthia talk together. Tess trails behind them, pinching off small stalks of asters flowering purple, white, and yellow along the road. Breanna lags behind. She wants to be as alone as she can be right now, which isn't very.

Up ahead, she sees the dirty white siding of the maintenance shed. Even worse: the green truck, idling on the gravel drive, a quick, hunched man behind it, slamming the tailgate shut. Her heart starts pounding and her stomach goes tight. She pulls a leaf off a bush and her fingers gently search out each segment separated by a vein. She takes her time, feeling each bit carefully. *Dogwood,* she thinks as her heart slows down and her gut unclenches. She knows it is not her dad's truck. It is not her dad, because he is not here. He is not here.

Coming up over a rise, they find Stacy standing in a wide field. Tall grass, fading from green to gold, shifts in the breeze, and swaths of purple flowers quiver but don't bend in huge patches dotted all around. The sun angles down in lines of visible yellow. It's beautiful here. It smells good, too, tangy, like some herb, sage maybe, that her gran might fold into the soft dough of her savory kolaches.

She thinks of her gran, her dad's mom, guiding her through the vegetable stalls and meat counters and flower sellers of Eastern Market in Detroit. Holding Breanna's hand, she bargained down the prices for beets and zucchini and giant sunflowers and dill gone to seed, all of it picked only hours before. Her gran's loud "Fine!" when she struck a deal with the man whose cucumbers made the best pickles echoed up into the building's high eaves.

She misses Gran. After everything went wrong with her dad, they didn't see Gran much. Gran didn't drive on the freeways and couldn't come to them. And they didn't go to Hamtramck—or even Detroit—very often. When she did see Gran, Gran was different— older, sadder, less full of life. What happened with Breanna's dad changed her, too.

Breanna stops on the road above the wide field. It is an amazing place, and she breathes it in. But she can't be thinking about Gran now. She needs to be on her guard.

Trevor runs past, lightly brushing her. "HONK," he blares. For a second, she thinks it might be something mean, about the green truck they just passed. But Niraj, coming behind, flaps his arms and sticks out his neck. A goose joke, of course! Breanna laughs, and it helps her tuck her thoughts about Gran away, before they lead her somewhere she cannot go.

Stacy stands in the middle of the field and motions all the kids to come closer. They move in. "Isn't it something here?" she says. "This is my favorite place at Camp Horizons. I love the view. I love how there's always flowers blooming." She motions all around. "Asters and goldenrod now." Tess, standing in front of Breanna, breaks off a little piece of swaying goldenrod. "But mostly, I love how we get to surprise you up here with a candescent challenge by choice." Looking around, her eyes rest, briefly, on Breanna, and it seems like they light up, just for her. But *candescent*? What the crap? "I hope nobody's ruined it for you and told you what it is. I know it's corny, but I love the surprise."

Most kids shake their heads. Like Breanna, they have no idea. But Cami looks smug, Rachel the Minion, too. They know. Probably Cami stepped on somebody's fingers to make them tell.

Marcos joins Stacy in the center of the circle. "Okay," he says. "On the other side of that rock cliff is a natural climbing wall that's straight and high. It's got marked routes, some easy, some not so easy. Everybody who wants to climb it can."

Breanna's cheeks turn icy, like all the blood is draining from her face.

This is an ambush.

"The climbing wall is good practice for the Sky Ropes," Stacy says. "If you want it." She smiles. "And there's a sweetener. At the top of the wall is a bell. Every time somebody gets all the way up and rings the bell, our cohort gets a point. Marcos and I keep track." Marcos gives them a thumbs-up. "At the end of camp, when all the teams have had a chance to come up here, the team with the most bell rings gets an ice cream party."

"No pressure," Marcos says, "but I love ice cream!"

That gets a big laugh.

Ha. Ha. Ha.

Breanna looks around for Cynthia, who has ended up somewhere in the crowd. Kids are talking. Plenty look twitchy, like they might be nervous, but they're smiling, too. She can feel the energy of the group. These kids, most of them, are interested, excited even. They're taking the bait. That's what this is—bait. No pressure, but you get rewarded for one choice, and your friends—not to mention the counselors—will be mad at you for another. The pressure for this is subtle but it's real, and in the end, it's pressure to do the Sky Ropes.

What a bunch of crap.

Breanna is not going up.

The whole team can be mad at her.

At least Cynthia's afraid of heights, too. And Max, who's injured anyhow. And Tess.

Solidarity.

But a long line of kids follows Marcos to the climbing wall, more kids than Breanna expected. Standing at the edge of the field, she watches them go. Behind her, she hears the hard smack of a car door, which is surprising up here. It's Max, on his crutches. James, cleaned up nice, walks beside him. She waves and they wave back, but they don't come to her. Instead, they join the line of kids heading to the climbing wall. It doesn't make sense for Max to do it, not with his ankle or his brain. He won't like this surprise, either. But James is going to climb. For sure he is.

The handful of kids not in line for the wall listen to Stacy explain the rules for Kick the Can, which she's starting up in the meadow. There aren't that many kids left to play.

Breanna isn't going to join some stupid consolation game. She makes her way to Cynthia, who stands alone by the trail to the climbing wall.

"Let's disappear," Breanna says.

Cynthia doesn't answer. She holds perfectly still, hand shading her eyes, staring at the kids following Marcos. *Phhht, phhht, phhht,* she sucks on her teeth. Breanna knows what that means. She's strategizing. This time, it is not good.

Slowly, Cynthia turns to Breanna, a patch of red spreading under the freckles on her cheeks. "Let's watch," she says, tilting her head toward the wall.

"Why would we do that?" Breanna asks.

"I just want to know what it's like," Cynthia says, "and whether it makes sense to try."

"It's a climbing wall," Breanna says, fear rushing in. "It's straight and steep and high and we're not doing it. We're scared of heights, remember?"

"We're not doing the Sky Ropes," Cynthia says firmly, already walking toward the wall. "This isn't the Sky Ropes. Maybe this one is possible. You know, maybe this is a challenge we could choose."

"No." Breanna is not going along with Cynthia on this. "No way."

"Come on. It won't hurt to watch."

Breanna panics. Her chest feels so tight it's like all the stuff inside, good and bad, is going to come squeezing out. Cynthia walks.

Breanna doesn't. Maybe a surprise climbing wall can breach Fortress Cynthia. But not her. She's not going near that thing.

"You know what?" Cynthia calls back. "I want to try. That's what my gut says. To try." She turns and walks backward, her face red now with whatever it is she's feeling. "Come on," she says, "You have to belay me. That's what Marcos said."

Breanna does not want to belay Cynthia. She does not want to hold the rope taut and watch while Cynthia climbs. "Let your best friend Pascale do that," Breanna shouts, not budging. She's mad now. Without warning, with almost no prompting, Cynthia has gone over to the dark side.

Cynthia stops walking and folds her arms over her chest. She looks mad, too. "Breanna, you're my camp partner," she yells back. "By the rules of camp, you have to do it." A breeze tickles the back of Breanna's knee and she reaches down to scratch it. "But you're also my friend. As my friend, I would like your support. I chased geese for you this morning." Her green eyes light up when she says that. "Now, I want you to do this for me. Okay?"

The two girls study each other across the grass. Cynthia must have crushed something in the field as she walked, because a smell, strong and sharp, hangs in the air between them. Breanna can almost taste it as she breathes in. She rubs the cuff of her clean green sweatshirt in her fingers. "Yeah," she says, shrugging her shoulders. "Yeah. I'll do it. But I don't like it. You owe me big-time."

CHAPTER TWENTY-NINE

KIDS ARE ON THE WALL ALREADY. IT'S HIGH, VERY HIGH. TREVOR'S moving up it like he's Spider-Man. Niraj, watching him, holds the belay line taut.

"You're a natural, man," he calls. "Keep going, man. You're almost there."

Up and up Trevor goes, hands and feet finding holds in the craggy face of the rock, till Breanna has to crane her neck back to watch him. At the top, he smacks the bell. A point for Team 17/18.

Marcos helps Cynthia into a harness and gives her directions. Above them, the bell rings two more times. He hands Breanna a rope. "Your job is to keep the belay line tight at all times. Feel the tension?" He tugs on Cynthia's line, and it gets tight in Breanna's hands. "Keep it like that. Can you do that?" he asks.

"Sure."

He looks at her funny, like he doesn't believe her.

"What?" she says. "I get it. I'll do it." She yanks the belay line.

"Hey," Cynthia says. "I feel that." She's staring hard at the climbing wall, her eyes tracing carefully up. She's really going to do this.

"Okay," Marcos says. "You ready?"

Cynthia reaches up to the wall and grabs two holds Marcos has recommended, then puts her feet on two others he points out. She's six inches off the ground and already her whole body is shaking.

Why is Cynthia doing this? She is so scared. Just watching her makes Breanna sick. The bell rings again. Breanna pulls the line tight, the way Marcos told her to.

"See the dark orange route?" Marcos asks, pointing up the wall to a jagged line of small, orange ledges, mixed in with ledges of yellow, blue, and purple, all just big enough to rest fingers or toes on.

Cynthia nods.

"That's the easiest way. Follow those all the way up. And don't hurry, okay? Take all the time you need."

Kids on either side of Cynthia mount the wall. They pass her before she's reached for her next grip. "Stay focused," Marcos tells her. "Do it your way. Don't pay attention to anybody else."

Marcos moves across the wall, coaching kids, shouting encouragement, cheering when the bell rings.

And it just keeps ringing.

Cynthia is shaking hard. It carries through the belay line. She's so slow, she's creeping. She's so much slower than everybody else.

It's painful to watch. Breanna is embarrassed for her. Why would she let everybody see how scared she is? All this time Breanna thought Cynthia was smart.

Cynthia finds holds for her next hand, her next foot. She pulls herself up and stops. She stops. Every time she makes a move, she stops. It's not like the other kids, who keep going, even if they're slow. Looking up, Breanna has no choice but to see those kids climbing higher and higher until they actually look small near the top.

This is crap. Her stomach hurts.

A girl on Cynthia's left, one of Cami's friends, who started climbing after Cynthia, rings the bell. Cynthia is only a third of the way up. Searching for a hold for her right foot, she has this look on her face. It's so intense, like there's nothing in the world but her and this wall and a foot that needs a place to land. She settles her foot. Slow, so slow, she pulls herself up.

Pascale is on the wall. Breanna didn't even see her get on. But here's Tess, standing beside Breanna, holding the belay line and watching Pascale, who goes up with no trouble, of course. She says something Breanna can't hear to Cynthia as she passes. Cynthia smiles.

Some boy rings the bell. Pascale rings the bell. She's rappelled down and Cynthia is just past halfway.

This is a bad dream, a long one.

Pascale, taking off the harness and handing it to Marcos, looks up to watch Cynthia's slow progress. She nods her head, like she thinks it's great, what Cynthia is doing, showing the world how scared she is of heights. Breanna grits her teeth and pulls a little slack out of the belay line.

Marcos helps Tess into a harness. Tess! Little Peanut is going to do the wall. Crap! What if Breanna is the only one who doesn't? It'll be so obvious. More and more kids keep coming over from Kick the Can. She might be the only one. How is she going to cover that?

"Good for you," she hears Marcos say.

"I want to go up twelve feet," Tess says. "So I'll be twice as tall as my dad. Then I want to come down."

"You got it."

"Tell me when I'm there."

"Deal."

By now, Cynthia has clawed herself up pretty high, high enough that it's absolutely terrible to watch. Breanna doesn't want to look anymore. But she has to. It's her job.

Cami is on the wall now. It's easy for her, of course. She's so fast, it hardly seems like she's using the holds. It's more like she's a lizard with a Leopards cap and sticky feet. She says something when she passes Cynthia and Cynthia's face turns redder than it already was. The belay line shakes harder. Cami rings the bell. *Mean girl.*

Back down in seconds, she asks Marcos, "When can I go again?"

"Let's get everybody up once and then we'll see."

She looks up at Cynthia and her lip gets that leopard snarl. "That could be hours," she says.

Marcos ignores her.

Cynthia is almost to the top. She's close enough that she stretches out her right hand to try and hit the bell. She can't reach it. She's close. But she can't reach.

"Cynthia," Marcos calls up, "One more short climb and you've got this!"

He glances over at Tess, who's made slow but steady progress. Pascale, holding the line, has been talking to her softly the whole time. "You go, Tess! Look at you. Way to go!"

"Hey, Tess," Marcos calls. "You're twice as tall as your dad, at least."

"Yes!" she shouts, looking so happy. She starts coming down, Pascale talking to her every inch. "That's it. Yeah, Tessie! You're doing great!"

Cynthia isn't moving. She's almost to the top and she isn't moving. Breanna knows she should call encouragement up to Cynthia, that it's the right thing to do. But she can't. The words won't come. Sweat prickles up below her sleeves. As a cool breeze blows, she shivers.

More kids mount the wall—Niraj, Rachel the Minion, James.

Max stands beside Breanna, holding James's belay line. He looks a little grim.

"You doing this?" Breanna asks.

"No. Even if I could." He looks down at his ankle. "And maybe I could. I'm feeling good. But I didn't know about this. I haven't done any research on fall rates or harness injuries or hold failures. So, no. Absolutely not."

"Solidarity," Breanna says, relieved that she won't be the *only* one.

James rings the bell. Niraj rings the bell and stays up there, pumping his fists in the air till a few kids give him a cheer. But Cynthia is frozen. Marcos watches her between getting kids harnessed and giving instructions. In a break, he calls up, "Cynthia, you can do this." His voice is calm and reassuring. "One more set of holds," he says. "Just one more."

Cynthia stretches out her hand, trying to reach the bell again, from the same spot as before. That's all she's been doing for a long time. She keeps doing it, like she's caught in some weird loop. Kids on the ground are watching her, whispering her name. More and more, they gather. More and more, they watch.

Cynthia is a moth caught in a web and nearly paralyzed and everyone can see. The nightmare of it is almost unbearable. Breanna's palms are slick with sweat. One at a time, she wipes them on her sweatpants. She grips the belay line so tight that her knuckles turn bloodless.

She shouldn't be watching this. Cynthia should never have done this. Breanna's chest aches. Her stomach burns. She does not want to be here.

"Nod if you can hear me, Cynthia," Marcos shouts up.

She nods.

"Great. You're doing great. You've got to do one more set of holds. Do you understand?"

She nods again.

"Can you do that?"

"There are no more dark orange ones." Cynthia's voice is shaky. "I don't know where to go."

"Got it!" Marcos says. "Got it. There are purple ones that you can reach. Do you see those?"

"Yes." Her voice comes small.

"Those are what you need. Use those now."

"Okay." Cynthia's right hand reaches for a purple hold. There's a crowd down on the ground staring up at her. It's terrible how everybody sees. Watching it makes Breanna dizzy. But she has to stand here, trying to keep the belay line tight in her sweaty, sweaty hands.

Cynthia grabs the purple hold with her right hand. Her left hand reaches for another. Her left leg. Her right leg. She's hoisting herself higher, shaking so hard you can see it from the ground. She climbs. All she has to do now is reach a hand up and smack the bell. It's only inches away.

Breanna is shaking now, hard. It's not just Cynthia shaking through the line. It's Breanna, too.

Finally, finally, Cynthia stretches out her hand and reaches it over the bell. *Smack!* It rings.

The kids on the ground erupt in cheers and clapping. Pascale whistles loud through her fingers. People clap Breanna on the back, congratulating her just for holding the belay line as Cynthia slowly rappels down. Everybody's smiling (not Cami). Cynthia, her face bright red, smiles biggest of all. Once she's off the wall, kids surround her and high-five her. Marcos helps her get the harness off, since her hands are shaking too hard to do it alone. All the time, Cynthia's eyes search past the kids around her. Finding Breanna, they light up.

"I did it," she shouts over the noise.

Breanna, who has dropped the belay line and is slowly backing away, gives Cynthia a tight smile. She knows she should be happy for her friend. What Cynthia just did? Amazing.

But watching it, every painful second of it, was too much, just too much, and Breanna has got to get out of here and she moves past the crowd and walks as fast as she can and her legs are shaking, even though she didn't go up that wall, because watching it, just watching it was bad enough and feeling Cynthia's fear through the line, her shaking through the line, that was bad enough.

Breanna doesn't know where she's going.

Away from the wall.

Away from the kids playing Kick the Can.

Away. That's all.

She finds a little rocky trail. It leads down the hill and around a giant boulder, pressed up tight against a stone cliff, almost as high as the climbing wall. There's a low, sloping overhang where the rock wall and boulder meet, and underneath, it's like a mini cave in the ground. She's sure that she is not supposed to be here. But this is where she needs to be, because this is a place where she can disappear.

She crouches down and slides in tight against the stone cliff. There's just enough room to lie, face to the wall, curled into the smallest human ball she can make. She rubs her fingers against the ribbing on the cuff of her sweatshirt, feeling the give of the elastic, the texture of the grain. It helps, a little. Eyes pressed shut, arms tight around her ears, she huddles on the stone-cold ground, willing herself to just stop shaking.

"Breanna?"

She hears her name. She doesn't know how long she's been curled up here. A second? A minute? An hour?

"Oh my gosh, I found you!" It's Cynthia.

Breanna curls herself in tighter, trying to make herself so small that she will disappear and Cynthia will go away.

Gravel crunches. Close by, Cynthia sucks on her teeth, *phhht, phhht, phhht*. Breanna can't move.

"Breanna." Cynthia's hand, warm and gentle, is on her shoulder, reaching into the little cave where Breanna has tried to hide. "Breanna, oh my gosh, Breanna. I've been looking everywhere for you. Everybody's leaving. I pretended you left something somewhere, that I knew where you were. But if you don't come, now, there's going to be two camp counselors and twenty-two kids looking for you. Get up." She tugs on Breanna's elbow.

Breanna groans.

"Hurry," Cynthia says. "You don't want anyone to see you here." She pulls harder on Breanna's arm. "Come on."

Breanna rolls over. Stones dig into her back. Cynthia stares at her, green eyes worried. Breanna lets Cynthia take her hand and pull her out and up. Standing on the rough trail that brought her to this hole, Breanna wraps her arms around her body and shivers.

Cynthia has tears in her eyes. "I didn't know," she says. "I didn't know that belaying me could do this. I'm sorry." She wraps her arm around Breanna's shoulders as they walk, slowly, back around to where the group is gathering beside the road. "I should have asked Marcos or found somebody else. I'm sorry."

Breanna isn't shaking so hard anymore. Her hands are cold, her legs stiff. But her heart isn't pounding and her brain isn't jangling and she feels okay, sort of, like at least whatever happened at the wall is over.

"Now you know," Breanna says, and she can hear that her voice doesn't sound right at all. "It's this bad."

CHAPTER THIRTY

THE REST OF THE DAY IS A BLUR. BREANNA CAN'T THINK STRAIGHT.
She can't bear to remember what happened at the climbing wall. In
flashes—like lightning—she thinks, *Sky Ropes, Sky Ropes. Sky Ropes
tomorrow.*

She has to show up. That's the rule.

She's got no plan to make herself look good. No prank to dis-
tract the other kids. Her fear will be right there, out in the open,
for everybody to see.

And they won't even be surprised, after what just happened—
or didn't happen—on that stupid climbing wall. Everyone must
have a clue already that Breanna Woodruff isn't fearless.

Camp has tricked her. It's made her weak in front of everybody.
She is cold and tired and numb, just numb.

All she has now is softball. She can lose herself in softball. At least there is that.

After dinner, Breanna stands on the pitcher's rubber. She is mad. Mad at Cami, who is up at bat. Mad at this stupid camp that is messing with her head. Mad at her memories escaping her lockbox. Mad at her dad. Him, most of all.

Cami does her stupid warmup and Breanna lifts a dangerous eyebrow. As soon as Cami steps into the box, Breanna throws. The pitch is high and slow, just like Max said. It drops neatly over the plate. Cami doesn't swing.

"Strike one," SheThor calls.

Cami's lips move. Breanna hopes the boring pitch bugs her, but she can't tell. Cami relaxes her wrists and lets the bat drop. She taps the ground a few times and wiggles her hips before lifting the bat and taking her stance again. Her eyes, in that familiar glare, are level and hot. She's got that leopard snarl on her lip.

Breanna couldn't care less.

She throws the same pitch. Same height. Same boring, beautiful drop. Too dull for Cami. She doesn't swing.

"Strike two," SheThor shouts.

Cami wipes sweat from her cheeks. Pascale shoots the ball back to Breanna, and it hits her glove with a good, hard *thwump*. Breanna curls it against her chest and holds it there, like a tender thing. Cami, ready, narrows her eyes in hate.

Right back at you, Mean Girl.

Breanna throws the next pitch low and fast and edging inside. Max, on the bleachers, shouts, "Hey, batta, batta. Swing!" Breanna watches Cami's eyes on the ball. She's spotting it right, and when it slow-drops to the inside corner, her wrists break. *Thunk*. She connects. The ball lops forward. Cami starts to run, but not hard. She knows the hit was bad. Pascale, calm and ready, gets underneath and catches it.

"Out," SheThor calls.

Out. Out! Cami is out!

It should be a great moment. But Breanna can't feel it. All she knows is that with her brain turned off and her body going through the motions, she is good, better. She walks James. She strikes out Rachel the Minion. She catches a pop fly when the next batter hits her first pitch. Four up. Three outs. James never gets off first.

At bat, the Wildebeests go wild. Trevor hits a triple. Niraj brings him home on a double. Even Tess gets to first base, probably for the first time in her life.

And that Tess—Max coached her today whenever he saw her. He told her that being small made pitching to her hard, told her to crouch down at the plate and never swing. She did it. She made her strike zone teeny tiny, and Cami never found it. Cami walked Tess. More like galloped her, because that's what Tess did all the way to first base. Pascale cheered at the top of her lungs.

How humiliating it must be for God's gift to pitching.

And, in fact, Cami is acting rattled. She yells when Rachel the Minion swings at a bad pitch. "Watch the ball. Geez!" Breanna strikes Minion out. Cami barks at James, "What is wrong with you? That was a simple grounder." The Roar plays worse and worse. James checks out. He makes error after error in right field. "You're better than this," Cami shouts. He gets sloppier.

"Not a good night for them," Cynthia, close by at shortstop, says quietly to Breanna. "More Whimper than Roar, wouldn't you say?" They laugh.

Breanna tries to feel the pleasure of the joke. Funny things usually reach her, no matter how bad things are. But not now.

The Wildebeests have played so well tonight that they've almost caught up with the Roar. They're down by one. One! This is a ball game.

Breanna wishes she felt excited about that, but she doesn't.

The sun has dropped behind the lake and there is a soft layer of violet light hanging over the field. It will be dark soon. This may be the last at bat of the night.

Breanna's going to make it count.

Cami, at bat again, is doing her stupid warm-up, rolling her hips from side to side, wasting time instead of taking up her stance. Breanna is sick to death of it. She walks off the rubber, over to Cynthia, who's playing shortstop like a pro. "You pitch," Breanna says, handing her the ball.

"What?" Cynthia says.

"Twelve feet up. Down at home plate. Think of home plate as a great big bucket you've got to land the ball in. That's all." Breanna is serious. It seems like a great way to mess with Cami. "You're a natural, remember? And if you can't do it, it's on me."

"This is dumb," Cynthia says. "You're on a roll."

"It *looks* dumb," Breanna says. "But it's smart. Because when you, a brand-new pitcher, get Cami out, she's going to go berserk. I want to see that."

"I won't get her out. This is a bad idea." Cynthia's eyes are wide. Fortress Cynthia is afraid.

"Play ball, ladies," SheThor shouts. "Let's go."

"Just try," Breanna says, patting the ball that Cynthia holds in her hand. "Walk her. That's enough. Your left arm is magic. Cami doesn't know that."

Cynthia takes the ball and steps to the rubber. She doesn't look confident. Cami, in the box, narrows her eyes at Breanna, who's at shortstop now. Then she fixes her eyes on Cynthia and lifts her lip in a snarl and her face is full-on deadly!

"Don't look her in the eyes," Breanna calls to Cynthia. "They'll paralyze you. Like that lady with snake hair."

Cynthia's laugh is a short snort. "Don't worry," she says. "I'm looking up her nostrils." And it's true. Cami's got her chin in the air, like the diva that she is.

Cynthia's first pitch doesn't reach home plate.

"Ball," SheThor calls.

"What was *that?*" Cami says, disgust in her voice.

Cami has to step back, so Cynthia's next pitch doesn't hit her in the arm. "If you're trying to insult me," Cami shouts, "it's working."

"You're doing great, Southpaw," Breanna calls over to Cynthia, and she means it.

Pascale, at catcher, throws the ball back to Cynthia, then turns to Breanna and raises her arms in a *what the heck!* kind of way.

Pascale is confused. That's okay. Probably Cami is confused, too, and that's what this is about.

Cami takes her position. Cynthia stands on the rubber, the ball in her glove. Cynthia's determined eyes, fiery under her navy cap, trace an arc between the rubber and home plate. Once, twice, three times.

Oh! This is great. This moment is enough to break through Breanna's numbness. Cynthia's brain, her beautiful brain, is strategizing. It's figuring out how to get the ball where she wants it to go. Something cool is going to happen.

Cynthia pitches. The ball arcs up. It drops slow, neat, right at home plate. Cami doesn't swing.

"Strike one," SheThor calls.

"Nice going," Breanna says.

Cami taps the ground three times with her bat. She wiggles her hips. This time, when she takes her stance, she's concentrating. Cynthia's next pitch is just like the last one. It drops at home plate and Cami swings and connects and it's a good, hard drive heading for the gap between between first and second. Cami flies for first as Cynthia sprints for the ball and she's reaching for it, stretching for it, her glove out, out, out.

Yes!

She snow cones it.

There's the ball, peeking out the top of Cynthia's glove.

"Out," SheThor calls. "It's getting dark. We'll pick this back up tomorrow." It must be clear even to SheThor that no one is giving up this game.

The Wildebeests cheer and crowd Cynthia on the field. She stares at the ball in her glove. Then at Breanna. Then at the ball. Her face breaks into a smile bigger than you'd think Cynthia could ever smile in a million years.

Cami is at SheThor's side in seconds, yelling. "It was too dark. I couldn't see. It's not fair." She's mad. She's whining. She's being the worst kind of bad sport, the real Cami all along, like Breanna always knew.

"If you couldn't see," SheThor says calmly, picking up bats and putting them in the equipment bag, "you needed to tell me before you took the pitch. It was darker than this last night when you were on the rubber. You were okay with that."

All the way down to the lake shore, Cami complains. "Grace is unqualified to ump." "In the Midwest Region Premier League, Grace wouldn't be allowed to set foot on a field." "Grace sucks."

Breanna should be enjoying this. She should be over the moon, bright and icy in the purple sky. But after that one jolt of excitement, she is back to feeling nothing. Even after getting within one point of the Roar in a softball game that was all she had to look forward to, she is numb.

Down on the beach, she watches the fire blaze high, crackling orange and blue, yellow and gold. She can see that Marcos has brought the roasting sticks and two bags of marshmallows. She loves toasting marshmallows. But tonight, she doesn't care.

Suddenly, Cami slides in behind the log where Breanna sits.

"Nice game," Cami says in her silky-smooth voice.

"Thanks," Breanna answers coldly.

"Your team's good. I mean really. I'm impressed."

"Okay." Cami is a liar.

"Soooo," Cami says. "Sky Ropes tomorrow."

Tomorrow. Sky Ropes. It feels like the fire blows out. Like every star in the sky turns off. One night. One night. Between Breanna and the Sky Ropes.

"You didn't do the climbing wall," Cami says, so smooth.

That voice. That silky-smooth voice. It makes Breanna think of her dad, every time. Breanna cannot handle this.

"Why not? You scared of heights?"

"No," Breanna says flatly, everything alive inside her extinguished now. "I'm not."

"Well good," Cami says. "Because I was thinking, we should go up together. You and me. We're the best athletes in this whole place." More poison lies. "We should race. See who's fastest up there. I bet it will be you."

Breanna sits, frozen. She can't answer. Cami's poison, lime green like her toenails, drips into Breanna's veins, turning her cold. She shivers. She wants to reach her icy hands out to the fire and warm them. But they won't move.

"I've already told the Roar," Cami whispers. "They can't wait to see us race." Drip, drip goes the poison. "Do you want to tell the Wildebeests, or should I?"

Breanna never saw this coming.

She means to say something, like, *Naw. One more night on the ball field is all I need to stomp you.* But Cami knows, has always known, and she is going for full-on humiliation, Breanna can tell. It's right there in that hard edge of her voice—mocking and mean and sure of victory.

Seconds ago, Breanna was numb and frozen. There was safety in that. Now it's gone. Cami's words have started something, like a low, glowing ember from the fire has flamed, hot and red, deep down inside Breanna and she is burning with fury and resolve: Cami will not destroy her. She will not.

"You tell them," she hisses.

And just like that, it's done.

Tomorrow, everybody will be watching—Cami will make sure of it. She wants every kid at camp to have a front-row seat to the *Breanna Woodruff Is a Coward Show*. Of course, Breanna can't beat Cami racing on the Sky Ropes. Cami will do them in ten seconds and beg for more.

But Breanna will do them. Cami isn't counting on that. She thinks Breanna won't dare, but she is wrong.

Breanna will do what she needs to do, like she always, always does.

Doing the Sky Ropes, just doing them, even if she's way slower than Cami, in front of all those watching kids, will protect her reputation, and that's everything. Knowing that everybody thinks she's gutsy is the one thing in her life that tells her every day that she is *not* that terrified little kid at the high-up window of the old house off McNichols anymore.

Losing that is the worst thing she can imagine.

Worse, even, than facing the Sky Ropes.

So fine. Yeah. She is doing the Sky Ropes.

CHAPTER THIRTY-ONE

THE CABIN IS INKY BLACK. THE MOON HAS DISAPPEARED BEHIND thick clouds. Not even a soft moon-gray shadow slips in through Breanna's open blind.

The darkness feels heavy, like dead weight on Breanna's chest. It feels like her lockbox is crushing her. Eyes open, she stares at nothing. Her brain jangles.

Tomorrow. Tomorrow. The Sky Ropes. Tomorrow.

How is she ever going to do them?

For as long as she can remember, even in the worst times, she could fight and think and scheme and find a path forward, some small, bright way shining in her brain, a flashlight beam in the dark.

Not this time. Not this time.

She can see the Sky Ropes in her head, glowing toxic in the darkness. It's too much. She kicks her sweaty legs out of her slippery blue sleeping bag.

Beneath her, Cynthia sighs and rolls and rustles on her bunk. Her finger pokes Breanna through the mattress. "You awake?" Cynthia whispers.

"Yeah," Breanna says.

"I can't sleep," Cynthia says. "My mattress feels like rocks. I think I twisted my ankle on that climbing wall. Maybe both my elbows and my biceps, too."

It's meant to be a joke and Cynthia doesn't try many jokes. But Breanna can't bring herself to laugh. "I can't sleep, either," she says.

From the next bunk, Pascale whispers. "I'm awake, too. I think it's the Sky Ropes. I'm excited but I'm scared and I can't stop thinking about them."

There it is. Out in the open.

The Sky Ropes.

They burn at Breanna's brain.

Seconds pass, and nobody talks. The weight on Breanna's chest settles heavier.

Cynthia takes a deep breath. "Are you doing them, Pascale?"

Pascale hesitates. "Yeah, I'm going to do them," she says. "They're so built up now. Everybody's talked about them so much." She shifts and her bunk creaks. "I feel freaked out. But I think I can do them, and I want to." She waits, but no one else talks. Carefully, slowly she says, "What about you two?"

There's another long pause. Cynthia's hands shuck across her sleeping bag, the noise loud in the silent cabin. "Yes," she says. "I've decided."

"What?" Breanna sits up. She can't believe what she's hearing. "What about solidarity?"

Cynthia doesn't know about Cami, doesn't know that Breanna, too, is doing the Sky Ropes. Breanna hasn't had the heart or energy to tell her. But all this time, even in the last terrible hour since Cami talked to her, imagining Cynthia and herself, together, saying no to the Sky Ropes the way they planned—that, that felt like a safety net. Now that's gone, too.

"It was the climbing wall," Cynthia says. "It was so scary. But it was kind of a mind game for me. I figured it out." She sounds calm and determined. "I know I made a pact with you not to do the Sky Ropes, Breanna. But doing the wall meant something to me." Breanna hears her swallow hard. "Now, I want to try the Sky Ropes. I want to face that challenge."

Holy crap. Cynthia's caved. This stupid camp has tricked her into what it wanted all along. Fine. She's not the Fortress Breanna thought she was. But so what? So what? Breanna never needed her anyway.

"Yeah," Breanna says. "I'm doing the Sk, Sk, Sky . . ." Her tongue feels raw. Her mouth sticks on the words. A corner of the lockbox presses sharp against her lungs and it's hard to breathe. "I'm doing the Sky Ropes, too."

Something hits Breanna's butt.

"Ouch!" Cynthia says. Clearly, that was her head.

Suddenly, Cynthia is on her feet, standing right up against Breanna's bunk. "Are you crazy?" she whispers. "You can't do the ropes!"

"Don't tell me what I can't do."

"Breanna, you're being an idiot!" Cynthia says.

"Hey!" Pascale jumps in. "Cynthia! Breanna wants to do the ropes. Good for her."

"Where have you been all week, Pascale?" Cynthia's whisper is as dry and quick as tinder catching. "Breanna can't do the Sky Ropes. She's terrified, like certifiably phobic, of heights. How can you not know that?"

Pascale's mattress crunches as she shifts in the darkness. "Well, in case you haven't noticed," and Pascale sounds annoyed, "I've been pretty busy this week. But heck, Cynthia, Breanna's trying to face her fears, just like you. It'll be great."

"Earth to Pascale! It won't be great. It will be terrible." Cynthia is almost panting. "Belaying me on the climbing wall made Breanna curl up and play dead. Did you see that? Did you know that?"

Pascale rustles louder in her bunk, like she's sitting up, but it's so dark in the cabin that Breanna can't be sure. "What do you mean?"

Breanna rolls over on her side, toward the wall, away from her friends' pointless conversation. She's made up her mind. She doesn't need to hear this.

She can't help but hear.

"When I came down the wall," Cynthia says, quiet and urgent, "Breanna took off, I didn't know where. It took me twenty minutes to find her. She was curled up in a *hole*, Pascale—shaking and curled up in a hole. That's how scared she is of heights. We're talking true phobia. She can't mess around with that."

"Ah," Pascale says. "Ah. Okay. Breanna, you should definitely not do the Sky Ropes."

Her back turned against her friends, Breanna says, "Shut up. Just shut up. I'm doing the ropes." Oh! But she'd been scared in that hole. She rubs the hem of her slippery blue sleeping bag between her thumb and first finger. The scar on her shoulder itches. Her chest hurts bad. The lockbox feels like it could bust open right this second.

"As your friend," Cynthia speaks quietly into Breanna's ear, "I'm telling you that you're doing the Sky Ropes over my dead body. If it will help, I'll skip them with you."

"Same," Pascale says firmly.

"Yeah?" Breanna rolls over. "How are you going to stop me?"

"We'll talk to Stacy," Pascale says. "She won't let you do them."

"No. We don't need to do that," Cynthia says. "We don't need Stacy's help. We're going to reason with you, even though you're a complete and total idiot right now and don't deserve it. We're your friends. We care about you. You know we do. So, you'll listen."

Breanna grunts.

"And if you won't," Cynthia says, "we'll wrestle you to the ground and sit on you till camp is over."

Pascale's laugh is too loud. These two, Pascale and Cynthia, are going to wake up the whole dang cabin. Breanna peers down the line of beds, just to make sure that Cami, on the farthest end, shows no sign of being awake.

Slowly, Breanna sits up. The moon has broken through the clouds. In a slim shimmer of light through the window, she sees

Pascale leaning forward in her bed and Cynthia standing up, too close. Breanna sighs. She feels tired. Tired. Tired. "You don't get it," she says.

The lockbox is crushing her heart. It's never been this heavy. Still, she will do her best to make her friends understand. The Sky Ropes, which she fought so hard to avoid, are now the only thing left. Because of Cami and her evil race, Breanna's reputation—which is everything—hangs on the thin, dangerous threads of the Sky Ropes. Those ropes have had it in for her from the start. She could feel it. They were always going to win.

"Look," she says. "I know that I can say, *The Sky Ropes aren't right for me*. Lame as that is, that was my plan. I never came up with a better one." She swallows hard and her spit tastes bitter. "But tonight, after the Wildebeests played so well, Cami decided to *bury* me. As in, she's telling everybody that we're racing on the Sky Ropes."

"That's messed up," Cynthia says.

"But you're not going along with *Cami*," Pascale says. "Not her."

"Of course I am," Breanna says, knowing that it's stupid, but also that there is no other way. "She's told everybody. Our whole cohort. Plus more, I'm sure. Everyone's going to be watching."

"She didn't tell me," Cynthia says. "She didn't dare." She sucks on her teeth, *phhht, phhht, phhht*. "But so what? So what? You can't give in to her."

"Cami will beat me. The ropes will be easy for her." Breanna says. "I think she's going for full-on humiliation. I'm nobody and she's a pitcher for the Lanton Leopards. My team, way worse than hers, is all of a sudden a real threat. One more night and we could beat them, and she can't live with that. She's the star." Breanna picks her words slowly. She wants to get this right, to tell the truth to her friends as best as she can. "I know I've hassled her, telling her to be nice to Tess and rubbing in how much she lost in team building and being super competitive in softball. And now she's getting me back. She's going to beat me on the Sky Ropes—the only thing that matters here—with everybody watching." Breanna swallows down the bitter taste again. "I can live with that, with losing. But if I don't go up there? Then everybody will know that I'm a big coward, which is what I am. I can't live with people knowing. I can't."

Breanna can't believe she's saying all this stuff out loud. She's telling her friends so much that she's scaring herself. But she doesn't know what else to do. Except she's done now. She's too tired to keep going.

"Breanna," Pascale says, her voice gentle. "No one will think less of you if you don't do the ropes. I promise."

"Wrong, Sweet Pea," Breanna laughs. "You can't make that promise true no matter how much you want to."

Slow, serious, calm, Cynthia says, "Breanna, sneaky Cami's outdone herself this time. But it doesn't change anything for you, except that now it will take more guts than ever to *not* do the Sky Ropes."

This is not what Breanna expected. She expected a fight, a straight-up yes/no fight. But something about Cynthia's words. They stop her. Last night, talking in the dark, Breanna told Tess that it was brave to say *no* to the Sky Ropes and she meant it. Now her friends are telling her that it's true for her, too.

"Standing up to Cami, here," Cynthia says. "In front of everybody. *That's* brave."

"I agree," Pascale says.

For a second, Breanna sits with that idea. They're right, her friends. They're right. She can feel it.

But she shakes it off.

"No," she whispers. "Think about this place. The Sky Ropes are everything. It all builds up to them. They're like the whole reason we're here. Yeah, it's fake. And sure, courage can mean saying no, like for Peanut. I get that." Sweat prickles along her forehead. She unfolds her legs and drops them over the edge of the bunk, so she's closer to her friends. "But for me, I can't show the whole world that I'm a coward. I just can't. Doing the ropes is the only way."

In the darkness, Cynthia rests her hand on Breanna's arm. "Breanna," Cynthia says, "you couldn't be a coward if you tried. I mean, I never thought you were fearless the way you said you were. I thought you were a jerk, sometimes. And a bully, sometimes, even though I don't think you meant to be. Loud, obnoxious, wild, funny. But not fearless. Nobody's fearless."

Cynthia brushes back a strand of curly hair. "Now, I know you. You've been my friend in a bad time. No matter what happens tomorrow, I'm going to be your friend. And you get to be afraid. Everybody's afraid. You know that, right?"

Cynthia is crying. Tears, delicate in the moonlight, run down her cheeks. Pascale leans over and hugs her. She is crying, too.

Breanna, feet dangling in the chilly night air, watches them. No matter what happens tomorrow, Cynthia will be her friend. Pascale, too. She thinks she believes that.

Cynthia dries her eyes on her pajama shirt. She looks at Breanna. "Cami is a bully," she says. "If you try the Sky Ropes, the bully wins. Because there's no way doing those ropes is going to work out for you. I won't let you do it." She folds her arms across her chest, in full-on Fortress mode. "I'll argue all night if I have to. I'll climb up there and fight you if that's what it takes." Close already, she inches toward Breanna's bunk, like she's coming up to fight right now. "Don't let Cami win. You're better than that. You're braver than that."

Cynthia's words sizzle in Breanna's ears. They hang in the air, like white smoke curling through the darkness. Breanna watches them rise, higher and higher past her bunk, up, up, up through the open eaves. They rise and grow and stretch themselves across the dark and Breanna knows, for sure, for sure, that Cynthia is right and that her friends, right here, right now, are giving her a small, bright way through.

"Okay," she says. "Okay. You're right. I'm done with the Sky Ropes. I'm done with Cami. I won't go up."

She's said it. The unbearable weight of the lockbox releases.

Suddenly, Pascale is off her bed and Cynthia is standing on the lower bunk and they have Breanna around the neck and they are squeezing her so hard it feels like they could crush her and it feels good.

DAY
FIVE

FRIDAY

CHAPTER THIRTY-TWO

SKY ROPES DAY.

Outside the cabin window, a thick cloud, white tinged with gray, brushes past a pine tree. The tip of the trunk shudders. It's windy today, Sky Ropes day.

It's okay. Breanna's okay.

A little sick to her stomach. Just that.

At breakfast, Cynthia and Pascale (and with Pascale, Tess) stick to her like bodyguards. Cami darts forward and hurries to one side and then the other, trying to get close to Breanna in line for food. Breanna is sure she wants to say something about their Sky Ropes race—the one that isn't going to happen.

But Cami can't get to her. If she comes on the left, Cynthia slips sideways. On the right, Pascale steps back. They keep Cami away. It doesn't even look like they're doing it on purpose. Their brains anticipate; their bodies are in sync. They move as easy as the wind carrying that cloud over the pine, but they are more wall than wind. Her hurricane wall—that's what they are.

She almost feels safe.

The cafeteria is crowded and loud. Outside the big window, gray clouds gather over the lake. The smell of old grease makes her stomach turn. Eric, filling up the bacon tray, lifts a thick black eyebrow at her and she knows that he is remembering yesterday's attempted goose prank. For the flash of a second, she feels defiant and proud of herself and her friends, and then the feeling is gone. She moves through the food line, glopping oatmeal into a bowl, adding in a spoonful of peanut butter, some chocolate chips, some coconut. Today, stomach churning, it feels like a better option than the stuff she would usually have.

Honestly, she feels a little sick. Maybe she's caught something. It feels like that, and she's glad about it, because sick is better than scared.

At the table, Cynthia sits on one side of her and Pascale on the other, then Tess. They don't pay attention to the sign in the middle of the table that tells them bottom bunks should be sitting at the other table. They are a team, an undivided team.

Breanna eats two bites of oatmeal, no peanut butter, no chocolate chips, no coconut. Something goes wrong in her gut.

Tess stares at her. "Your face is turning green," she says. "Are you sick?"

Breanna is sweating. She stands up so fast that her chair leaps back. "I've got to get to the john."

Cynthia jumps up, ready to come with her.

"No," Breanna says. "I'm sick to my stomach. It might be gross. I don't want you in there."

Cynthia scans the room. Cami sits far on the other side of the cafeteria at the other cohort table. Her back is to them. She and Rachel the Minion are deep in conversation and she's not paying them any attention. Cynthia frowns but sits back down. "Hurry," she says.

Breanna rushes out. She'll only be a minute. Passing the closed door to the infirmary, she thinks she ought to get some Imodium or Pepto or something on her way back. She wouldn't mind seeing SheThor, the camp nurse, this morning.

She hits the bathroom and runs into the first stall. Kneeling down in front of the toilet, she vomits. Holy crap. She really is sick. What else could this be? She has thrown up, once or twice, when she's been really upset. But she's not doing the ropes, so what's there to be upset about? Sweat soaks her hair and trickles down her face. She shivers, then vomits again.

The bathroom door opens.

Somebody's here. Great. Just great.

They'll see her on her knees or hear her retching and then everybody's going to know that she's in here sick. It'll look like she's scared, which she is, but nobody can know that, because *not* doing the Sky Ropes is gutsy and *she* is gutsy and that's the only vibe she can give off right now.

Whoever's in the bathroom doesn't go into a stall. Breanna twists around to look. Whoever it is stands against the sink, facing her. Whoever it is has toenails painted lime green.

It's Cami. Freakin' Cami.

Holy crap.

Breanna spits into the toilet and pulls herself to her feet. She looks at the latch on the door. There's a door with a lock between her and Cami. That's good. She can stay here as long as she needs to. She tears off some toilet paper and wipes her mouth. She tears some more and wipes the toilet seat. She flushes and when the flush is done, she sits herself down.

"Pre-race jitters?" Cami asks, her voice silky smooth and fake as a plastic turd.

Breanna squeezes her eyes shut hard. "I'm not racing you on the Sky Ropes. I changed my mind."

"*What?*" Cami says. "Why not? Don't tell me you're scared." Her feet move closer. "Not you."

Breanna swallows hard. She grabs the ribbed cuff of her sweatshirt between two fingers and takes a deep breath. It's time to take her stand. She practiced the words in her head ten thousand times since last night. All she has to do now is find the courage to say them. She takes one more deep breath and forces the words out of her mouth. "The Sky Ropes aren't right for me."

"HAHAHAHA." Cami's shrill laugh echoes along the white tile walls of the narrow bathroom. The sound is cold and sharp as a winter wind on a negative-fifteen-degree morning. It hurts. Breanna covers her ears.

Cami laughs and laughs. Her feet move across the cracked gray floor until they're inching close to Breanna's locked door.

Breanna tries to focus her brain on the messages scratched into the wood of the stall.

Rose and Trudy 4ever.
Camp Horizons sucks.

Cami is talking through the door, but Breanna is not listening. She can hear. The words are entering her auditory canal, vibrating her tympanic membrane, signaling the auditory nerve and all that fancy stuff she learned about in science last year. But she is not listening.

"I can't believe it," Cami says. "Tough girl Breanna! I heard all about you. You're famous in Beecham, do you know that? People know about your pranks. Kids say you used some boy's glass eye to take down your whole school. But here you are, in the bathroom puking your guts out on Sky Ropes day like a coward."

Cami knows. She knows. Her lime-green toenails inch even closer. "Tough girl Breanna not even going up. I don't know. I just thought you'd be better competition. I thought I'd respect you even if I didn't like you, which I don't. But you're all show, a phony."

Breanna hears that word in Cami's silky-smooth voice. Leaning forward on the toilet, she pushes up her sleeves and crosses her arms and digs her fingernails into the skin above her elbows. Her whole body shakes.

Cami's feet shuffle even closer. "All I mean," Cami says, "is that I expected *you* to really be something." She rubs her foot along her ankle. "But it turns out you're nothing. Breanna Woodruff is nothing at all."

Nothing. Breanna hears that. *Nothing.* She covers her ears, imagining herself sealing them off so tight that no sound wave, not even one, can leak through. But even if she could seal them now, she can't unhear what she has just heard. The words are stuck. In her ears. In her head. In her unprotected heart.

There is a door and Cami is on the other side of it and Breanna doesn't feel right and she's alone and she told her friends to stay put and she doesn't think they're coming, though she wishes they would and she does not know how to get out of this.

She tries to stay cool and think. That's what Pascale would tell her to do. *I am not a coward. I am not a phony. I am not nothing. I am not.* But the damage is done. The memory of the moment in her life when she honestly felt like nothing is leaking out, again. Her dad. That high-up window in the old house off McNichols. "Fly, baby. Fly!"

It is like a terrible nightmare, but it actually happened to her.

Her stomach is roiling again. It feels dangerous again, even though there's nothing left to puke up. She grabs on to the toilet seat, gripping it so hard that her knuckles burn.

"Are you going to hide in there all day?" Cami asks, sighing in a disgusted sort of way.

"I'm sick," Breanna says.

"Scared sick."

"No. Just sick. I'm really sick."

"That's good. Keep telling yourself that," Cami says. The door rocks. Cami must be leaning right on it.

If only Cynthia was here. Pascale with her. They would block out Cami like the world's best hurricane wall. But they're not here and Breanna needs to think, because if she doesn't, she might do something stupid and this seems like the wrong time for stupid.

The bathroom is silent. Breanna can hear Cami's sharp, quick breathing. Breanna needs to think. Cami is mean. Yeah. Cami is mean. If Cynthia were here, that's what she'd say. Cami is a bully. Truth. Truth. Why did Breanna tell Cynthia not to come in here?

Breanna's teeth are chattering and sweat is soaking through the neckline of her sweatshirt. Decent kids don't talk like Cami. They don't think like Cami. The stall is too small. She's sitting on a stupid toilet. She's got to get out of here. Cami's toenails look like chewed-up Laffy Taffy. They are poison. Breanna's body is soaked with sweat. She snatches at the words she knows, that she has practiced, that are supposed to keep her safe. *The Sky Ropes aren't right for me. The Sky Ropes aren't right for me.*

The memory of Cami's cold laughter echoing down the tiles fills her brain. The safe words dissolve before she can claim them and she knows that they are useless anyway. She buries her sweaty head in her hands.

Her heart hurts. It's everything. Cami. The Sky Ropes. Green trucks. Her dad. Her dad.

Her heart hurts. It's beating way too fast and it feels like the lockbox is finally busting, everything escaping, tilting, tipping, dripping, falling out, like garbage, just garbage and all the good things, too, her sweet, safe little basket, the doe, the chickadee, the stars on the beach at night, and James, beautiful James, and there are Cami's toenails pushed right into the stall like she belongs in this private place and Breanna's fears and her good things, too, are all mixed up and on the floor and everything, everything is inches thick with lime-green poison.

Her feet twitch. They want to go. They want to move. They want to *do* something! She stands up. She flips the latch on the wooden stall door. She shoves it open and knocks Cami back. "Get out of my way," Breanna says.

"Where you going?" Cami asks, her silky-smooth voice startled.

Breanna blows right past her, out of the bathroom, shouting back before the door slams shut, "Sky Ropes, Mean Girl. Let's go."

CHAPTER THIRTY-THREE

BREANNA TEARS PAST CYNTHIA AND PASCALE AND TESS, WHO WAIT for her in the hall outside the bathroom.

"Hey! Wait up!" Cynthia calls.

Breanna doesn't wait up. She runs out of the building and off the porch and up the trail without looking to see if her friends are coming after her.

From somewhere behind, Cynthia shouts, "What are you doing? You promised you wouldn't. Stop! Breanna, stop!"

Breanna knows what she promised. But Cynthia wasn't in that bathroom just now. Wasn't sitting on the john while Cami, vicious Cami, clawed right through to that little holding place above Breanna's heart. Now everything she dared to put inside, birds and bugs, girls' voices in the dark, James, even that silly rhinoceros dream, everything sweet and precious about camp, has been ruined by the bitter poison of Cami's words.

Cami said *Coward.* Cami said *Phony.* Cami said *Nothing.*

Cami knows. She knows.

That cannot be how this all ends.

It doesn't matter what Breanna and Cynthia and Pascale decided back in the cabin, cozy in the dark. She is going to do the Sky Ropes. She has to.

Breanna slams along the trail. It's steep. Her body feels electric and jangly, like she's riding lightning. Pebbles roll out from beneath her sneakers and she slips and catches herself, her hands bleeding against loose rock. She wipes them on her sweatpants as she runs. Branches snatch at her ponytail and she yanks her hair free. She knows she's going too fast, but she can't stop, because if she does, she might chicken out.

That cannot happen.

She passes other kids, but she doesn't notice who.

The trail is so steep. Her legs burn. Her heart pounds. Sweat runs off her forehead and down her neck. Her lungs feel shredded.

Doesn't matter. Three bounding steps up a slippery rock and she's here. At the top. Face-to-face with the Sky Ropes.

Holy crap.

They are worse up close. Way worse.

Rising out of a hard-packed clearing, massive tree trunks reach up and up and up. Breanna cranes her neck back to see how far up they go. They disappear into gathering clouds. Twiggy bridges stretch from tree to tree, too small to hold a squirrel.

A dangerous web of narrow white rope shivers in the wind. Some kid, too far away to recognize, clings to the web without going forward or back, up or down, like a paralyzed fly. Silver cables flicker high up in the leaves, like rabid dog drool catching light.

It's too much.

Breanna finds a rock to sit on beneath a giant oak. She touches her fingertips to the tree's rough bark and strokes it, softly. Her racing heart slows down. The tree's leaves rustle. Air fills her aching lungs and her brain says, *Think this through*.

Topping the trail, Cynthia leaps into the clearing. She looks around wildly, spies Breanna, and runs toward her. Cami comes behind her.

That's all it takes, the top of Cami's head cresting the hill, and Breanna's legs are moving again, taking her straight to the shed where Roger is passing out safety harnesses.

"Where's your partner?" he asks. Big, tan arms burst from the sleeves of his Camp Horizons T-shirt. The blond of his hair is unnatural.

Cynthia, red-faced and panting, gets there.

"Right here," Breanna says, pointing at her.

"You're not doing this," Cynthia says.

"Hey, now. That's not what we do at Camp Horizons," Roger says. He's got a wad of gum in his cheek. "We encourage! We cheer on! We don't say, 'Don't do it.'"

"She shouldn't do it," Cynthia insists. "She's terrified of heights."

"Good for you," Roger says, turning to Breanna. "Facing your fears like this."

Thank goodness he's dumb.

Panting hard, Cynthia looks at Roger. She looks at Breanna. Already Breanna has the safety harness buckled on. Cynthia opens her mouth.

Breanna holds up her right index finger, like mean Mrs. Codger in second grade. "Don't. Don't, Cynthia," she says. "That's not how things work at Camp Horizons." She can hear the mean edge in own voice. But she can't help it. She can't let Cynthia stop her.

Roger is talking again. He's holding a clipboard now, which he reads from. Breanna's ears buzz, but she nods when he looks at her.

"Verbal confirmation," Roger says. Breanna doesn't know what he means. They stare at each other. "Repeat back to me what I just said, so that I know you understand how to do the ropes safely."

"One more time," Breanna says.

Roger starts reading from the clipboard again. His paper flaps in the gusting wind. Breanna listens. It takes everything she's got, because behind her, she feels the trees holding up the Sky Ropes turn suddenly treacherous as they flex and stretch and reach their skeletal branches down to pull at her.

Every time Roger stops and looks at her, she repeats what he's just said. She can say the words back, even if she doesn't know what they mean.

The trees are pulling at her brain.

They're magnets.

She's metal.

It's harder and harder to keep her feet on the ground. Strange electricity thrums through her fingers and toes. It's the trees;

they're making her heart fluttery. It won't beat right. She's got to settle down. She runs her fingers over the straps of her safety harness, searching for a texture that will calm her. They are slick and synthetic and unpleasant to touch, but there is a grain and she finds it and it helps her heart beat slower.

Roger is talking to Cynthia now. "Verbal confirmation," he says. She's got to show she knows how to be Breanna's partner on the ground, safety-checking Breanna at every point. Breanna remembers this from their Sky Ropes pre-instruction on Wednesday, a million years ago. Cynthia's repeating words back to Roger, her face so pale that her freckles glow. She looks atomic. Maybe it's the trees, messing with her, too.

Roger puts check marks on his clipboard, and it's done. They are safety-checked and free to go.

Breanna lets the trees pull her.

Cynthia yanks on the back of Breanna's safety harness and stops her cold. "Talk to me. Talk to me," she says. "What happened? Why are you doing this?"

"Cynthia, I have to. If you're my friend, don't stop me." Breanna's left eyelid ticks up. It's got its own electric pulse.

"I am your friend." She still holds the harness tight from behind, but she's leaned around so she's right in Breanna's face. "I can't let you do this. Talk to me."

Breanna twists hard, pulling the harness clean out of Cynthia's hand. She lets go to the magnetic trees. They pull her, feet not touching the ground, straight to the base of a mounting ladder.

CHAPTER
THIRTY-FOUR

EXCEPT FOR THE ELECTRIC BUZZ IN HER EARS, THE TICK OF HER LEFT eyelid, and her feet floating just above the ground, Breanna feels good. She can do this.

Stacy is here, standing at the right side of the ladder. Cynthia stands on the left. She hasn't blabbed to Stacy about Breanna being scared of heights. She's keeping her mouth shut, like a real friend.

Wind blows somebody's half-full water bottle across the clearing. Breanna wants to get going, before this wind gets worse.

But she can't start yet. Stacy has to say all the words that Roger said, all over again. Maybe different words. "Line" this. "Line" that. "Line." "Line." "Line." Breanna doesn't know.

"Got it?" Stacy says.

Got what? Breanna has no idea. She nods her head anyway.

"Check in with Cynthia on every line," Stacy says. "Okay? Yell loud. It's a long way down."

Long way down. What terrible words! They sizzle through Breanna's nerves. For a second, her feet touch down. What is she doing? She can't do this! She looks up the ladder, up, up, up into the red and orange and yellow treetops, flailing in the wind. Of course she can't do this!

But there's Cami. Already up on the next course over, dancing over a twig-thin bridge.

It's enough to make Breanna start.

She puts her foot on the first rung of the silver ladder. It trembles under her weight. It's flimsy and hollow and its hollowness vibrates from the arch of her foot to the back of her molars. Cynthia grabs the ladder and steadies it.

The trees pull Breanna to the next rung.

And the next.

And the next.

All the way up to the top of the ladder.

She clambers onto a plywood platform built into the trunk of a giant tree. She's off the hollow, vibrating ladder, but she's still vibrating inside, a secret buzz, from the trees. Already, she's higher than a two-story house on a platform that tips with wind. But she's only partway up. There's a new ladder bolted into the platform that goes up so high she can't see the top through the cover of leaves.

She hears Cynthia shout, "Line on."

She doesn't know what that means. The trees tug at her. They pull her on to the new ladder.

"Line on!" Cynthia yells, something panicky in her voice.

Breanna steps on the second rung of the second ladder.

"Stop! Stop!!" Stacy is yelling. She's rushing up the first ladder. Here she is on the platform, grabbing the second ladder. Breanna puts her foot on the third rung.

"Come. Down. Now," Stacy shouts, with no Stacy sweetness. Her voice is stronger than the pull of the trees. Breanna steps down.

The platform, with two of them on it, feels too small. It rolls as the tree trunk sways in the wind and there is nothing to grab on to. Stacy takes Breanna firmly by the arm and steadies her. She looks hard into Breanna's eyes. "You copacetic?" she says. "You seem really scared."

"I'm okay," Breanna says.

"Are you sure? You don't have to do this. You can go down that ladder now. I'll help you, nothing lost." She's staring at Breanna. "You took a shot. You're terrified of heights and you took a shot. That's a victory."

Cynthia! That rat! She did tell. So much for trust. So much for friendship.

"I'm fine," Breanna says coldly.

Stacy keeps staring. Breanna's fingers and toes are thrumming again. The trees are pulling her again. Eyeball to eyeball with Breanna, Stacy says, "Okay. If you're going to do this, listen to me. If you can't do this right, then you can't do it. Are you listening?"

"I'm listening." Breanna summons every scrap of energy in her whole, entire body. She frees her brain from the trees and listens.

"There are steel rods on each side of this ladder," Stacy says, pointing. "The rods follow the ladder all the way up. Did you hear me talk about this?"

Breanna shakes her head no.

"Are you listening now?"

Breanna nods.

"Good. The first two rods have a line of cable attached. Each cable ends in a clip. Find the clips. There's one on each side. Clip them to your safety harness, here and here." She touches sturdy hooks on each side of Breanna's waist. Whoa! Where did they come from? "Clip one on. Call down to Cynthia, 'Line on.' Wait for her to answer, 'Line on.' Got it?" Breanna nods again.

"Do the exact same thing for the second clip. After that, you move each clip, one at a time, to each new set of rods. You have to clip on and off, twice, every four rungs, all the way up." Stacy's face is so fierce that Breanna has to pay attention. "Again, up on the course, at every platform and every obstacle. You have to tell Cynthia every time and she has to answer before you move on. Do you understand that? Can you do it?"

"Yes," Breanna says, clearly. The trees pull at her. It's all she can do to keep her feet on the platform.

"If you don't," Stacy says, "I'll haul you off these ropes myself." She sounds ferocious enough that Breanna believes her. "The cables are your safety net. They keep you from falling. Do you get that?"

Breanna nods. She gets that.

Stacy frowns. "We'll do the first one together," she says. Reaching for a length of cable on one side of the ladder, she clips it onto Breanna's harness.

"Line on," she shouts down.

"Line on," Cynthia calls.

"You do the next one," Stacy says.

Breanna reaches for the second cable. She clips it to her safety harness. "Line on," she yells.

"Line on," Cynthia's voice rings up. "You can do this, Breanna. You're going to do great."

Whatever. Cynthia told Stacy. Cynthia is not her friend.

The trees tug and pull. The gray sky darkens. High up, kids move across strange, swaying formations of white rope and silver cables. Somewhere up there is Cami, balancing, dancing, floating like this is nothing. Breanna wants to move, now!

Stacy, finally done talking, tells Breanna she can go. Breanna gives herself over to the trees and lets them take her up the ladder.

One step.

Two steps.

Three steps.

Four.

She stops. Her hands are shaking so hard she can't undo the first clip. Already she has climbed through the cover of quivering red leaves and she is next to the sky, where gray clouds pulse around her. The wind blows hard up here. It rifles her hair and buzzes her ears and the ladder shakes beneath her. She shouldn't be up here, not in wind like this. It's not safe.

The clip is slippery from her sweating hands, but finally, finally, she gets it off. "One line," she calls down.

"Line off," Stacy, still on the platform, corrects her. Stacy is a biting, black fly.

"Line off," Breanna shouts down.

"Line off," Cynthia answers.

She clips on. "Line on," she calls down.

Cynthia answers. They do it again for the second clip. It's slow. It's aggravating.

Still, there's something solid about it. Like when she shouts and Cynthia answers, it reminds her of the call and response at her cousins' church, in Detroit, Sundays and Wednesdays when she was a little kid. Call and response. Call and response. Now she can feel how her feet connect to the ladder.

She moves up each length of the upper ladder, clipping and unclipping. She calls. Cynthia responds. She's climbing straight at a storm growing in those darkening clouds. Leaves, orange, gold, and red, whirlwind from the trees. She wants to grab one, to feel each vein against her fingertips, but she takes her hand off the ladder only when she has to.

Up and up and up she climbs.

And then she's there.

All the way up.

On the Sky Ropes.

She edges herself off the ladder and stands on the platform. The trees sway and the platform bucks. Breanna grabs the tree trunk and holds on tight.

She sees her friends. Two trees over is Pascale, climbing up to the second platform. There is James, slowly moving across dangling rope steps. He is not smiling. His eyes never leave the platform he is aiming for. Her friends. They are up here with her, showing her how. She will do what they do and it will be okay.

She lets go of the trunk, only her hand resting against it. Carefully, she looks all around, wind blasting at her cheeks. She is on top of a high, high hill, standing high in a tree ten times taller than the comforting oak in her front yard. She can see everything. Out across gray and foaming Lake Ojibwe, past the tossing sea of trees around camp, out to the town they passed on the way in, out to the freeway. Out, out, out, till the world dissolves at the edges.

It is a terrifying sight.

She closes her eyes and breathes, breathes. She will ground herself up here. Take herself back from the trees. She opens her eyes. Reaching up as high as she can, she plucks one red leaf free. It is cool and dry and every vein stands out beneath her fingers. She holds it between her thumb and first finger and rubs it back and forth and back and forth.

The trees release her. She feels the platform solid underneath her feet. She's going to be okay. She lets go of the leaf and watches it flurry down.

She stretches up to the rod that runs along the ladder, unclipping one cable. "Line off," she calls down.

"Line off," Cynthia returns. There is something hopeful and strong in her voice. It is good to hear that voice, even though Cynthia told.

With call and response, Breanna gets herself unattached from the ladder and attached to the two thick wire cables that run from the ladder, across the platform, to the first obstacle. As she edges across the platform, the lines drag behind her, *swish, swish*, along their cable. Her heels, through her sneakers, thud against the wood, connecting with every step.

Facing the first obstacle, she clips on to a new set of overhead cables. Obstacle 1 is simple, a narrow wooden plank, with loose rope handrails along the side. All she has to do is walk from this platform to the one in the next tree, across this plank.

From the platform below her, miles away, Stacy shouts up, "Don't look down. Keep your eyes zeroed in on the next platform. That's it."

That's it. She can do that.

Breanna shuffles her feet across the narrow beam, never lifting her heels or toes. Shuffle. Shuffle. She wants to feel that board beneath her feet every second. Shuffle. Shuffle. So the trees don't get any ideas. Shuffle. Shuffle. She looks straight ahead. Her eyes don't leave the platform, which is coming closer. The beam sways. It rocks in a gust of wind. Breanna totters and leans into the rope rail and she balances. Shuffle. Shuffle.

She makes it. All the way across.

Lungs burning, she scrambles onto the platform and sucks in a world of air. She must have been holding her breath that whole time. She sees Niraj, waiting at the start of the beam she's just crossed. He smiles at her, a big, sweet, happy Niraj smile, and it's enough to help her smile back at him and mean it.

It hits her hard.

She's just done an obstacle on the Sky Ropes!

And if she's done one, she can do another. And another. And another . . .

But first, she needs to breathe. Her legs feel wobbly and her ears are buzzing. She rests her hands on her knees and pulls air hard into her lungs. Niraj is waiting for her to clip off, she knows, but she is not ready. Not yet.

Before she can clip off, she has to walk three or four steps along the platform to get to the spot where she clips onto Obstacle 2. She fills her lungs with cool air one more time and walks. The wire cables on their overhead tracks swish along with every step—one, two, three, four.

Here she is, at the edge of the platform, facing Obstacle 2. Her legs feel like Jell-O. "Line off," she calls, disconnecting one cable.

"Line off," Cynthia returns. Cynthia, who stands on the ground. Cynthia, whose feet touch dirt.

Breanna clips herself to Obstacle 2. Behind her, she hears Niraj and Trevor's call and response as Niraj clips himself to Obstacle 1. She turns to watch his first wobbly steps on the beam. He doesn't make it look like nothing. Bless him.

Obstacle 2 is a net of narrow white ropes, stretching wide between two trees. It looks like something off a pirate ship, and it's a whole lot more complicated than Obstacle 1. Niraj is almost done with the plank. He's close behind her. She's got to get going.

From somewhere far below, Stacy shouts, "Stay high! If you go low on the net, it's harder. Take your time. You're doing great."

Breanna wipes her hands off on her sweatpants. The scrapes on her palms sting. She sits down on the edge of the platform, like she saw the girl ahead of her do, and edges herself forward. Her heart pounds. Her ears roar. She leans and clenches the top row of the thin, slick net with both hands, then wiggles her feet into two holes not too far down. Her butt is at the very edge of the platform and she knows she's got to shift her weight but it's scary and she's shaking hard and she forces her heels down against the ropes and her butt lifts and she is on.

Wind blusters and the net pitches. For seconds, all she can do is squeeze the net, tight, tight, tight. Her fingernails draw blood. But the net quiets. She hangs where she stands, feeling her feet and hands against the ropes, up, up, up in the air.

Niraj waits at the edge of the platform for her to finish this obstacle that she has barely even started. She forces her hand to move. She clenches a new handhold of net. Slowly she drags her foot into a new spot.

"Stay high! Stay high!" Stacy shouts.

Breanna moves her foot higher. Her legs are quaking. She's so scared. She makes herself move. One hand. One foot. Slowly. One hand. One foot. She's doing it. She thinks the trees are helping. One hand. One foot. All the way across the net.

Her left hand touches the platform, and she is so happy she thanks God, who she doesn't even know if she believes in.

Stacy has scrambled up, here, on the platform with Breanna. She crouches down, talking softly. "This dismount is tricky," she says. "You can grab the platform and kind of pull and squirm yourself off the net or give me your hand and let me drag you." She looks worried. "It can feel really unsteady, this part."

Breanna understands. She's already unsteady and trying to climb up the net and pull herself over to the platform at the same time is too much. She reaches out a trembling hand to Stacy, tiny Stacy, who drags her off like a beached whale.

"You did that like a swashbuckler," Stacy says, sitting now on the platform next to her. "Take some time here to catch your breath."

Breanna lies with her right side pressed against the cool wood of the platform. She doesn't want to get up. Ever. The thought of getting up and doing another obstacle makes her want to cry.

"Two down," Stacy says. "That's amazing. You're almost halfway—if you want to keep going."

Not even halfway. Holy crap.

She has to keep going. Cami is probably done by now. Breanna knows she's going slow, sloth slow, and that's embarrassing. But as long as she does it, as long as she finishes, that's enough. Cami can never call her *nothing* again. She gets to her feet.

Sweat pools behind her knees, in the crooks of her elbows, under her hair. The platform is narrow, and Stacy stands close. In a rush of wind the trees sway and the platform tilts and Breanna grabs hard for Stacy.

These trees. These tricky trees.

Stacy holds Breanna by her elbows and looks at her. "You're doing great," she says. "You're a rock star. But are you sure you want to keep going? You're shaking really hard."

Breanna studies her fingers. They're not really shaking. They're thrumming, just thrumming. The trees are pulsing through her, playing tricks. She doesn't think Stacy would understand if she told her. "I'm fine," she says. "I want to keep going."

"Okay," Stacy says. "I'm going to stay with you and talk you through." Breanna nods.

For the third obstacle, she has to walk across a series of looped rope steps while holding on to rope cords overhead. It's the one she saw James doing. It helps to know that James has done this. He even looked a little bit scared. Stacy stays with her while she clips on and off.

Cynthia's voice carries up strong when Breanna calls down. "Line on."

"Line on."

"This one isn't hard," Stacy says. "But it's wobbly and that can feel scary. Hold on tight up top. That's key to helping you balance."

"Okay," Breanna says.

She feels the arch of her foot firm against the first loop. She looks only at the next loop and goes on, holding tight to the ropes above her. It feels like everything inside her has turned off but her buzzing ears, listening to Stacy's shouted words. "Step. Hold. Step. Hold." Breanna moves from loop to loop not thinking and not feeling and by the time she gets to the last loop, her feet are floating again. That's okay.

The loops led her up. Now, on the other side, she's further off the ground than ever, the new platform lodged even higher in the giant oak. She doesn't care. She's hardly even shaking, except for her teeth, which are chattering uncontrollably.

"You're doing amazing," Stacy says. "Past halfway." She rests a hand on Breanna's shoulder. "Want to take a break?"

Of course she doesn't want to take a break. She's almost done. She shakes her head. Cold sweat drips into her eyes.

Two more obstacles. Two! She is going to finish the Sky Ropes.

She should be listening carefully to Stacy describe Obstacle 4, but Breanna is looking for her friends. Even though she is close to the end, seeing them would feel good. Niraj, who must be somewhere on the spider web, is blocked by a swishing cover of yellow leaves. Cynthia, on the ground, is hidden by a tangle of thick branches, but she is there anyway, answering, always answering, when Breanna calls. And Stacy is here, her voice calm. Breanna doesn't pay attention to everything Stacy says, but her body is doing what Stacy tells it to do and that is all she needs right now.

"To clip on to Obstacle 4," Stacy is saying, "you have to step up on that board." Breanna listens as Stacy points to a rickety piece of 2×4 hammered into the tree trunk. "You have to do it twice, to clip both lines. Then you have to mount a higher platform. It's a little scary. Do you think you can do it?"

Wind hurls yellow leaves from the trees and raises goose bumps across Breanna's cold arms. Her teeth knock. This looks hard. Twice, she has to walk maybe two yards and then step up on a rickety board. Each time she steps up, she'll only be clipped to one cable. She doesn't like that. But she's almost done. She's done all the rest and they were hard and she didn't think that she could do them but she did.

She can do this.

Heidelberg Street, that place she went on a field trip in Detroit, flashes through her brain. Heidelberg Street. That's what the rickety board makes her think of. She sees plywood painted to look like clocks nailed into the trunks of big oak trees. She sees a plastic Superman flying out the window of the Polka-Dot House. She sees a naked half mannequin driving a kiddie car and knocking the head off a teddy bear.

But the trees help her. They lift her foot to the rickety board. "Line on," Breanna calls.

"Line on," Cynthia answers. Her voice feels so faint and far away that Breanna looks down just to make sure that Cynthia is still really there. She is a universe away, her face a fingernail. There are black gnats in the corners of Breanna's eyes. Heidelberg Street is in her head. Clocks painted on the rickety board.

Even though her brain is somewhere else, her body keeps doing what Stacy says, and somehow, she is up on an even higher platform walking over a swaying wood bridge in the tops of these tall, tall, trees. She must be so high. She wants to call to Cynthia, to hear her right now and see if Cynthia's voice calling back will help Breanna's feet touch down. But she doesn't. She keeps going, her floating feet moving, this one, then that one, every time Stacy, on the platform behind her, shouts, "left," "right," "left," "right."

And then it's done.

One more obstacle and the Sky Ropes are over.

Stacy crosses the bridge and is with her on the last narrow platform. Gently, she takes Breanna's arm. "How are you doing?" she asks. "Your skin is icy. You're sweating. Want to stop and let Niraj pass through before you do the last one?"

Breanna shakes her head.

"Okay," Stacy says. "This last one looks dangerous. It's scary that way. But it's simple." She points to a wooden frame built above the platform and says, "First you step up, into that."

The frame has a base and two long sides. It looks like a window, a high-up window. Breanna's whole body starts chattering.

In front of the frame that looks like a high-up window, she clips off, then on. "Line on," she calls, her voice chattering now, too.

"Line on," Cynthia calls back.

"Step up into the frame," Stacy says, squeezing Breanna's shivering arm. "Once you're there, look straight over and a little way down, to the platform below. See?"

Breanna sees, but there are gnats in her eyes.

"It's not far," Stacy says. "You have to jump. It's only a mind game. You can't miss."

Breanna isn't moving. She is in front of the frame, her hands holding both sides, and Stacy is telling her to lift her left foot and she knows her feet are floating and that she doesn't have to lift her foot far, but it won't come. All this time, the trees have been helping her and now, when she needs them most, they've stopped.

"You've got this," Stacy says, and the trees lift Breanna's feet and wild and victorious, she stands in the frame.

All around her fierce wind blows and the giant trees writhe and moan. She holds tight to the frame with both her hands, but the frame is quivering and she is shaking and shaking and she reaches high to tear a leaf from the blustery oak that she can run her fingertips over and she pulls one away from the closest branch and holds it between her thumb and first finger and feels only leathered dryness. Her shaking doesn't stop and her ears still roar and the gnats are gathering in the corners of her eyes.

"Only a tiny jump." Stacy's voice comes slow and mumbly, like she's chewing socks. "Imagine you can fly."

Fly. Stacy said *fly.* All the gnats come now, pooling dark in Breanna's eyes and she shakes her head to scatter them.

She sees the old house off McNichols and she is there at the high-up window with her dad and he is holding her out, high, high over the way-down sidewalk and she knows that any second now he is going to let go and she is biting and screaming and fighting and scrabbling to get inside and sirens are shrieking and footsteps are pounding and her mom is screaming, "There, he's there," and her dad's silky-smooth voice laughs out over everything, "Fly, baby. Fly!"

He lets go.

He lets go.

She is falling and Stacy screams and something tugs hard against her waist and her head jerks and she remembers strong arms grabbing at her pajama shirt and pulling her in.

From somewhere far away, Niraj calls, "Look. Look. She's doing her prank!"

Breanna is falling.

The world is black, black as she hurtles through space, arms and legs flailing. The ground lights up and it's coming fast and her friends are lost and all she can see is the crumbling sidewalk of that old house off McNichols and the flashing police lights and the yard coming so, so fast and it doesn't make sense but on the ground what she sees is the yellow smiley-face pillow that she got with the giant claw at Quality 16 Theaters, its black eyes staring at her, watching her, sighting her as she falls.

Falls.

Falls.

He let go.

CHAPTER
THIRTY-FIVE

BREANNA'S EYES OPEN. SHE IS IN A BED, IN A ROW OF EMPTY BEDS.
Old linoleum curls up in the far corner. Sun comes in through dirty windows still wet with a spattering of rain. Some are open, and a cool breeze rustles her sheets. From far, far away, laughter floats in.

Click, click, click.

She turns to the sound. Her neck hurts.

SheThor. The noise is SheThor, Grace, that cool camp nurse, sitting in a white plastic chair pulled up right next to Breanna's bed. Grace is knitting. Her needles click. Her yarn is shocking pink.

"You're awake!" Grace says. "How are you feeling?"

Breanna closes her eyes. "How am I alive?"

Knitting clattering to the floor, chair scuffing back, Grace stands. She leans over Breanna, her sunburned forehead creased into worry. "It can't be that bad," she says. "Where does it hurt?"

"I fell off the Sky Ropes. How am I alive?"

"What do you mean?" Grace says. "You passed out. The cables caught you. You didn't fall."

"Oh."

What the crap? She remembers falling through that wooden frame that was just like the high-up window at the old house off McNichols. She remembers flailing down. And now Grace is saying it didn't happen and here she is, alive and not injured, except for a sharp pain in her neck.

She didn't fall?

She didn't fall.

Grace stares at her.

Breanna looks past her. She sees, half hidden by an open door, a water stain spreading from ceiling to floor on the old wood paneling lining the wall. The longer Breanna stares at it, the more it looks like a monster, half dragon, with flaming eyes and open, dripping jaws and little stumps of arms halfway down its strange body twisting through the wood grain, until, at the floor, it gathers into coils like a roiling snake.

Breanna rolls on to her side, away from Grace, away from the wall stain. She pulls the top sheet, soft and worn, up over her shoulders and then the light blue blanket folded once at the foot of the bed. The blanket feels nice. Holding it between her thumb and first finger, she rubs it back and forth. It's a loose weave, each strand distinct. She closes her eyes. She feels tired. She feels sick of Grace.

Grace leans over her, so close that Breanna can smell her breath, like stale coffee. "Do you want to talk?" Grace asks.

"No," Breanna says, burying her face in her pillow. Talking is exactly what she doesn't want to do.

"We'll talk when you're ready," Grace says. Breanna hears her settle back into her chair. "Get some sleep. Then you can go back to the cabin, eat some lunch, find your team. Whatever feels right." Her knitting needles click.

None of those things *feels right*. "I want to go home," Breanna says.

"Oh!" Grace sounds surprised. "Oh." Her needles stop. "Okay. You can do that. Let's talk. And then you can call home. Work it out with your mom. She knows you're here, with me, in the infir-mary. She knows what happened. I just . . . I didn't tell her that you might come home. I didn't think . . ." Her voice trails off.

Breanna finishes the sentence in her own head. Grace didn't think that Breanna would be a double coward and leave.

But what else can she do?

How can she face Cynthia and Pascale, who tried to protect her?

How can she face Cami, gloating at Breanna's complete failure? Epic failure, frankly.

How can she face the kids in her cohort who saw her fall? And every other kid at camp who would have heard by now? She can just picture it, one person telling another, all along the hiking trails, at the climbing wall, down on the beachfront, in the cafeteria, kids laughing their heads off, imitating how she looked hanging in the harness when she thought she was falling, and of course she must have looked ridiculous, passed out, her brain tricking her, telling her she was dropping to her death, and probably she was thrashing, unconscious but thrashing, because she remembers her arms and legs flailing as she thought she fell. Everybody had to know by now.

No. She cannot face those kids.

She's going home.

If Grace is shocked that Breanna is this kind of coward, it doesn't matter. Breanna never has to see her again. If she could never see any of them again, that would be perfect.

She knows that can't happen, but for now, she needs Grace to get her regulation green garbage bag out from underneath her bunk in cabin 17, so she can leave from here, from the infirmary, while everybody is out doing something they'll call fun and nobody will see her go. That's what she wants.

But at the moment, even that seems too hard.

"I'm gonna sleep," Breanna says. The words just come out of her mouth. She hadn't meant to say them. "But then I'm going home."

CHAPTER THIRTY-SIX

SCRITCH. SCRATCH. A FRESH SOUND WAKES BREANNA UP.

She's still here, in this long, dull room.

Not tired. Not confused.

Angry.

And whatever it is scratching around in this room is making her angrier. She glares at the wall monster. It's only a stain. It isn't scratching.

Scritch. Scratch. It must be a mouse. Stupid mouse. She looks under the bed. Nothing. She looks for Grace. She's gone—some nurse.

Breanna's mouth tastes bitter. Her gut feels sick and heavy, like she's swallowed a fifty-pound weight, the cheap metal kind with the silver peeling off that her cousins used to lift in their basement in Mexicantown.

Scritch. Scratch. Holy crap! What is that noise?

It's coming from the open window behind her bed. She twists around to look.

It's a kid. Some idiot kid who's snuck down here to mock her. He's wedged himself behind a bush that grows right up next to the window. His face is blurry behind the rusty screen that he scratches at with his finger. *Scritch, scratch,* like a rat.

"Get lost," Breanna says.

"Breanna? It's me. Max. I have to talk to you."

"Go away, Max."

"That nurse, the scary one with asymmetrical hair. She said I could come talk to you if I gave you space and stayed here at the window. I asked thirteen times before she said yes. I *have* to talk to you."

Stupid Grace! Breanna does not want to talk to Max. Not to anybody.

"I want to thank you," Max says, "for what you did up there on those ropes."

What a jerk! She can't believe he's here, making fun of her like this. Breanna glares at him through the screen. "For passing out? For falling? For making a fool of myself? You're welcome."

"Yes," Max says. "No. Wait. You didn't make a fool of yourself. You were perfect. A perfect data source."

Data source? What the crap? Oh, Max. Of course. It clicks who exactly she is talking to. "You're such a weirdo," she says. "What do you even mean?"

"I studied everything about the Sky Ropes before I came here," Max says. "I searched online. I went to the library, the main branch, downtown. You know, where the nonfiction section takes up the whole second floor." His words come fast and it's hard to keep up. "I went to the university, to the undergraduate library. I read everything on ropes courses I could get my hands on."

She has no idea what Max is talking about. What are you supposed to say to crap like this? *Congratulations for finding so many ways to waste your own time?* She says nothing, just glares at him.

"Listen, Breanna." Max puts his hands up against the screen and moves in so close he looks like he might come through. "I'm serious. I read everything. Nothing told me what I needed to know, which was what happened on this exact course when you fell. I knew about the cables and the lines and all the safety measures. But I couldn't figure out how *far* you'd go before the cables caught you. A millimeter? A meter? Seven meters? I couldn't do the ropes because I didn't know."

Breanna wishes she could stop listening. But she is too disgusted to do anything but lie here on her side and watch Max's mouth move. Every word is more weight in her gut.

"Breanna," he says. "When you fell, I got to see that the cables caught you fast and that there was no way you were going to hit the platform or anything else. It was exactly what I needed to know." He is grinning through the screen. "It's like you saw my data deficit, and you coded the answer straight to my brain."

Breanna squints at him. "You know you don't make sense, right?"

"Breanna," he says, "I did a part of the Sky Ropes. Me. Max Barrett! My ankle is okay today, so I could choose, and I did them because I saw you fall. I saw how it worked. That's what I had to tell you. Thank you."

"Fine. You told me." She turns away and lies down flat. She is glad about Max's ankle, but she is done talking.

But now there's more thrashing around in the bush behind her bed.

"Geez, Max! There you are. I've been looking everywhere for you."

Breanna recognizes the voice. James. Beautiful James. The last person on earth she wants to see right now. She freezes in her bed. Maybe if she doesn't move, he'll think she's dead.

"Hi, Breanna," he says, his voice like a poem. "How are you doing? That was intense, what happened on the ropes. You're tough."

How dare he! How dare he! He's worse than Max. Such a liar! Breanna sits back up. She faces James. The weight in her gut turns molten, gurgles up her throat, and flames into words. "Don't you dare lie to me. Don't you dare!" she shouts. "You think I don't see through that? You think I don't know what you think of me?" She tastes something burning in her mouth.

"Hey. Stop." James rests his arms on the upper frame of the open window. "Breanna. Are you okay?"

She slams herself back against the bed and folds her arms over her chest. She thinks she might burst into tears, and she can't let that happen, not in front of James. Not after everything else.

"Breanna," James says. "That must have been scary for you. Geez, it was scary to watch. But you were totally strong. You wouldn't quit." Breanna listens. "Like, Stacy was unbuckling your harness and you buckled it back up. Remember?" She does not. "You tried to go back up the ladder. You kept pulling her back toward the ropes saying, 'I'm not done yet.' You wouldn't stop. Really, you wouldn't." Breanna lies on her bed, listening hard. "It was crazy," he says, "but it was cool."

Breanna can't remember any of what he's describing. But his words make her whole body shake. It remembers.

Tears flood her eyes. She can't stop them. They run down the sides of her cheeks and into her ears as she lies there, listening to James. He's being so kind. His words have zapped her rage and stolen her fight. She can't think of one thing to say.

"You were tough up there," James says. "So tough. Like, like, I don't know, like my grandad's steel-toe Red Wing boots that he wore at the factory and won't throw away. Like that, only, you know, pretty."

James just called her pretty. Why is he being so nice? Max, too? If they'd been mean, she'd have been ready. She could have handled that. But not this. Not this.

Nobody says anything for a long time. Breanna watches the breeze pick up the corner of her sheet. She hears leaves rustle outside.

"Okay," James says. "We should go. Kids are excited to see you, Niraj especially. He's telling everybody that you did it on purpose, that it was your epic prank. Was it?"

Breanna doesn't answer. She has no idea what to say about that. But she is so glad for Niraj and the way he is trying to give her cover, again.

James stands there and part of Breanna doesn't want him to go. "See you," he finally says.

"Bye, Breanna," Max says. "Thank you. I mean it."

Breanna says nothing. She hears their footsteps crunch away. She hears branches snap back and ping lightly on the window screen. She lies there in a slant of light sifting through the window, her eyes looking up, tracing the uneven lines of the ceiling tiles through her tears.

CHAPTER THIRTY-SEVEN

BREANNA HEARS GRACE'S KNITTING NEEDLES, *CLICK, CLICK, CLICK*. The angles of sun tracking across the room are soft. It's less bright than before. She must have slept again.

Kids' voices filter through the open windows. Breanna wonders, vaguely, what everybody's doing. But she feels a million miles away from those kids, from camp, from everything.

She studies the wall monster. It's something to do. Of course, it's not a monster. It only makes her think of one because her brain's not right after the Sky Ropes. The more she stares, the more she feels mad at it for pretending to be what it's not.

After a while, she looks over at Grace. Her cheeks and forehead are sunburned. The short side of her hair barely covers a bright red scalp. She looks tired.

"Hey. How are you feeling?" Grace asks.

"You sent Max and James to see me," Breanna says.

"Max. I said Max could come."

"That was unprofessional."

"What do you mean?" Grace laughs. "It was highly professional, a mental health emergency. Max was nuts. He would have been in one of these beds himself if he didn't say what he needed to say to you. Trust me, I've kept plenty of kids away." Grace's needles stop clicking. Her eyes move slowly over the knitted lines before she nods and they start clicking again. "That Cynthia's a dog with a bone. She tried to sneak down here fifty times. And your friend Pascale's just as bad."

Cynthia? Pascale? They want to see her? Great. Just great. She can just imagine that conversation. *We told you not to do it. What is wrong with you?*

Either that or pity and lies, like Max and James.

No thank you.

Breanna props up her head and faces Grace. "I don't want to see them," she says, her voice quiet but steady. She's thought hard about this. "I don't want to talk to any of them. I want to go home." Grace stops knitting. "You said we'd talk about this after I rested," Breanna says. "I've rested all day. I want to go. Now."

"Do you?" Grace looks intently at Breanna, her thin eyebrows high on her sunburned forehead. "Huh." She shrugs. "I thought you'd want to stay. I really did."

"Why? So everybody can lie to me?" Breanna feels that molten fury coming back. "Like Max? James? Or, I don't know, tell me how stupid I was? Or that I'm a big fat coward? I don't need that crap! I'm going home."

"Look," Grace says. "I didn't know James had come down here. I don't know what *he* said to you." Her gaze is serious. "But Max? You think Max *lied* to you? You think that kid can say anything but what he believes to be real and factual?" She leans back in her chair and takes a deep breath. "Come on, Breanna, you're smarter than that."

"Oh great," Breanna says. "So now I'm stupid, too?"

"Breanna. Where are you? What universe are you living in?" Grace pulls her chair right into Breanna's personal space. "Max had an experience watching you. He learned something when the cables caught you, something that helped him do the ropes. That was powerful for him. Do you get that?"

Breanna doesn't *get that*. And she doesn't care. "I want to call my mom."

"First," Grace says, "I need to hear what you think happened today." Her fingers rest on her knitting as she sits, waiting.

"Fine. But then I go."

Grace nods.

"I tried to do the Sky Ropes," Breanna says, sitting up, locking eyes with Grace, showing her that she's serious. "I passed out." At the words, her body trembles and she's sure that Grace can see. "I'm a coward. A phony. Nothing. Just like Cami said."

"Wait. Wait a minute." Grace puts up a hand to stop Breanna. "What does Cami have to do with this?" Her voice is suddenly alert.

"Oh, come on. You've watched us play softball. You know we hate each other." Breanna's talking all calm, but she would like it much better if she could be screaming right now. "She's been on my case since the first day. She thinks she's so much better than me. Miss Junior Olympic Pitching Commando."

"Sure," Grace nods. "I've seen you two duking it out on the field. It isn't pretty." She leans forward in her chair. "But Breanna, the Wildebeests are holding their own against a better team. What's the problem?"

"*That's* the problem!" Breanna shouts this time. "She's not crushing me out there so she decided to do it on the Sky Ropes."

Grace watches her. Breanna can see in her face that she doesn't understand.

"Look. It's personal between us two," Breanna says. "Cami's cocky about the Lanton Leopards and she picks on Tess and that's not okay with me and I think she likes James and James likes me."

Grace smiles at the James part.

"Cami's had it out for me since day one," Breanna says. "She's been watching me for weakness. And she found it. She found it. She snuck inside my brain when I wasn't paying attention and she saw that I'm afraid of lots of things." Breanna's nose drips and stupid tears leak from her eyes. "I've been a disaster here. Cami saw everything. She got it. And last night, after the game, she told the Roar that she and I were going to race on the Sky Ropes." Breanna's voice cracks. "Because she knew I was afraid. And Cami's a ninja on those ropes. It was her chance to show me up big time, in front of everybody."

"Oh, Lordy," Grace says quietly.

"Last night," Breanna can't stop talking. "Pascale and Cynthia helped me. They made me promise that I wouldn't do the Sky Ropes, because I'm not the normal kind of scared, I'm way past the normal kind."

Fingers kneading the skin of her forehead, Grace listens.

"I practiced saying *The Sky Ropes aren't right for me* all night long. But this morning, in the bathroom, Cami found me. I was alone and sick. I said the safe words and she laughed. She said I was nothing. Nothing! It was terrible, like she was killing everything good inside of me." Breanna is saying way too much. She forces herself to stop talking.

"Oh, sweet girl," Grace says, shaking her head. "I'm sorry." She sighs. "So very sorry. That must have hurt you bad."

Breanna nods and wipes her nose on the sleeve of her sweatshirt.

They sit in silence. "I don't know about Cami," Grace says. "If she's as cruel as you say, that's just sad."

That *if* makes Breanna mad. Grace should know about Cami by now.

Before Breanna can set her straight, Grace rests her hand gently on top of Breanna's hand. "I don't know who Cami is, really. I suspect there's a reason for this cruelty of hers and it's probably something hard. Don't get me wrong, I'm not excusing her. Cruel is cruel, no matter the why. But I need to say one thing about her, and please trust me on this." Grace's hand on Breanna's is warm and comforting. "Breanna, Cami is wrong about you. Absolutely, completely wrong."

"She's not." Breanna jerks her hand away, like Grace has burned her. "That's the thing. I am coward. I'm scared out of my mind all the time. I'm not Fearless Breanna Woodruff. That whole thing is phony. And now everybody knows." She can't stop a sudden, single sob. "Which leaves me nothing. I'm nothing."

The room is silent, except for their breathing. The breeze through the windows lifts a strand of Breanna's escaped hair.

"Okay," Grace says, looking at her intently. "I need to tell you some things. For one, you went up those ropes and showed Max how the safety system worked. You know that, right?"

"So?"

"Stay with me." Grace leans forward, her face determined in a way that Breanna can't help but pay attention to. "You showed Stacy raw guts like she's never seen before. You made her cry, a seasoned counselor. She told me how you wouldn't quit, how you wouldn't give up." Grace's eyes are shiny bright. "Niraj thinks you pulled off the world's best prank and he's telling everybody. Cynthia and Pascale and Tess only care about whether you're okay." Breanna lies down and stares at the ceiling, so she won't have to look at Grace, who has tears in her eyes. "I don't know what it meant for James to watch you, but I'm guessing he had good things to say." Grace's voice rises. "Are you with me here?"

"Maybe."

"Okay then. I need to ask you something." Grace runs her hand across her mouth. "Everybody who saw you on the Sky Ropes has their own version of what you did. Max, Stacy, Niraj, all your other friends. Why choose Cami's, Breanna? Why believe the cruelest story?"

Breanna is listening. Grace is saying something important, something big. Breanna knows that, but she does not understand.

"What do you mean?" she says, quietly. "I went up the ropes and passed out. I don't get to choose that. It happened." She can feel tears running down her cheeks. She hates it.

"Look," Grace says, chin resting on two balled up fists. "We're getting philosophical here, but okay. Let's go. Here are the facts. You're terrified of heights. You went up the Sky Ropes and you passed out, just like you said. Those are facts." She stops and pushes back her chair. Her hands clench and unclench as she talks. "But everything else? You decide! You. *You* get to choose for yourself what the facts mean, Breanna. Do you get that?"

Breanna is listening. But she still does not understand. "No," she says.

"Okay," Grace says. "You can say to yourself, 'I was an idiot for going up in the first place.' Then you're an idiot. Or you can say, 'I proved Cami right because I passed out on the ropes.' Then you're a coward and a failure."

Breanna gives a hard, bitter laugh.

"But what about this?" Grace says, sitting on the very edge of her chair, hands curled to fists in front of her chest. It feels like all the energy in her strong body is right here, in this conversation. "How about you say, 'I faced an overwhelming fear, and I did four obstacles successfully. Four!' Then you're a gutsy kid. A very gutsy kid. You get to take your pick, Breanna. That's your privilege. The same facts support all three versions and a whole lot more. *You* choose the story you tell yourself."

Breanna is listening with all her might. She doesn't know why. Maybe it's the hands. Maybe it's how strong Grace's voice is. Whatever it is, Grace believes what she's saying, Breanna can tell. And this time, somehow, the words spark straight to Breanna's soul.

They sit in silence. Faint voices glide in on the breeze. Grace studies Breanna, then takes a deep breath. "Know this, Breanna," she says. "It matters what you pick. It matters for today. For tomorrow. For every day for the rest of your life. You have to decide what meaning you assign to facts, all the time, over and over." She pauses. "I'm telling you the truth. Choose meanings that are generous to you and other people, kid, and you'll be okay."

"But what about Cami?" Breanna's voice is a ragged whisper.

"What about her?" Grace says, slapping her hands against her knees. "The world is full of Camis. Believe me, Breanna. Cami's going to have to walk her own hard road." Her eyes meet Breanna's. "And if she's the person you think she is, I don't envy her that." Now Grace's voice cracks. "But for you? Right here? Right now? It is *powerful* not to care what Cami thinks."

Tears drop down Grace's sunburned face. It's surprising—she's so tough. But Breanna likes it. It makes Grace's words feel even more like truth. Breanna wants to believe her. So bad. She thinks of Max, that weirdo. Of sweet Niraj. Of beautiful James. What if James wasn't lying? What if James really does think she's pretty in a work-boot kind of way?

He said it. Why not believe it? He hasn't given her a reason *not* to. Grace, too. Why not believe her, too?

It's strange, but she feels a little happy. Somehow a tiny bit happy, here in the infirmary after falling off the Sky Ropes in front of the world. She can feel that little basket, the one she keeps above her heart. It's still there and Grace's words are in it, Breanna sees them. She looks around for the lockbox, but she doesn't know where it's gone. Somewhere. She knows that. But for now, at least, it isn't heavy.

Grace's knitting needles are clicking again. "Grace?" Breanna says.

"Yeah, sweetie?"

"That water stain behind the door looks like a monster."

"Water stain?" Grace stands up. She walks to the corner and pushes the door closed, so the whole stain is clearly visible. Staring at the lines in the warped paneling, she slowly reaches out her hand. "Well, this is new," she says. "I don't know what this is."

Her fingertips move above the surface, tracing the contours of the stain without touching it. She puts her face up close, studying the wall. She looks over at Breanna, her forehead wrinkled into worry. Then, she turns back. Softly, so softly, she brushes her hand against the stain, touching one spot, then another. Here, then here. Suddenly, she jerks back. "It's alive," she screams. "Run, Breanna! Run!"

Breanna jumps straight up on the bed, too confused to know what to do.

But Grace is laughing. "I got you! I got you!" she says. "The bravest kid I know, and I got you!" Grace is laughing her head off.

That was a dirty trick. Breanna should be mad, but she isn't. Arms around her belly, she is laughing, too. Grace goes quiet.

She's watching Breanna, her gaze so kind. Tricky tears leak from Breanna's eyes. She climbs down off the bed, turns to Grace and puts out her arms. Grace holds her, holds her, holds her, as she cries about the black scar on that doe and Cami and the Sky Ropes and the high-up window of that old house off McNichols and her dad, oh, her dad.

CHAPTER THIRTY-EIGHT

BREANNA FINALLY STOPS BAWLING.

It's time. She knows.

Time to figure out what's next.

She slips her sneakers back on and wraps the blue, nubbly blanket from the bed around her shoulders. She and Grace sit at the old metal desk, its plasticky wood top curling up at three edges, eating the lunch that Eric made up special for them.

"I know," Breanna says, a bite of peanut butter sandwich still in her mouth. "You can call my mom on that big old landline phone right there and tell her she needs to take a job in Manitoba, in Canada, on Monday. I'll be at a new school next week."

"You tell her." Grace picks up the bulky handset. "You'll speak Canadian if you do that. You'll wear a toque."

"What's a toque?"

"Exactly."

Breanna smiles. She knows she's not moving to Manitoba. "School choice!" she says. "I can transfer to Lincoln Consolidated. I've seen the billboards—they're a school of choice. No one will know me there." She licks the coating off a sour cream and onion chip before she eats it.

"Excellent idea," Grace nods, taking a bite of a chocolate chip cookie when she hasn't touched her carrots. "Fresh start. Make new friends. How long did that take you the last time?"

Breanna shifts in her chair. "Five years."

"Perfect. You'll have friends your last two years of high school."

That is not okay. She is not going back to no friends. That is, if she still has friends. She thinks she does. She hopes she does. She can choose to believe she does, if Grace's theory is right. Cynthia, Pascale, Niraj, and James. She chooses to believe in them, at least.

"Or," Grace says, putting down her cookie and looking hard at Breanna, "you can go back to cabin 17. It's closer than Manitoba. You have actual, real, not just in-the-future friends there."

Breanna knows this is what she has to do.

But it sounds so hard.

Cami is in that cabin. And other girls, Rachel, and Cami's other friends, who Breanna never bothered to know. They were there when she passed out. They think she's a chicken. Or maybe they think she's been gutsy enough to try. Or maybe they think that she pulled off an epic prank. Breanna doesn't know what they think.

That's what there is to go back to in cabin 17. All these people—Cami included—who she doesn't actually know. All these judgments that she doesn't actually know. It's going to take real guts to go back there.

"Sooner is easier," Grace says. "Once you're there, enough kids will be kind. It won't be as bad as you think." Finally, she's eating her carrots.

Sweat prickles along Breanna's forehead. She swipes at it with her napkin.

"I trust those girls," Grace says. "Enough of them." She brushes her hands off over the garbage can. "Pay attention to the kind ones. They're the only ones you need."

The kind ones. The kind ones. Okay.

"It's almost time for dinner," Grace says. Geez, no wonder Breanna was starving. "Once everybody's in the cafeteria, we'll slip out and get you back to your cabin. It will be hours before anybody comes in. You can join the night activities if you want or deal with the girls when they show up later. Whatever you can manage."

Breanna is going back to cabin 17.

She is afraid.

It's okay. Everybody is afraid. She's learned that at camp.

Voices are coming now, closer and closer. Shouting. Laughing. Talking. So much talking. Breanna pushes her chair hard into the corner, even though she knows nobody can see her here. The floor rumbles with pounding feet. For a few seconds, the walls shake. Then they are all past, all gathered in the cafeteria, contained in a known place.

It is time for Breanna to go. "I'm ready," she says.

"One more thing," Grace says. She drags open a crooked desk drawer and pulls out two full-size boxes of Nerds. "My last two contraband boxes." She reads from the label. "'Double Dipped Lemonade/Wild Cherry and Apple/Watermelon.' They're the best." She hands them both to Breanna. "For fortitude."

"Thanks," Breanna says. It feels like a solemn thing.

Outside, the air is cool. The sun hangs low to the west, out over Lake Ojibwe, tinging the clouds in the blue-gray sky red and orange. Walking the trail, not talking to Grace, Breanna looks east, up the high, high hills, to the giant trees and the Sky Ropes.

There they are, shadowed this late in the day, reaching into the evening light.

Breanna stops. She remembers the strange pull of the trees and shivers. "I can't believe I was on those ropes," she says quietly.

"Well, you were," Grace says. "Believe it."

At the cabin, Breanna walks down the aisle of bunks till she gets to her own. The sign is still there, BREANNA WOODRUFF, in black marker and gold glitter. Stacy made that sweet sign. She drags her garbage bag out from under the bottom bunk and slips one box of Nerds inside. The other one stays in her hand.

Grace stands just inside the door, looking at the big timbers, where names and dates and hearts are carved into the wood. "Look at this one! *1995*. And this one. Do you think *Linda* still *loves Allen*? Wouldn't that be cool?"

Breanna, about to climb on to her bunk, notices that the old, soft University of Michigan sweatshirt that she crumpled up to use as a pillow Wednesday night is neatly folded at the head of her bed. Her smiley-face pillow rests on top of it.

Tess has given it back.

Of course she has.

Tess doesn't want any proof that she and Breanna were ever friends. Breanna is the fool of camp, and even the tiniest, most babyish kid here wants nothing to do with her. Breanna cannot stand this.

There's a note, a piece of paper, torn from the spiral notebook Tess sometimes writes in at night, poking out from under the smiley-face pillow. Breanna feels the sweat bead up on her forehead. She doesn't want to read it, but her shaking hands unfold it anyway.

The handwriting is loopy and careful, like it's written by someone still practicing her cursive.

Dear Breanna,

After lunch, without you, camp was boring. Camp is more fun when you are here. Cynthia and Pascale both said so. I miss you. You were brave on the Sky Ropes. I tried after you. If you could try, I could, too. I walked across the beam. Then I went back down. It was scary, but it was good. I thought you might need your pillow tonight. Thank you for letting me use it. It helped me.

Your friend,

Peanut

Breanna stands at the bunk, holding the paper in her hand. Peanut missed her. Said she was brave. Tried the ropes. Said she and Cynthia and Pascale liked camp better with Breanna in it. Breanna's tears are at it again. Geez, oh geez. What is wrong with her?

But oh! What a good, sweet, kind little kid.

"What's that?" Grace is looking at her, eyeing the note in her hand. "Everything okay?"

"Yeah," Breanna says, wiping her eyes on her arm. "Everything's good."

Breanna climbs up into her bunk. The slippery blue sleeping bag rustles beneath her. She picks up the yellow smiley-face pillow. An image flashes into her brain, an image of this pillow in the yard of that old house off McNichols, where it never was, of course. It had eyes that fixed on her as she thought she was falling. She remembers.

But she wasn't falling.

She knows that now. She didn't fall. That night when it all happened, her dad let go and she started to fall and it was the most terrifying thing in the world. But somebody caught her as he let go, somebody who came with all those flashing lights and sirens, who her panicked mom guided fast up the stairs, who had quick hands and strong arms. They caught her and pulled her in. They did.

She studies the pillow. It's only the yellow smiley-face pillow that she got with the giant claw at Quality 16 Theaters. She touches the black eyes, runs her finger along the curve of the thick thread smile. A stupid, soft smiley-face pillow.

Better to sleep on than a crumpled-up sweatshirt.

She wiggles her legs into her sleeping bag and rests her head on the yellow plush. She opens the Nerds and pours half the box into her mouth at once. The sour coating rings her taste buds, and she lets the sensation trickle to her fingertips and toenails. She thinks she might sleep. It would be good to rest a little more, before everybody comes pouring in for the night.

Grace still stands at the other end of the cabin.

"I'm okay," Breanna tells her. "You don't need to stay with me anymore."

Grace's footsteps move away, over the wood floor. They stop. "Breanna, you're one gutsy girl," she says. "I'm glad you didn't go home. It's going to be okay. It's going to be better than you think."

Breanna listens, her heart grabbing at the words. She wants to hold on to them, to have them for the minutes and hours ahead. She pictures the word *gutsy* hanging over her body, stretched out on the top bunk. She sees it dissolve into powder, like delicious sour coating, and then sprinkle down to soak deep into her skin.

CHAPTER THIRTY-NINE

SMACK! THE CRACK OF A BAT, CRISP AND CLEAR, CLAPS BREANNA out of sleep.

Softball!

She doesn't think. She flies off her bunk and drags out her garbage bag and searches for her glove.

There!

She's got it.

She shoves her feet into her sneakers and runs out of the cabin, the screen door smacking behind her.

Her feet slam down the trail. A sandhill crane bursts up in a beat of wings.

She runs, pulling the glove on as she goes, past the pale-yellow main building, down the boardwalk, through the marsh to where the trail opens out into the cut-grass field.

She stops.

Here, shadows gather, blue and gray in the early twilight. Peepers chirp in the marsh. Drums beat. Kids' voices rise on the wind.

Up there in the darkening hills, the Sky Ropes rustle.

Let them.

Let them.

Breanna watches the Wildebeests, spread out across the softball field, glowing in the last rays of the day's sun. She sees Niraj playing second base, Tess in right field, Trevor in left field, and Max, in far-left field, staring up at the purpling sky.

Cynthia, on the pitcher's rubber, sends the ball flying over home plate. A bat cracks. Pascale steps under the spinning yellow ball, catches it, and throws it hard to third. James, beautiful James, is out.

Oh, Cynthia. Oh, Sweet Pea. They make her proud. This whole stupid camp makes her proud.

She stands, breathing in something sweet and tangy in the wind and watching the game, her team—her friends. Then she runs to them, full out and wild.

THE
END

ACKNOWLEDGMENTS:

I want to begin by saying thank you to three people who simply gave this book—and my writing career—its fighting chance. The first is my friend and longtime writing partner, Mylisa Larsen. In our earliest, aimless writing years, we tried to help each other, but knew nothing. I would have given up without Mylisa's support and her understanding that we needed serious training. She found Patricia Lee Gauch and *made* me come, terrified, to Patti's Highlights workshop. Patti is the second person who made this book possible. Somehow, she believed I could be taught to write, and she taught me—about concrete objects, weather, ecstatic scenes, and voice. Voice, to hear and follow that. She's an extraordinarily generous, good-natured, and rigorous teacher. And last, this book wouldn't have happened without Nathan Soderborg, my husband, who shouldered greater responsibility so that I could pursue this quixotic dream of writing. He's a statistician. He had no illusions about the long odds of my success. But he did it anyway, and he did it graciously and for a long time before there was any glimmer of hope. I am indebted to all of you.

Thank you to friends who shared stories and skills with me. Laughing hard, his hand bandaged, Nicolas Foster told me an unforgettable tale about what happened when he caught a baby raccoon at camp. Angie Bautista-Chavez told me hair-raising El Chupacabra stories as we road-tripped through Maine. Shauna Sylvester acted out softball scenes in my kitchen late at night, so I could get the details right.

Thank you to my early readers. Cora Mitchell, who was a kid

back then, finished reading and simply said, "This book is important." That helped me keep going. Susan Wheeler, my friend and colleague, asked pointed questions that made me think. Mylisa Larsen read everything, a lot.

Thank you to the Highlights Foundation, which gave me a place to learn, write, and gather with colleagues. Honestly, it feels like Highlights gave me the oxygen to breathe this book alive. It started as a short story written in preparation for a class there. I fully imagined the Sky Ropes there. And the crisp fall air of Milanville feels like the air Breanna breathed, slipping out of her cabin early, before almost anyone else was up.

Thank you to my dear colleagues, who I met through Highlights: Lisze Bechtold, Shari Becker, Christine Carron, Tara Carson, Sharon Dembro, Louisa Jaggar, Stella Michel, Chester Perryess, and Susan Wheeler. We have been on this journey together for a long time. Your ongoing courage, humor, and hard-won progress teach and inspire me.

Thank you to Whale Rock Workshops, where, beside glorious Lake Huron, I was able to test out chapters I wrote after selling the book. I'm grateful for the kind feedback I received from skilled writers who laughed but also worried as Breanna rode the bus to camp. Patti Gauch was there, inviting me to cut, but with a feather. Gary Schmidt was there, with his precise eye for what belongs where and what doesn't belong at all, and with his sense of humor. It's fun when a scene makes Gary laugh.

Thank you to Erin Murphy, my steady, smart agent. She's discerning. She sells books. Her kindness in hard times is imprinted on my heart.

Thank you to Taylor Norman, my visionary editor. A generous champion of *Sky Ropes* from the start, she saw the beating heart of the book and invited me (a few times) to reveal it more fully. She also listened, which is something I never take for granted. We've worked hard together, and it's been a joy.

Thank you to Ryan Hayes, the book designer who put that wonderful bark inside the pages. Thank you to Ginee Seo for helping me through the final stages and to Claire Fletcher, Lucy Medrich, Debra DeFord-Minerva, and Kevin Armstrong, who made *Sky Ropes* real and beautiful. And to Andie Krawczyk, Mary Duke, Carrie Gao, and the rest of the Chronicle children's marketing team for their care and attention in bringing the book to readers.

Thank you to Chaaya Prabhat for her sensitive, alive cover illustration. What a gift.

Finally, thank you to my family. There is Nathan, of course and always. There is my mom, Carol Healey Sumsion, and my dad, Jerald Andrew Sumsion, who aren't here anymore to celebrate. But they would be so happy! I love knowing that. My kids, Seth, Sarah, and Hannah, are honest critics. I appreciate those times when they think that I've gotten it right. I also appreciate their tolerance of my frequent, context-free references to characters who exist only in my head. During the writing of this book, my sister Elizabeth Sumsion Graul, my brother-in-law Ed Graul, my aunt and uncle Linda and Allen Sumsion, and my cousins Bill Darden, Stefani Sumsion, Laura Sumsion Barila, Matt Sumsion, Mike Sumsion, and Amy Sumsion Paulson, supported me when I needed it. Their kindness and humor surely seeped into these pages.

Clearly, I have been beyond lucky in my book and life journeys. I am grateful.